Bad Blood

A Young Jesse McDermitt Novel

Tropical Adventure Series
Volume 2

Wayne Stinnett

Copyright © 2024
Published by DOWN ISLAND PRESS, LLC, 2024
Beaufort, SC
Copyright © 2024 by Wayne Stinnett
All rights reserved. No part of this book may be reproduced, scanned, or distributed in any printed or electronic form without express, written permission. Please do not participate in or encourage piracy of copyrighted materials in violation of the author's rights. Purchase only authorized editions.
Library of Congress cataloging-in-publication Data
Stinnett, Wayne
Bad Blood/Wayne Stinnett
p. cm. - (A Jesse McDermitt Novel)
ISBN: 978-1-956026-75-7
Cover and graphics by Aurora Publicity
Edited by Marsha Zinberg, The Write Touch
Final Proofreading by Donna Rich
Interior Design by Aurora Publicity
Published by Down Island Press, LLC

This is a work of fiction. Names, characters, and incidents are either the product of the author's imagination or are used fictitiously. Any resemblance to actual persons, living or dead, businesses, companies, events, or locales is entirely coincidental. Many real people are used fictitiously in this work, with their permission. Most of the locations herein are also fictional or are used fictitiously. However, the author takes great pains to depict the location and description of the many well-known islands, locales, beaches, reefs, bars, and restaurants throughout the Florida Keys and the Caribbean to the best of his ability.

If you'd like to receive my newsletter, please sign up on my website. WWW.WAYNESTINNETT.COM.
Once or twice a month, I'll bring you insights into my private life and writing habits, with updates on what I'm working on, special deals I hear about, and new books by other authors that I'm reading.

The Gaspar's Revenge Ship's Store is open.

There, you can purchase all kinds of swag related to my books. You can find it at

WWW.GASPARS-REVENGE.COM

Also by Wayne Stinnett

The Jerry Snyder Caribbean Mystery Series

Wayward Sons Voudoo Child Friends of the Devil

The Charity Styles Caribbean Thriller Series

Merciless Charity Enduring Charity Elusive Charity
Ruthless Charity Vigilant Charity Liable Charity
Reckless Charity Lost Charity

The Young Jesse McDermitt Tropical Adventure Series

A Seller's Market Bad Blood

The Jesse McDermitt Caribbean Adventure Series

Fallen Out Rising Storm Rising Tide
Fallen Palm Rising Fury Steady As She Goes
Fallen Hunter Rising Force All Ahead Full
Fallen Pride Rising Charity Man Overboard
Fallen Mangrove Rising Water Cast Off
Fallen King Rising Spirit Fish On!
Fallen Honor Rising Thunder Weigh Anchor
Fallen Tide Rising Warrior Swift and Silent
Fallen Angel Rising Moon
Fallen Hero Rising Tide

Non Fiction

Blue Collar to No Collar No Collar to Tank Top

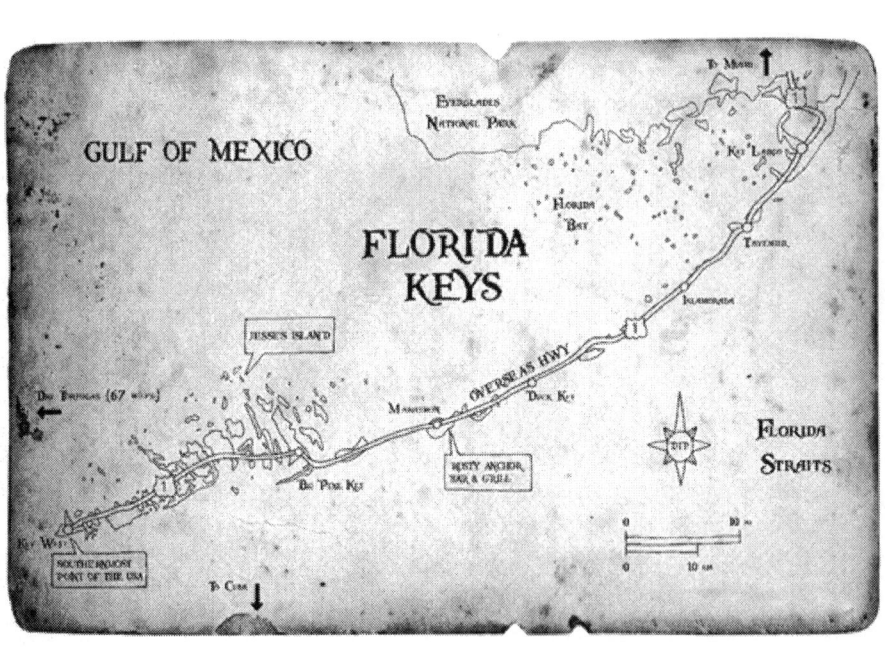

Chapter One

❖━━❖━━❖━━❖

December 27
Camp Lejeune, North Carolina

The oak tree was ancient. Its thick branches, some covered with moss and resurrection ferns, reached out more than a hundred feet in all directions, and two of its enormous limbs rested on the ground before bending upward toward the sun. When this happened, the live oak was referred to as an angel oak.

Live oaks didn't lose their leaves in the fall like the water oaks and tupelo trees in the area. Instead, they shed leaves year-round, replacing the canopy with new growth all through the winter. Hence the name live oak.

Spanish moss seemed to drip from the branches, and the exposed roots of the tree covered the ground almost as far as its canopy shaded it. In that shade, nothing else grew, and the ground between the roots was covered with a dense layer of fallen brown leaves.

And though the sun was near the tops of the tall pines and bare hardwood trees to the west, it brought little warmth to the landscape.

It was a picturesque scene.

A young man—still in his teens and full of the exuberance of youth—sat cross-legged on the thick bed of leaves beneath the old live oak. He held a pad of paper and pencil in his hands, and his frustration was evidenced by the cloud of vapor appearing in the cold evening air, produced by the sigh he emitted as he furiously erased something on the pad.

He wasn't sketching the scenery. Instead, he was trying to compose a letter to a girl he'd met four months earlier but had barely had any contact with since.

He used a pencil instead of a pen because he often had to erase whole sentences, never really sure of what to say to girls. The eraser on his current stub of a Yellow #2 was almost gone.

He'd spent several days with her in the Bahamas, and they'd had a lot of fun—diving the fringe reef on the west side of the Tongue of the Ocean, or TOTO, snorkeling the patch reefs in the shallows and walking along the shoreline by day.

They'd had some memorable nights, as well, staying in a small beach house owned by a family friend.

But since then, he'd only managed to write a few letters to her. He'd just started his new career, and his studies and training filled nearly every waking hour.

The Marine Corps School of Infantry at Camp Geiger had challenged young Jesse McDermitt in ways he didn't think imaginable. During that whole two months of training, he'd only written to Gina twice.

After that, since being assigned to 1st Battalion, 8th Marines at Camp Lejeune, he'd only been able to write to her a few more times.

Maybe six letters in four months. But he *had* called her once.

They'd talked until he'd run out of change for the phone booth outside the enlisted club. She'd told him about her sister's recovery, the trial of the man who'd nearly killed her, and who *had* killed another woman.

During the call, Gina had talked even more about things going on in the Keys—artsy stuff. Gina Albert was interested in a lot of things and seemed to be on the go all the time.

Jesse liked listening to her voice, especially when she laughed.

"What's up?" a voice called from behind, interrupting Jesse's train of thought.

"Trying to write a letter to Gina," Jesse replied. "I'm just not sure where we are in our relationship."

Jesse had first met Jim "Rusty" Thurman on a Greyhound bus headed to Parris Island late the previous spring. Being the only two in their platoon from Florida, they'd naturally become friends.

After boot camp, they'd spent part of their leave time scuba diving in the Florida Keys, where Rusty lived. That was where Jesse and Gina had met; she was close friends with Rusty's girlfriend, Juliet. While there, he and Rusty, and especially Rusty's dad, Shorty, had been instrumental in the capture of a killer by the name of Norbert "Bear" Bering.

When that incident was over, Rusty's dad had suggested they go somewhere else for the last few days of their leave, so they'd taken Gina and Juliet to Andros Island in the Bahamas.

"I'd say you're 'bout four months into it," Rusty replied, sitting down on the ground next to Jesse. "Total time, that is. You're still in the first week of actual time together. Lemme see what ya got there."

Jesse relinquished his writing pad.

"'Dear Gina, hope you're doin' well.' That's it?"

"I started the next line a few times," Jesse said. "But I don't know what to say."

After their leave, Rusty and Jesse had gone through SOI together, even being assigned to the same unit after graduating. In just a short time, Rusty felt like an old friend.

"McDermitt! Thurman!" a voice boomed from the office behind them. "Get your asses in here!"

They both scrambled to their feet and ran inside to find Sergeant Livingston waiting by the clerk's desk with the company roster in his hand. He was the duty NCO for the night.

"You wanted to see us, Sergeant Livingston?" Jesse asked, standing at parade rest in the office.

Russell Livingston was Jesse's fire team leader and was also his and Rusty's squad leader, but Rusty was in a different fire team. Of the four squad leaders, Livingston was the senior Marine. He was tough but fair.

Nobody in third squad got away with a second of "malingering."

"At ease," the sergeant said, then looked at the two of them. "You two haven't been home since boot camp, is that right?"

"Yes, Sergeant," they both replied in unison.

"We didn't want to miss the ball right after SOI," Jesse said, referring to the Marine Corps Birthday Ball, a ceremony that Jesse would remember forever.

"Two of Sergeant Redmond's guys, Lance Corporals Davis and Burlington, were busted with grass," Livingston went on. "They're restricted to the barracks, pending office hours as soon as the major gets back from Christmas leave."

"Office hours," or NJP—non-judicial punishment—was meted out by commanding officers at the company and battalion levels in lieu of the more serious court martial for lesser infractions.

It didn't surprise Jesse. The two men were basically terminal lances, meaning they'd made the highest non-rated rank of lance corporal, but lacked the skill, knowledge, or ability to be recommended to NCO school and promotion to corporal, and would likely leave the Corps as a lance corporal.

"They *were* scheduled for a week's leave, starting tomorrow morning." Livingston looked up from the roster. "That's obviously been shit-canned. Can you two turd-fondlers be packed and ready to go right after zero-six-hundred formation?"

"Go where?" Jesse asked.

"Wherever the hell you want, Lance Corporal McDermitt. The Corps don't like non-rates saving up leave time. Go home, go mountain climbing, go get the clap from a Wilmington hooker. What do I give a shit?"

"Not really much use going home," Jesse said. "My grandparents are going on a ten-day cruise for all of next week. They're leaving tomorrow."

Rusty glanced up at Jesse. "We could go to my place and do some more divin'. Water's cold, but the season's open."

Sergeant Livingston looked up from his paperwork again. "You two knuckleheads dive? Scuba? For lobster?"

"Yes, Sergeant," they both replied.

"Lance Corporal Thurman lives in the Keys," Jesse added. "I'm from Southwest Florida. Everyone in South Florida dives."

Sergeant Livingston looked back and forth between them. "Either of you interested in a lat move to combat diver? There's a slot open."

A lateral move from a basic infantry rifleman MOS, or military occupational specialty, to Reconnaissance Platoon was unheard of in such a short time. Both he and Rusty had only graduated infantry school less than two months earlier.

"You both scored high on last week's PFT," Livingston said, looking back down at his papers. "Real high. And McDermitt, you were the top shooter in the whole damned battalion, first time on the combat course." He looked up again. "There's gonna be two openings next month, and familiarity with scuba is a huge plus."

"Recon?" Jesse asked.

"*Force* Recon, numbnuts," the sergeant replied. "I'm headed back in a few months, myself—Third Force Recon, Onna Point,

Okinawa."

"Well... yeah," Rusty stammered. "I mean, yes, Sergeant, I'd sure jump at it."

"Me too," Jesse replied.

Livingston turned to the clerk, a young PFC Jesse had seen around the mess hall a few times but didn't realize worked in the battalion admin office.

"Get me two leave request forms, Walkley," he ordered.

The pretty redhead scurried off to the file cabinet and Sergeant Livingston turned back to face his two squad members.

"So you're going scuba diving in the Keys for New Year's, huh?" he grumbled. "And I'm taking the wife and rugrat to Myrtle Beach."

"You dive, Sergeant?" Jesse asked.

"Since I was fourteen," Livingston replied. "Advanced open water as a civilian and Recon combat diver instructor after this."

"Same here," Jesse said, grinning. "AOW, I mean. And Rusty's probably logged more dives than half the Navy."

"Ya don't say," Livingston said, appraising the shorter Marine a little more closely. "I'll be leaving in the spring for a one-year unaccompanied tour in Oki. Maybe we can dive a couple of wrecks off the OBX before then."

"OBX?" Rusty asked, puzzled.

"Outer Banks," Livingston replied, then turned to the clerk. "Get me two lat move request forms while you're back there, Walkley."

He turned back to face the two younger Marines. "My wife and I have a little vacation house on Pamlico Sound, not far from Hatteras Inlet. Got a dock there, and a decent dive boat. Lots of gold's been lost in the Sound and just offshore. There's a long history of piracy in that area."

"You're askin' us to go divin' with you, Sergeant?" Rusty asked.

BAD BLOOD

"You can never have too many dive buddies," Livingston replied, "and there aren't many sport divers in the battalion; you two make six, and the other three are more interested in dive destinations and bikinis than diving deep and local."

"Sure," Jesse said. "Diving for treasure sounds like fun."

"My house out there has an extra room and I'll be there for a month's leave before I ship to Oki. If you don't mind putting up with the offspring, my wife makes the best shrimp and grits anywhere. She's from the Banks. The house is one of about a dozen that have been in her family for generations. Cousins everywhere along the Sound."

The clerk returned and handed the forms to the sergeant, then smiled at Jesse before returning to a stack of forms on the counter.

"Here, fill these out and I'll see they're approved first thing," he said. "Lieutenant Brooks is always here by zero five hundred."

Jesse fished the stub of a pencil from his pocket. "Got a pencil right here, Sergeant."

PFC Walkley smiled at Jesse again as she placed two ballpoint pens on the counter. "It has to be in black ink."

"Give it some thought," Livingston said, as Rusty and Jesse filled out the forms. "You guys come out on the weekends while I'm there with the missus, and we'll search for treasure, spear some fish, and hoist a beer or two to Chesty."

"Now you're talkin'," Rusty said, looking up from his paper. "They really findin' gold there?"

The sergeant reached down his white undershirt and pulled his dog tags out, then a gold chain with a coin of some kind hanging from the end.

"Found this in a hundred and ten feet of water," he said, holding it out away from his neck.

They leaned forward so they could see it closer.

13

"That's a doubloon!" Rusty said. "I've seen a few down in the Keys but ain't never found one."

"Not a lot of bottom time to search when you're that deep," Livingston said. "And it's darker than a Manila hooker's heart. Three of us could cover three times as much area."

"Me and Jesse… er, Lance Corporal McDermitt here," Rusty began. "We did some dives that deep. He even speared a whopper of a bluefin."

"That's good," he said. "Deep is dangerous enough without experienced dive buddies." Then he leaned in conspiratorially, tucking the doubloon and dog tags away. "There's more there and I'm the only one who knows where to look. Anything we find, we split four ways with each of us and my boat getting equal shares."

Jesse understood the math. The sergeant would get half and he and Rusty would split the other half.

"What about those other three guys?" he asked. "Won't they be put out?"

"Like I said, they're not interested in working dives," Livingston replied. "Besides, they're all butter bars."

Jesse had learned the semi-derogatory term for a second lieutenant fresh out of Officer Candidate School long before boot camp.

"You should be *chargin'* us, Sergeant," Rusty said. "Back home, I'd make twenty bucks a head to do the same thing."

"That's why the boat gets a cut," Livingston replied, with a nod of his head. "I'm not interested in making a buck taking divers out. For me, it's all about the hunt. And I'm onto something big."

Chapter Two

❖❖❖❖

Jesse and Rusty hurried back to the room they shared with another lance corporal in the enlisted barracks. Though they were equal in rank, Tyler Anderson had more than a year of time in grade, so was senior to Rusty and Jesse. He would likely be promoted to corporal in the coming year. Currently, he was home on leave for Christmas and wouldn't be back until Monday.

"What do I do about the letter?" Jesse asked, pulling a seabag from his wall locker.

"Screw that," Rusty said. "I'll call Jewels and tell her we're on the way and to let Gina know. Hey, how we gonna get there?"

Jesse looked up from his bunk, where he'd deposited what little civilian clothing he had. "I don't know. The bus?"

There was a knock on the door and being closest, Jesse grabbed the knob and flung it open, turning to face PFC Walkley, the redhead from Headquarters Company.

"Oh... hey," he stammered, stepping back. "Would you like to come—"

"Off limits," she replied, then smiled, and held out a small piece of paper. "Here. Call this number. My uncle's a loadmaster at New River—Staff Sergeant Virgil Walkley. He's loading a Hercules tonight that's taking off at ten hundred, heading to Gitmo. They'll stop in Homestead on the way."

Jesse glanced over at Rusty. "What do you think? It'd be a free ride."

"Um, no," Walkley said. "You'll have to pay him twenty dollars each. Tell him I gave you his number."

She turned and started to walk away.

"Wait," Jesse said. "What's your first name?"

She turned and smiled again. "Linda."

Jesse lifted the piece of paper in salute. "Thanks, Linda."

He closed the door and went back to his bunk.

"And you think you have trouble with chicks," Rusty scoffed under his breath. "Ya don't even have to *talk*, ya dumb grunt."

Jesse went back to packing his seabag. "What are you muttering about?"

"She smiled at you twice and you didn't notice," Rusty said, standing up and staring at him.

Jesse looked up. "Everyone smiles," he said. "It's called being polite."

"They call her the Ice Queen, bro. Every Marine in the battalion's been shot down in flames. Until just now, nobody even knew her first name!"

"She was just being helpful," Jesse replied. "And she'll probably get a cut from her uncle."

"You better go call him," Rusty said.

Jesse nodded, then headed out the door.

The sun had set, and an orange glow from the streetlights spilled into the grass along the side of the barracks. Their room was on the second floor, as was the rec center. There was a phone booth there he could use if nobody was there first.

Jesse got lucky, and a tall, sandy-haired guy was just ending a call when Jesse walked in. It was Sergeant Redmond.

As he stepped past him, the sergeant nodded. "Heard you lucked into a vacant leave spot."

Jesse nodded. "Next up on the roster, I guess."

"No. You weren't," Sergeant Redmond replied. "I was. But because two of my guys screwed up, Sergeant Livingston told the gunny he should pass over me on the roster."

"I'm sorry," Jesse said, and meant it. "That's not right. Did he say why?"

Sergeant Redmond cocked his head slightly, giving Jesse an odd expression. "Who the heck are you, man? Dudley Do-Right?"

"Maybe if I talked to the gunny, he'd—"

The anger on the sergeant's face stopped him mid-sentence. He hadn't planned on taking leave until spring in the first place, and he certainly had nothing to do with it being offered.

Redmond calmed. "You would, wouldn't you?" He said. "Talk to the gunny, I mean."

"Well, sure," Jesse said. "You were next on the roster, so you should get it. I was saving up my leave time for spring, anyway."

The sergeant grinned slightly. "Nah, man. Russ is right. My guys screwed the pooch, so that falls on me. Besides, my family's right here."

"I heard it was marijuana," Jesse said. "Why would they get messed up with that?"

Redmond gave him the odd look again. "It's *pot*, man. And I don't know. I've been working extra with them, but they're a coupla shitbirds."

"I don't think you should give up on them, Sergeant Redmond," Jesse said. "Maybe after their office hours, they'll straighten up and fly right. You have a lot of experience to share."

Again, the odd expression.

"I will," Redmond said. "And thanks. I can see you as a squad leader one day. And it won't be a long time from now, neither."

"Thanks, Sergeant," Jesse replied, then turned to the phone.

Sergeant Gray Redmond was almost as tall as Jesse, and though most would call him lanky, Jesse knew he had great strength in those long sinewy arms.

He was also from Florida, a little fishing town in the panhandle called Apalachicola. Jesse had worked with him a couple of times in the past two months, and they'd exchanged backgrounds—the typical Where ya from? What'd you do before the Corps? He'd been an oysterman, a very labor-intensive job, he'd said.

He didn't like that Redmond had been passed over for leave, but figured the gunny and Sergeant Livingston knew better about these things. Maybe while they were restricted to the barracks, Redmond could work with them and counsel them. Jesse *knew* he could motivate his Marines.

Besides, he didn't believe that anyone who'd survived Parris Island *and* Camp Geiger could ever go far enough adrift to be unsalvageable.

He dropped a coin in the slot and dialed the number on the piece of paper Linda had given him.

"Staff Sergeant Walkley," a man answered, almost before the first ring ended.

"Hey, Staff Sergeant," Jesse said. "This is Lance Corporal McDermitt with Alpha, One-Eight. Your niece, PFC Walkley, said you might have room on a flight down to South Florida tomorrow. Is that right?"

"She tell you the terms?" he asked.

"Yes, Staff Sergeant."

"I'll meet you at the main gate at zero nine hundred," he said. "I'll make a U-turn and if I don't see you, you're not flyin'. So be early. UD is Charlies. I'm in a yellow Dodge Charger."

"We'll be there," Jesse said.

"We? How many?"

"Just two," Jesse replied. "Me and Lance Corporal Thurman."

"Don't be late," he replied. Then there was a click and a dial tone.

Jesse went back to his room and told Rusty they had seats on a cargo plane.

"Cool!" Rusty said. "And only twenty bucks?"

"Yeah, twenty each," he replied. "He said the uniform of the day is Charlies."

"We gotta be in uniform?"

"And we gotta be there at zero nine," Jesse said. "We should probably just go to formation in Charlies then catch the bus into town."

Of the dress uniforms they were required to wear periodically, the Dress-C or Charlie was the most comfortable to Jesse. No tie and short sleeves. But the morning temperature would probably be below forty degrees, which to him, was bone-chilling.

"I'll go call Jewels, now that we know we got a ride," Rusty said, clipping his seabag closed. "She can pick us up. What time we gettin' there?"

"Aw, geez! I forgot to ask. He didn't sound like a pleasant guy."

Rusty looked over at him. "He's scalpin' room on a military transport. Not somethin' ya wanna chit-chat about."

Jesse's head came up. "We could get in trouble?"

"Naw," Rusty said. "The wingers do it all the time. But we need to know what time we're gettin' there."

By "wingers" Rusty meant those in the Marine Air Wings.

"Okay, okay... let's just figure it out," Jesse said. "It's flying from here to Guantanamo Bay with a stop in Homestead, and it takes off at ten hundred. How fast is a Hercules?"

"Do I *look* like a friggin' Airedale?" Rusty asked sarcastically, using the slang term for those in Marine aviation.

Jesse shrugged, holding his hands out. "A guess."

"I dunno," Rusty said, "Two-fifty, maybe?"

"I'd say it's probably less than a thousand miles," Jesse said.

"Way less," Rusty said, nodding. "The drive's only nine-fifty. I measured it on a map, and it ain't no straight line like a plane flies."

"Okay, so nine hundred, divided by two-fifty..." Jesse said, trailing off as he did the math in his head. "A little over three-and-a-half hours. I don't want to call him back."

"I'll tell Jewels fourteen hundred," Rusty said. "That's four hours. If anyone's waitin', it's better if it's us."

"Waiting an hour for a ride in South Florida beats hanging around here in the cold." Jesse agreed.

Chapter Three

◆━━━◆━━━◆━━━◆━━━◆

At 0600, Jesse and Rusty fell in with the others in Alpha Company, wearing short sleeves in the cold, late-December air. Everyone else was in camouflage utilities and field jackets.

The predawn temperature was hovering close to freezing.

Sergeant Livingston came down the rank from his spot at the head of third squad and stopped to face Jesse.

"Flying out of New River?" he asked, picking at a non-existent thread on Jesse's shoulder.

"Yes, Sergeant," Jesse replied. "To Homestead. Thurman's fiancée is picking us up there."

"Here's your leave papers and request for Recon school," the sergeant said, extending one of two clasped envelopes he held. "Both approved by the XO. You and your buddy Thurman are going back to Geiger when we return from Fort Drum."

"Thanks, Sergeant," Jesse said, taking the envelope.

"The LT wants to see you both after formation."

He continued down the rank to where Rusty stood in the third fire team, while Jesse wondered what Lieutenant Brooks wanted to see them about.

Gunnery Sergeant Bramble came out of the duty office and strode to his spot in front of the formation.

"Company! Ah-ten-shun!"

For the next ten minutes, the gunny went through a list of

training exercises and work parties for the day. As his voice droned on, Jesse became colder and colder. Finally, the gunny dismissed the platoons, and Jesse and Rusty hurried toward the duty hut.

The XO was talking to the admin chief, Sergeant Blake, and when he saw Jesse and Rusty enter, he motioned them back.

"This way, Marines," the lieutenant said. "I won't keep you more than two minutes."

He led Jesse and Rusty into a small office, and moved behind the desk, as the two young Marines stood at attention.

"At ease," the lieutenant said. "Sit down."

They did as they were ordered and the lieutenant opened two service record books on his desk, glanced down at each for a moment, flipping pages in both, then closing them and looking up.

"I just want you two to know, I'll be joining you at Camp Geiger in March," the lieutenant said. "I was also accepted to Reconnaissance School."

He paused and looked at Jesse. "Sergeant Livingston told me you had the highest score in the battalion your first time at the combat range and I looked in your SRB and saw you scored perfect on the rifle range at Parris Island. I don't think anyone's ever done that before. Based on that, as well as the coolness I've seen you exhibit under tough conditions, I've recommended you for scout/sniper training."

Then he turned to Rusty. "Have you ever used a rebreather?"

"A couple of times, sir," Rusty replied. "Way out of my price range, though."

"When we finish recon training, you're going on to parachute and combat diver school."

"Ooh-rah, sir," Rusty said.

"Yut-yut," the lieutenant grunted. "Now get out of my hootch."

Jesse and Rusty rose and quickly exited the XO's office, went through the outer office, and double-timed back to their barracks.

"We have two hours," Jesse said. "Piece of cake."

"Never assume that," Rusty said, rubbing his arms as they walked up the ladderwell. "Damn, I wish I had a wooly pully."

He was referring to a wool pullover that could be worn with the Charlie uniform. It wasn't standard issue, but they could be bought at the MCX, or Marine Corps Exchange.

"Only lifers wear those," Jesse said, opening the door to their room.

"So where's yours?"

"Yuck, yuck," he retorted, sitting on his footlocker. "What should we do for the next two hours?"

"It's a twenty-minute walk to the bus station at Mainside," Rusty suggested. "Another twenty to the Jacksonville bus station. We could just hang out there for an hour, play some pinball, then grab a cab to the air station."

"Let's do it," Jesse said, getting to his feet, and opening his footlocker.

He dug beneath stacks of neatly folded white T-shirts and withdrew a rolled-up sock.

"Whatcha got there?" Rusty asked.

Jesse looked over and grinned. "Fish money."

An hour and fifty minutes later, the taxi pulled over to the stand just before the gate, getting in line behind two more cabs, and the two young men got out.

"What do I owe you, Gus?" Jesse asked, having noted the man's name on his taxi license displayed on the dash.

"Seven dollars," the driver replied.

Jesse handed him a ten and told him to keep the change, as Rusty hoisted both their seabags from the trunk.

Jesse had taken two twenties and two tens from his stash, putting the rest in his seabag, since he didn't want to have to pull out a large roll of cash in public.

His seabag would get no farther away from him than it had been in the trunk of the cab.

Both Marines shouldered their bags and walked to the gate. Because they were in uniform, the guard just nodded, and they continued to a parking area just inside.

Rusty checked his pocket watch. "We're ten minutes early."

They grounded their seabags at their feet and waited. Once in the fleet, they'd learned very quickly that the Marine Corps did a lot of waiting.

"I don't know what I'm gonna do when we go to Fort Drum," Rusty said. "North Cacka-lacky's too cold for me as it is."

"You'll do fine," Jesse said, then snickered. "Just don't wear your Charlies there."

"Bro, we're gonna be outside in the snow!" Rusty snapped. "For four straight weeks! That ain't nothin' to laugh at for us Conchs."

Jesse noticed a yellow car in the distance. "I think that's him."

A moment later, Jesse recognized the car as a Charger. Not a new model, but not very old. Maybe three or four years. He waved to the driver, who turned a complete circle to pull into the parking area next to them, facing the way he'd come.

A staff sergeant in cammies got out and moved around to the back of the car, then opened the trunk. "McDermitt?"

Jesse nodded. "Staff Sergeant Walkley."

"Put your bags in here," he said. "The Herky Jerks are anxious to get in the air on time."

Rusty lifted his in, then Jesse put his seabag on top. "Herky

Jerks?"

"What we call C-130 Hercules drivers," he replied, slamming the trunk. He held out his hand.

Jesse and Rusty both dug folded twenties out of their pockets and handed them over.

Walkley pocketed the bills and moved toward the driver's side. Jesse got in front and Rusty climbed in behind him. As Walkley pulled out onto the road, he turned to Jesse. "If anyone asks either of you anything, just say you're Recon, then don't say another word. Clear?"

Jesse nodded.

"Those Recon guys hitch rides down to Gitmo by ones and twos all the time."

Twenty minutes later, they hustled across the apron to a massive airplane that had all four engines running and the ramp down. A line of wooden crates extended into the gloom of the plane's interior.

The staff sergeant stopped at a cart, where he handed them both a set of headphones. "Remove your piss cutters and put these cranials on before boarding!" he shouted over the engines. "There's two empty jump seats on the port side, halfway along the stack of pallets. Stow your seabags under the seat, run the shoulder strap through the webbing, and strap yourselves in. Nothing goes on my aircraft that isn't secure, and everything and everyone stays secure until the plane stops, whether that's on its wheels or in a nosedive to the ground. Understood?"

Jesse and Rusty both nodded, then removed their covers, tucking them under their web belts before putting the "cranials" on. Then they followed Walkley to the back of the plane, where another Marine in a flight suit waited. The two put their heads next to each other's and said something Jesse couldn't hear before Walkley turned and strode back toward the hangar.

The guy in the flight suit motioned to them to come aboard, then pointed to a pair of jump seats. There were three other people sitting adjacent to the two seats, and Jesse nodded at them as he folded one down, then slid his bag under it. He quickly threaded his bag's strap through the seat's webbing and clipped it back onto the ring at its top.

Jesse sat next to a major, wearing alphas with a wool overcoat. He was busy looking over paperwork from a briefcase on his lap.

Unsecured.

The ramp started going up and the guy in the flight suit took the last remaining jump seat on their side, putting a U-shaped pillow around his neck and getting comfortable.

There were no windows, and as the ramp closed up, it became dark inside. Jesse's eyes grew accustomed to it quickly, but when he looked around, all he could see were his fellow passengers on that side, a wall of crates, all stacked on pallets and strapped securely, and the right side of the large ramp. Forward was an empty bulkhead.

The plane began moving, swaying slightly as it rolled off the apron onto a taxiway. Several minutes went by, and even though there was a sensation of movement, Jesse couldn't tell how fast or how far they were going.

Suddenly, the engines roared, and Jesse could feel the acceleration as the giant plane started down the runway. They didn't go far and couldn't have been going very fast when he felt the plane rise and the nose point skyward, as if the belly of the beast were empty.

He wondered what was in the crates and how much everything weighed.

The major beside him continued his paperwork, ignoring the

surroundings. Beside him, a woman in an Air Force uniform, also wearing a heavy coat with second lieutenant bars, did pretty much the same.

Occasionally, the two talked and shared a document.

I should have brought a book or something, Jesse thought, as the plane climbed higher and higher.

After noting that the crewman in the flight suit looked to be asleep, and with nothing else to do, Jesse stretched his legs out and closed his eyes.

Chapter Four

Relaxing his neck muscles, Jesse found a comfortable spot in the webbing that supported his head, then consciously relaxed his shoulders and arms. He didn't need sleep, nor would he get any. But he'd found that any time he could relax his body and let everything go on autopilot, the better he felt afterward.

As the engines droned on, Jesse realized he'd forgotten to ask Rusty if he'd talked to Juliet about whether Gina was joining them.

He'd written so few letters to her, but she'd answered each one with two of her own. As he'd explained to Rusty, he had no idea what their relationship was, or if there even was one. He knew she hadn't been dating anyone when they'd met and then spent a week in the Bahamas together. He liked her, and he felt sure she liked him too. They'd had a lot of fun on Andros. They'd dived one of the blue holes, waded along the shallow shoreline, and had made love countless times under the stars.

She liked a lot of things Jesse did and like him, she wasn't big on crowds.

But he'd been gone for over three months.

When they'd talked on the phone a couple of weeks earlier, she'd seemed excited about his coming back to the Keys in the spring and had even asked if she could come to Jacksonville for a weekend, just outside Camp Lejeune.

As much as he would have loved for her to do that, their training schedule often included weekends. Especially if it rained.

Sergeant Livingston had a thing about rain.

He often scheduled something at the last minute, superseding the work details, whether that was class work, PT, field, or range exercises—whatever. Even if it was on the weekend.

If there was bad weather in the forecast, they'd be training in the wet lowlands or up in the pine forests.

The plane seemed to level off, with no change in the constant whirr of the engines. When exactly they'd leveled off, he couldn't be sure, since there hadn't been a sudden change in the plane's attitude or motion.

Jesse visualized the map in his head. Would they follow the coast?

Probably not, he decided. A straight line would take them over the ocean soon after take-off, and probably all the way to the east coast of Florida, then diagonally across Central Florida and the Everglades to turn left, into the prevailing wind.

The shortest distance between two points was always a straight line.

It'd been three months since he'd seen Gina. It had also been three months since Bear had brutally beaten Gina's sister, Rachel, and murdered another woman. The murder had happened within hours of Jesse's altercation with the man, and he felt that Bear's anger at the skirmish might have led to the woman's abduction and murder. At times, it weighed very heavily on him.

The trial was held at the courthouse in Key West and word of it had even reached the local NBC News station down in Wilmington.

In her last letter, two weeks ago, Gina had said that Bear had been found guilty of murder and sentenced to life at the state prison in Raiford.

He got off easy, Jesse thought, wondering how difficult it might be to spread a rumor in the prison that Bear was also a pedophile.

Inmates didn't like child-molesters, he'd heard.

The gentle sway of the airplane's cabin felt almost like being on Pap's old sloop at night out on the Gulf of Mexico.

It'd been his parents' boat before they'd died. His dad and Pap had built it together when Dad was home on leave. It had taken more than five years to complete it.

Jesse remembered sailing the sloop with his parents for the first time, all the way down the coast to Cape Sable during Christmas, then Key West for the new year.

There was a bump, and Jesse opened his eyes. The engines sounded different. He must have dozed off. He looked over at Rusty, who was checking his pocket watch, and tilted it toward Jesse.

It was a little over two hours since they'd taken off. Even if he had dozed off, they couldn't possibly be arriving already.

He could hear a whirring sound—hydraulics—and he could feel the plane slowing, sensing the nose drop.

The crewman sitting at the end was up, putting his pillow away.

It'd been cold when they'd taken off, but not too uncomfortable during the flight. Now it felt warmer.

The sound of the engines dropped even more, barely audible with the headphones on.

Jesse could sense that the plane was in a shallow dive. They could be descending from as far away as Daytona Beach, for all he knew.

He and Rusty had just guessed at the speed, but neither of them knew how high or how far a C-130 could go.

They didn't need to know. They were infantry.

There were more hydraulic noises and the plane slowed even more, then started rocking from side to side.

Suddenly, the giant plane banked steeply to the left and Jesse felt as if he were looking up at the massive stack of crates.

They were at an impossibly steep angle, and it seemed to Jesse that the plane was going to fall sideways out of the sky.

Walkley's comment about the nosedive caused a lump in Jesse's throat.

Then the engine power rose, and the plane's nose came up slightly as it leveled off, creating the sensation of an elephant sitting on Jesse's lap.

There was a soft bump before the engines roared as the plane began to slow very quickly.

A few minutes later, the C-130 stopped, and the ramp began to descend. The crewman signaled to Jesse, who elbowed Rusty, then started unbuckling his harness.

The crewman followed them down the ramp and Jesse spotted a fuel truck pulling up. He glanced back as he stepped off the end. Nobody else was getting off. The crewman tapped Jesse on the shoulder and pointed to his own headset.

Jesse removed his, as did Rusty, then handed them over.

The guy leaned in close, lifting one side of his headphones. "Who are you guys?"

"We're Recon," Rusty replied, stone-faced, then turned and walked away.

"Oh," the crewman said, wide-eyed, as Jesse hurried after his friend.

"Or we *will* be," Rusty added with a chuckle when Jesse caught up to him.

They carried their seabags into what looked like the main building to get directions to the gate. An airman showed them how to get to the arrival area, telling them that was where anyone coming to pick them up would be directed.

Rather than sit inside, they both strode through the building and out into the parking lot and warm sunshine.

"Hot damn!" Rusty declared. "It's good to be home!"

"Yeah, it is," Jesse replied, breathing deeply.

Neither of them was home, but the mixture of scents in the air told Jesse they were close to both their respective homes. He didn't know what the exact mixture of flowers and plants was that he was sensing, but the only place he'd ever smelled it was in South Florida.

"That was some flight," Rusty said. "It'd cost two or three times as much on a regular plane."

"And probably take twice as long," Jesse added.

Rusty pulled out his pocket watch. "Guess we were a little off on how fast that big-ass bird can fly."

"What time is it?"

"Not even thirteen hundred," he replied. "Jewels won't be here for more'n an hour."

Just then, an older Corolla pulled in and a horn honked. It was Juliet in her "no keys Keys car."

And Gina was in the passenger seat.

Jesse grinned as the car came toward them, both girls laughing and pointing. Juliet pulled up to the curb and they both got out and jumped into the arms of the two young men.

"Have you been waiting long?" Juliet asked, when Rusty put her down.

"We just walked out the door," Jesse said.

"Yeah, you're an hour early," Rusty added.

Gina kissed Jesse's cheek and then stepped back, looking him up and down. "You look good in that!" she said with a smile.

"How'd you know to come early?" Rusty asked.

Gina turned toward him. "When JJ told me you were guessing at your arrival time based on it taking four hours to fly here in a Hercules, I checked with my dad and he said it'd probably only take three, if that."

"Let's get out of here," Rusty said, hefting his seabag. "I need some vitamin sea therapy."

33

Chapter Five

They quickly tossed their bags in the trunk, and Jesse opened the back door for Gina on the passenger side. Then he went around and got in beside her and behind Juliet.

It wasn't a conscious thought. At under five feet, Juliet had the driver's seat all the way forward. Jesse'd been over six feet tall since the seventh grade and he knew the limitations of his body. And the backseat of an import was one of them.

"How would your dad know how long it took?" Jesse asked Gina.

"He used to be in the Air Force," she replied. "He was a radio operator on cargo planes. Where are you staying?"

"In the rum shack," Rusty replied.

"I have a better idea," Juliet said, taking Rusty's hand, after shifting. "You're twenty-one now. Why don't we get two rooms over at Blue Waters with a connecting kitchen? We can move your boat over there and be steps away."

Jesse leaned forward. "I'm only—"

"Only the last one of us that would be carded," Gina said, cutting him off. "Cool idea, JJ. Besides, you only have to be eighteen. Don't tell me you guys never got a room before."

Jesse knew why Juliet still lived at home, and why Rusty had until he'd shipped out. They both lived as frugally as they could, saving every nickel possible. Each of them wanted the same thing—a house and family. And they both chased that dream with a single-minded purpose.

"I had the same thought," Jesse said, winking discreetly at Gina. "I still have a good bit left over from that tuna money, Rusty. I was going to surprise you guys, but Juliet just stole my thunder."

"I don't know, bro," Rusty said.

Though he'd only known Rusty a short time, Jesse knew his friend was too proud to take a handout, especially since he actually had the money himself.

"My treat," Jesse said. "To make up for blowing right past your birthday last month. As soon as you suggested we swoop down here, I decided I'd spring for a late birthday present."

"Yeah, well..."

"There is one little catch," Jesse said, grabbing Juliet's seatback and pulling himself forward. He gently patted her left shoulder as he turned to Rusty. "I'm not feeding you, devil dog. You put twenty pounds of filets in the freezer, and a case of beer in the fridge for your stay."

Rusty laughed as Juliet used an actual key to start the car. "Okay, bro. You got a deal."

"Hey, your no keys Keys car needs keys now!" Jesse exclaimed, happy to get what everyone wanted and change the subject.

"It was stolen last month," Juliet explained, putting the car in gear and steering toward the exit. "Whoever it was brought it back two days later with more gas than when they took it. But I was still without my car for two days. So, I bought a new switch and keys from the auto parts store and my dad helped me put it in. It wasn't all that hard."

When Juliet turned right, Gina leaned into Jesse's shoulder and whispered, "I've missed you."

"I'm sorry I didn't write more."

"JJ told me you guys were super busy. She also told me you both got promoted at the end."

"Rusty maxed the PFT," Jesse said. "You shoulda seen him. Kept right up there with the taller guys on the three-mile run, then whipped all our butts in pull-ups and sit-ups."

"Oh, hey!" Rusty shouted, turning in his seat toward Juliet. "I forgot to tell ya the news. Me and Jesse been selected for Recon School! Just this mornin'."

"What's recon?" Gina asked. "Sounds like a big deal."

"Imagine the Marine Corps as a big ol' spear," Rusty began, recalling something Sergeant Livingston had said to them. "It's flung far ahead of the main force—first to fight. Says so in the hymn. And Force Recon is the pointy tip of that spear."

"So, if there was a war?" Gina asked. "You would go first? Ahead of the rest of the Marines?"

Jesse sensed concern in Gina's voice.

"Reconnaissance goes in days or weeks ahead of the main force," Rusty replied. "To locate and identify enemy forces, positions, and equipment."

"*With* a lot of support," Jesse added, trying to downplay it. "And plenty of training."

"Our company XO... er, executive officer, Lieutenant Brooks, recommended me for parachute and combat diver school," Rusty told Juliet. "Can you believe that?"

"Fighting underwater?" Juliet said, taking her eyes off the road for a second. "In a bulky dive suit?"

Rusty laughed. "Nothin' like that, babe. We'll use those fancy rebreathers to get ashore without detection, snoop around, and let the Airedales know where to drop the bombs."

She turned her head toward him again. "And parachuting?"

"Yeah, well, there *is* that," Rusty replied. "The idea of jumpin' out of a perfectly runnin' airplane don't sit real well."

"Are you also going to this... school?" Gina asked Jesse.

"Recon School, yes," he replied, sensing a negative feeling in the car. "But not Combat Diver School."

"Jesse's goin' to scout/sniper school!" Rusty exclaimed.

Gina's eyes widened slightly. "Sniper?"

Rusty's head jerked around, glancing at me. He also seemed to sense the negativity, though a little late, and he started back-pedaling.

"Scouts move around undetected," he said. "Usually at night and with a spotter and backup."

Gina looked over at Jesse. "On a scale of one to ten, how dangerous will this be for you?"

Jesse thought about it for a moment. He was under no illusions about what his new job was going to be like. He'd heard both his father and grandfather speak about the "fewest of the few" and the impossible tasks they performed. His dad hadn't talked to him directly about it, though; he'd been too young. But he'd overheard his father and grandfather talking one night, when he was supposed to be asleep.

"In training, there's a little danger," Jesse said. "The training will be tough. Maybe a one or a two. I'd guess it could be a five or six when actually in combat. For me, maybe a four or five, I'd say."

She sat back a little. "You're that sure of yourself?"

"He oughta be," Rusty said. "He did somethin' nobody else has ever done—a perfect score on the rifle range."

"I'm that sure of the training," Jesse replied. "The Marine Corps doesn't take shortcuts there. And I enjoy the hard training."

"I used to know a guy who lived here," Gina said. "He left and went into the Navy and got hurt earlier this year."

Juliet looked at her in the mirror. "You're talking about Scott Ingersol, right?"

"Yes," Gina said, nodding. "You heard what happened?"

"I know him," Rusty said, turning toward Jesse. "He's prolly ten years older'n us. Tech MOS—never gets sea duty."

"It happens," Jesse said. "People get hurt on other jobs, too. Even executives."

"Yeah, well," Gina began. "Since he got home after his accident, three months ago, Scott's had someone try to kill him three times."

"Why would someone want to kill him?" Jesse asked.

"I've only met him a few times," Rusty replied. "Pop knows him better. But he's always seemed like a decent guy."

"The police think it has something to do with his job in the Navy," Gina replied. "He has a top-secret clearance or something."

They continued across the long causeway, with thick mangroves and marsh on their right and shallow flats on the left.

Jesse wasn't worried about anyone coming after him for what he knew, and doubted he'd ever have any kind of security clearance. Yet, he couldn't help but wonder what the guy did that made him a target multiple times.

And why would one of America's enemies want to kill him? Capture and torture maybe, to get information he had. But killing him would be pointless.

When they crossed the bridge into Key Largo, Jesse could sense the mood change. It was like the worries of the world were dropped when you left the mainland.

"Bam!" Rusty said as soon as the car came off the bridge. "Back in the Conch Republic."

He and Juliet reached up and put a palm against the headliner.

Rusty looked back, grinning. "Ya gotta touch the roof. It's tradition."

Gina and Jesse looked at one another, then reached up and touched the car's roof.

"Whose tradition?" Gina asked. "I was born here too, and I never heard of this."

Juliet leaned to one side to see Gina in the rearview mirror. "It's *his* tradition; he just made it up one day. Whenever we cross this bridge, or when we cross any borders in the future, it's what we do."

"We crossed three state lines on the way down here," Jesse said, leaning toward Rusty. "I didn't see you reaching for the C-130's overhead."

He turned in his seat and shook his head. "We never crossed any borders. We was over blue water just a few minutes after we took off."

Jesse laughed and sat back in his seat again. "You have a point there."

Juliet drove at a decent speed, sometimes over the limit—keeping up with the flow of traffic. She didn't tailgate, slam on brakes, or have a lead foot, and she seemed to know when the cars ahead were slowing down before Jesse saw any brake lights.

Her little Keys car ate up the miles, and once they were through Key Largo, Juliet turned her head toward Rusty. "Did you tell him yet?"

"Tell me what?" Jesse asked.

Rusty turned around again. "Pop's been havin' some work done on your car, bro. In his last letter, he told me it's runnin'."

The Mustang...

Jesse had felt really bad telling Billy that the car he'd spent so much time building had been torched. He'd called him from Rusty's dad's bait shop before they'd flown to the Bahamas.

Billy had shrugged it off, as was his way, saying it was just a material thing.

Pap had insurance on the car, but what they paid didn't cover what his grandfather had put into it. Though he knew the old man would never ask for it, Jesse still owed him a little over three thousand dollars.

As soon as he'd arrived at Camp Geiger, Jesse had opened an account at the Navy Credit Union. Since then, nearly all of his pay for the last six months had gone into it. He was planning to repay his grandfather for the loss when he went home in the spring.

"It's a different motor," Rusty continued. "Pop shipped the 427 and transmission to your buddy, Billy, then picked up a used 289 and automatic."

More money, Jesse thought.

Maybe Billy had the better idea. He didn't own a car.

Jesse didn't need one at the base, either; everything was within walking distance. If he needed to go into town, the bus was only two dollars.

Everyone in the Keys drove clunkers. They called them "Keys cars" and they probably didn't pay more than a few hundred for one, the general consensus being that a new car would rust apart before you could even pay for it.

Even Pap had never owned a new car. He'd buy a two-year-old, low-mileage car and drive it for a few years, then sell it and buy another.

He'd explained to Jesse that as soon as a new car is sold and titled, it becomes a used car and loses a third of its value. Even if there was only one mile on the odometer.

"Think he can sell it for what he's put into it?" Jesse asked.

"You don't want it?" Rusty asked, as Juliet slowed, coming into Marathon.

"Cars are a lot of work and responsibility," Jesse said. "I don't need one at the base."

"But what about when you go home?" Gina asked.

Jesse shrugged. "My friend Billy always has a pickup lying around."

Juliet slowed and turned into a one-story motel on the Gulf side. It had a small swimming pool in front, and a long canal with dock space on either side behind the pool. There were rooms facing both the pool and dock areas, with lots of tropical plants and tall palm trees.

Juliet parked by the office and started to get out.

"Y'all wait here," Rusty said, putting a hand on her arm, then turning toward Jesse in the back. "You sure you wanna spring for this, bro? I mean, all three of *us* live here and got beds. There's plenty of room."

Gina squeezed Jesse's hand and he smiled at her, remembering those Bahamian nights. "Let's go get the keys," he replied, opening his door.

As he and Rusty strode toward the office, Rusty looked around. "I feel real conspicuous in these uniforms."

Jesse nodded. "We're probably the only two in the Keys wearing Charlies."

"No, my recruiter's prolly around somewhere. He always wore the Charlie."

Five minutes later, they returned to the car, each carrying a key attached to a foam float buoy with the name of the motel on it.

Jesse noted a dive flag on a tall flagpole at the business next to the motel and asked Rusty about it.

"Hall's Dive Center," Rusty replied. "They teach advanced classes and instructors there. Even got a resort management course, where you learn how to run a whole dive op."

After they pulled their bags from the back of the car, Gina took the key from Jesse, then grabbed his hand as she pulled him toward their room.

"Give us an hour to freshen up," she said to Juliet, then inserted the key and smiled up at Jesse.

Chapter Six

Later that evening, the four of them went to Juliet's parents' house on Big Pine Key, so she could get some clothes. They lived way out on the north end of the island, and Jesse saw more than a dozen Key deer on the slow drive through the mostly vacant neighborhood.

Jesse and Gina waited by the car. He'd changed into a pair of shorts and an Eighth Marine Regiment T-shirt.

"Your shirt's too tight," Gina said, hugging Jesse around the waist.

Jesse moved his shoulders. She was right. The shirt had fit fine when he'd bought it in early November. That was only eight weeks ago, and he'd only worn it a couple of times before it got too cold. It shouldn't have shrunk with just a couple of washings, but it felt tight under his arms.

"I only bought it two months ago," he said. "Guess it shrunk."

"We should go shopping while you're here," Gina said, lifting her head from his shoulder and looking up at him. "If you prefer T-shirts, I know a great little custom shop right here in Marathon."

"Sure," he replied, liking the feel of her body leaning against his and the taut muscles at the small of her back as she arched it. "Most of my civilian clothes are at home in Fort Myers."

"Pick a day," she said. "I have Rach's car keys, and we can bring her car back to the motel when we go get my things."

When Rusty and Juliet came out, they all piled back into her car and drove to the City Marina, where Gina and Rachel had their boat docked.

"You guys go ahead on back," Gina said to Juliet. "We'll be along in a few minutes. I have Rachel's car for the week."

As they drove away, Jesse and Gina walked out onto the dock where Gina's boat was tied up. The water was still and reflected the lights from across the harbor.

She opened the companionway hatch and stepped down into the cabin. Jesse followed, careful not to bang his head on anything.

"Sorry," Gina said, giggling at him bowing his head down. "It's kinda small inside. The headroom is only six-two."

"I remember," Jesse said. "I'm used to it. I went over six feet the summer before eighth grade."

"Make yourself at home," she said, disappearing through a narrow passageway beside the steps. "I'll be just a minute." She paused and looked back, smiling. "But, you know, we could just stay here."

Jesse looked around at the small salon and galley. There was a narrow hatch forward, which he assumed was Rachel's cabin. Neither could be very big.

"The motel has a lot more room," he called down the passageway.

Five minutes later, Jesse carried Gina's small, cloth duffle bag over his shoulder as they walked out to the parking lot.

"Rachel's gone for the week," she told him again. "Won't be back until next weekend."

"I wouldn't want to make Rusty uncomfortable," Jesse said. "Our room's huge, there's a big shower and a big kitchen."

"Then we should stop at the store and get some things," Gina said. "I want to cook for you and I'm off for the whole weekend." She slipped an arm around his waist and leaned against him. "And next week is nothing but a question mark."

BAD BLOOD

"What about your job?" he asked.

"Oh, I only fill in for others when I want to," she replied, then skipped ahead of him and turned around to walk backward. "And since this afternoon, I don't want to."

"I meant your job as a reporter," Jesse said.

"That's just something I do on the side sometimes."

"You have to make it your focus if you ever want to be a newspaper editor," he said. "That's what you told me you wanted."

"There's not a lot of newsworthy things going on around here."

"What about the three attempts on your Navy friend's life?" Jesse asked. "I wonder who would want him dead."

"Russia, China, Cuba, North Korea..." Gina replied. "That's what everyone thinks, anyway."

"What do *you* think?"

She stopped her backward walking and looked up at Jesse. "I wonder why they wouldn't torture him for what he knows first."

"Exactly," Jesse replied, taking her hand. "Which one's your sister's car?"

"Guess," Gina said, standing on the curb. "If you get it right, you get a kiss."

Jesse looked down at her and grinned. "That's it?"

She smiled back. "Well, there's no telling what that kiss might *lead* to. But the kiss is the prize. Which one?"

Jesse had already surveyed the parking lot when they'd arrived and gotten out of Juliet's car. There were seven vehicles in the mostly vacant parking lot.

His eyes scanned the cars again, ignoring two that had out-of-state tags. Two more looked like rental cars. That left three—a thirty-three percent chance with just a wild guess.

His eyes moved from one of the three cars to the next.

"The white Pinto."

45

She looked up at him. "Lucky guess," she said, taking his hand and leading him toward the small Ford.

"Not really," he replied. "Two are from out of state, and two more are almost new, probably rentals. That left the pickup, the Chrysler, or the Pinto."

He paused beside the car and tapped the Bob Marley sticker in the bottom left of the back window. "One Love."

On his first time to the Keys with Rusty, right after they'd finished boot camp, they'd gone out to a little island he and his friends called Party Island, to meet a bunch of them. A guy had a guitar and Rachel had sung the Marley tune.

Gina opened the back door and took her bag from Jesse. "You remembered."

"I'm cursed with an eye for details," Jesse replied.

"I wouldn't call that a curse," she replied, as he opened the driver's door and she got in.

He walked around the car and opened the passenger door. "What if I were to tell you the tag numbers of all seven cars parked here?"

Without thinking, he reached down and pulled the seat release lever, moving it back a good four inches before getting in.

"You can do that?" she asked, as he pulled the door closed.

Jesse felt cramped with the seat all the way back, but he felt that way in a lot of places, even the backseat of Pap's land yacht.

"The guy at the desk at the motel is named Craig," Jesse said. "Saw it on a letter he was reading. His car's parked near the entrance, a 1972 Chevy pickup, license plate 38WW-261. There's a dent in the right front fender with no rust around the exposed metal, so it was recent. Things rust fast here."

She started the car and looked over at him, amazed. "All that stuff stays stored in your head?"

He shrugged. "I wouldn't say stored," he replied. "It's just there if

I need it. I can't really explain it."

The car was a four-speed manual, and Gina drove it with no trouble at all; it responded nimbly in her hands.

"Do you remember everything with such clarity?" she asked, glancing over at him as she turned left through a yellow light onto the highway.

He grinned at her, one corner of his mouth higher than the other. "I remember every detail about this afternoon. And I remember you owe me a kiss."

When they pulled into the motel, Gina parked beside Juliet's car and the couple came out of their room before Jesse even got out.

"Did you get everything you need?" Juliet asked Gina as they met outside her and Jesse's room.

Gina grabbed Jesse's arm as he put her bag next to the door.

"Everything and then some," she replied.

"I don't know about y'all," Rusty said, "but I'm starved. Where're we gonna eat?"

"How about Dockside?" Jesse suggested. "We want to go to your dad's place and get your boat anyway, right?"

Rusty shook his head. "I just got off the phone with Pop. He's gonna bring it around this evening for us. About 2100, he said."

Jesse nodded at a small table between the rooms. "We have a grill; is there a store nearby? We could grab a few things and make our own food—save a little money."

"Just past the marina," Gina replied. "I like that idea. Do you know how to cook on a hibachi grill?" Gina asked. "You don't seem the domestic type."

Jesse grinned. "Cooking meat over a fire is about as far removed from domesticated as you can get. I vote burgers and fries by the pool."

Chapter Seven

◆━━◆━━◆━━◆━━◆

An hour later, dripping wet and wearing only his bathing suit, with a towel draped over his shoulders, Jesse was turning burgers on the grill.

When they'd returned from the store, he and Rusty had dived into the water at the end of the dock and raced one another a couple hundred yards out into the Gulf while the girls put the groceries away and changed into bathing suits.

The little kitchen between the two rooms had a deep-fryer and Rusty was inside, making French fries, while the girls lay beside the pool, catching the last of the sun's rays.

Jesse looked over the grill at Gina, reclined in a lounge seat.

She was wearing big white sunglasses and her sun-streaked blond hair hung loose around her shoulders. A white bikini contrasted sharply with her dark tan.

Jesse looked down at his white legs and feet. The whole summer's sun had been lost to boots and utility uniforms. He had tan lines halfway down his biceps and around his neck.

He promised himself he'd correct that while he was on leave and try to get outside more—without boots and utes—just as soon as it warmed up enough at Camp Lejeune. He'd heard about a great beach near the base.

He looked over at the girls again as Gina turned onto her side to say something to Juliet, propping her head on a cocked elbow with one leg scissored over the other. The position greatly accentuated the swell of Gina's hips and the narrowness of her waist.

Though not legally an adult for another three months, Jesse was a man in every physical sense, and the view excited him. Gina wasn't the type he'd dated in high school. He'd mostly dated girls who were taller, and she was barely more than Juliet'a height.

"Fries are done," Rusty said, as Jesse flipped another burger onto a plate with a folded paper towel on it to absorb the grease.

"Carry them on out," Jesse said. "One more minute with the last two burgers."

Rusty continued out to the pool as Jesse flipped the burgers on the small grill. The girls had said they only wanted one each and one of the grills was busted so he could only do four at a time. His and Rusty's second burgers were slowing him down.

Finally, he slid the last one onto the plate, laid the spatula on the sideboard, and started toward the pool, leaving the small fire to burn itself out.

That's when he saw the two guys with Rusty.

They were trouble. Jesse sensed it immediately from his friend's posture.

Behind Rusty, Gina and Juliet were sitting on their lounge chairs, facing one another, but heads turned and looking at Rusty and the two men.

One of them said something and Juliet started to stand.

Jesse sized the two men up instantly. Both were tall, nearly six feet, though one was slightly taller. Both were half a foot taller than Rusty and Jesse guessed their weight at less than two hundred pounds.

Two hundred was Jesse's benchmark.

If an opponent was more than fifteen pounds under his 215, it wouldn't matter if they were armed or not. His early training in martial arts, and subsequent Marine hand-to-hand combat training, coupled with his size, strength, natural agility and speed, meant the outcome was a foregone conclusion.

"Here," Jesse said to Juliet, as he passed between her and Gina.

Without thinking, she took the plate of burgers.

Jesse didn't slow his stride and in three steps, he was beside his buddy. He smiled at the two men. "If I'd known you were inviting friends, Rusty, I'd have made more burgers."

Jesse could tell the man standing in front of him was the leader of the two, simply by his stance.

Still smiling, Jesse said in a low, calm voice, "So you'll have to come back later. After we've eaten."

Rusty was only small in stature. At just five-six, and tipping the scales at a buck-sixty, he was lean and solid, with powerful legs and shoulders. He could hold his own against much bigger Marines, so Jesse wasn't worried about these two.

And Rusty's heart was as big as the ocean. He'd give the two guys his shirt and his food, if he felt they needed it.

The bigger of the two, the dark-haired guy standing in front of Jesse, started to say something, but Jesse raised a hand.

"I'm not going to say it *two* times," he said in a low and menacing tone, the smile gone as he glared at the man in front of him. "At the count of three, no matter what else happens, I'm going to break your nose."

"One," Rusty said, scowling up at the other man.

He'd understood Jesse's signal.

Neither man made a move, but the bigger one's expression changed slightly. Jesse saw it in his eyes. The fight or flight instinct.

A tiny part of the human brain controls the instinct to run away from danger or stand and face it. The trouble with most people was they didn't follow their instincts.

Their chance to run had come and gone.

"Two," Jesse said, softly.

Instantly, both he and Rusty unleashed their right fists, catching both men flush in the middle of the face.

Behind them, one of the girls screamed.

Jesse followed through with his punch, stepping forward with fists ready to deliver another blow.

But it wasn't necessary.

The two would-be assailants staggered back a step, dropped to their knees with blood flowing from busted noses, then toppled over, out cold.

Jesse glanced around, taking everything in and processing it in a microsecond.

There was nobody else around.

Rusty looked up at Jesse as they turned and started back toward the girls. "Mine hit the ground first, bro."

Jesse grinned. "Mine was a little taller."

"Oh, my God," Gina said. "Did you—"

"They'll get up in a minute and scurry away like a coupla palmetto bugs," Rusty said. "Might have to get their noses straightened, but they'll be okay."

Jesse turned as he heard a groan. The two men were slowly getting to their feet, pinching noses and shaking heads to clear the cobwebs.

The shorter guy was helping the other one onto all fours. They both glanced once toward Jesse and his friends, eyes open, but brains still partially shut down. The bigger guy blinked his eyes hard—probably still seeing double after the crashing blow to his face. Then they hurried off, staggering toward the highway fifty yards away.

"See?" Rusty said. "A coupla roaches."

BAD BLOOD

Jesse followed the men's movements until they disappeared. He hoped it was over.

Sure, they were bullies, picking on one smaller guy, maybe just to show off to the girls. That didn't mean one of them didn't have a screw loose in his head and a gun in his car.

He turned toward Gina and forced a smile. "Maybe we should just eat inside."

Chapter Eight

◆━━◆━━◆━━◆

There weren't many places better than Key West in the dead of winter. At least that was Chuck's perspective. He'd come down to the island city five years earlier and decided it was the place for him.

The Allegheny Mountains around Pittsburgh could get damned cold in wintertime. But here, even on the coldest days, the girls could still wear skimpy outfits.

Chuck stood on the dock at Mallory Square, looking out toward one of the coolest sunsets he'd seen in months. His customers were back aboard their cruise ship, now almost a mile away, and probably flying high over the wave tops, mesmerized by the distant orange ball.

And Chuck's pockets were full of cash.

He relit a joint and took a long drag, then quickly snuffed it out on his tongue. It was far too expensive to allow a single tendril of smoke to curl away from the tip.

His cousin's pot had been every bit as good as what he was forced to buy now, but his cousin had only charged half the price.

For years, they'd made a killing, growing it and selling it by the joint, mostly to tourists and cruise ship passengers.

Chuck knew the average Midwesterner wouldn't take the risk of bringing a stash from home on a plane prior to boarding their ship. So for many of them, when they got off the ship, they were looking to score.

Chuck figured if they were paying all that money for a floating hotel room, and twenty dollars for a crummy Key West T-shirt, then ten bucks for a primo doobie wasn't asking too much.

"Hey, Chuck," a young blonde said as she approached.

Carly was about Chuck's age, tiny, fit, and as cute as they came. She worked part-time during the day, while her kids were at school and her husband at his job over on the Navy base.

Chuck nodded at her. "Hi, Carly." He noted her downturned expression. "Hard day?"

She blew out her breath and looked toward the south at the ship now on the horizon. "Almost all European tourists."

Chuck understood. Many visitors from Europe didn't tip. It's not that they were assholes or anything; they just didn't do that over there. He guessed French and German waitresses and bartenders were paid a regular salary like any other job. But in Key West, they survived on tips.

"Sorry to hear that," he said, taking a rolled joint from his pocket and offering it to her. "On the house."

Sometimes Carly paid him, sometimes she didn't. The joints cost him a little over a buck apiece, and he sold them for two to locals and ten to tourists.

She'd catch up when she could. And if she didn't, no big deal. The markup to the tourists was a thousand percent and covered his philanthropy.

"Thanks, man," Carly said, accepting the gift, then breaking a cookie in two and offering half to him. "How was your day?"

He smiled at the tiny blonde and accepted the morsel. It was still warm.

"Not great," he replied, popping it into his mouth. "Mmm, that's good. You just made my day a little better."

"Thanks again, Chuck," she said and started to turn away.

"Carly, wait," he said, reaching into his twenty-dollar pocket. He handed her one of the bills and said, "You forgot your tip for the cookie."

Chuck always wore nice clothes, but one thing he insisted on was four pockets. He kept singles in one, fives in another, tens in his left hip, and twenties in the right. If he had to make change, he didn't want to pull out a wad of bills. Especially in his business.

She looked up at him for a moment, then glanced at the bill.

"Go ahead," Chuck said. "If it helps, my mom was from France. Let me make it up a little. For my people."

Carly smiled and nodded, taking the offered money. "Thank you, Chuck. It's not easy here."

"Believe me, I know," he replied. "It's very easy to lose faith in people, though. Am I right?"

She offered a sad smile. He'd heard about what had happened with her husband.

He shrugged. "Pothead wisdom."

Carly giggled, thanked him again, and turned toward Duval Street, her short ponytail bouncing from side to side.

Just then, the pager on Chuck's Italian belt vibrated, so he plucked it out of its holder, pressed the button and saw a local number followed by 911.

It's always an emergency, he thought, as he turned away from the sunset and headed toward the corner phone booth.

He considered ignoring the page. He only had about half an ounce left, and his new supplier was sometimes sporadic on the weekend. He smoked too much of his own product.

So had Chuck and his pals back in the day. And still now, Chuck could party all night with the best frat boys. Just not as often. Those days were mostly behind him; he was almost thirty.

He stopped and looked at the phone booth on the wall for a

moment, then sighed and stepped toward it. He picked up the receiver and dropped a coin in the slot, then dialed the number on his pager.

"Hello," a man said.

"You paged me," Chuck replied, his tone flat and composed. "Who is this?"

"It's Gary, man. Gary King. Up in Marathon. I used to run with your cousin."

Chuck remembered the guy. Gary had sold quarter ounces for Chuck's cousin back in the day.

"What ya need, Gary? I'm pretty tapped out right at the moment."

"Nothin' man," the guy replied. "Got some four-one-one I think your cousin probably wants to know, though."

"Yeah, what's that?" Chuck asked, watching two very attractive young ladies crossing the street toward him.

He smiled. *Dancers from Key West Bar.*

"Remember those two jarheads who got your cousin busted?" Gary asked, as the girls smiled back at Chuck. "They're back in town."

The smile at the prospect of the evening's entertainment dissolved from Chuck's face.

"Where?" he demanded.

"A quarter ounce?" Gary asked. "Times are tough since he went down, man."

The two strippers stopped and stood just off the curb, smiling up at Chuck. Both were dressed in snug-fitting club dresses that barely covered their crotches.

"Yeah, whatever," Chuck said, wondering if he needed to act right away on the information he was about to learn. "Where are they?"

"Blue Water Motel in Marathon," Gary said. "I dunno what rooms, but they're there with two chicks and one of them's the sister of the bitch who testified."

Rachel Albert's little sister, Gina, Chuck thought.

He smiled at the girls, but it wasn't a happy smile.

The shorter of the two guys who got Bear busted and burned their crop was a local named Thurman, so the other chick would be his girlfriend, Julie something.

Both girls had disappeared the same day as the two jarheads, even while the reporter's sister was in the hospital.

If Gina was with the tall one and they were all staying at a motel and not at Thurman's place, then they'd be busy long enough for him to sit on the information for a few hours.

He smiled at the strippers again. *Maybe just sit on it until morning.*

The enticing looks from the two girls sealed his decision.

"Thanks," he said, then hung up the phone without taking his eyes off the girls.

"We wanna party, Chucky," the shorter brunette said.

Chuck remembered her name was Crystal, though it was probably her stage name.

Chuck stepped off the curb and put an arm around each woman's waist, pulling them toward Duval and his apartment at La Concha.

"Well then, Crystal, I don't think we should delay it any longer," he said, as his hands roamed farther down, feeling the taut muscles of the dancers' asses as they walked.

The jarheads could wait.

Chapter Nine

After dinner, and more importantly, after enough time had passed that Jesse was certain the two men weren't returning, the four of them went back outside to the little porch to talk and wait for Rusty's dad.

Jesse thought the motel was nice. It was clean, looked organized and well-maintained, and each room had a small, covered porch, with an outdoor love seat, two chairs, and a low rattan coffee table.

Gina took the love seat and pulled Jesse down beside her.

"How did you know Jesse wasn't counting to three?" Juliet asked Rusty, as she sat down on one of the chairs.

"He said *two* instead of twice," Rusty replied, taking the remaining seat across from Juliet. "When he was warnin' the guy. Most folks woulda said something like, 'I'm not sayin' this *twice*,' but Jesse said he wasn't gonna say it *two* times."

"I was hoping you picked up on that," Jesse said. "Otherwise, mine definitely would've hit the ground first."

Rusty laughed, but the girls didn't.

Another young couple was in the shallow part of the pool, splashing with a little girl who looked to be about four or five. The young parents glanced over occasionally and said a few words in whispers.

"They're talking about you," Gina said quietly, leaning against Jesse on the small love seat. "You stand out in any crowd."

Rusty chuckled. "And of the three of us Conchs, I'm tallest, and still nine inches shorter'n this big ape."

"Who? Who?" Jesse grunted like a gorilla.

The girls giggled and Rusty laughed. "I said ya'd fit right in down here, bro."

Jesse looked toward the couple again. "I think they're wondering if that blood on the pool deck's from one of us."

"I didn't think about that," Juliet said. "Why'd you have to go and hit them? You could've just said 'Boo!' and they'd have run off."

"They deserved it," Gina stated flatly. "After what they said."

Jesse glanced over at Rusty. "What did they say?"

"The one I dropped made a nasty remark about Jewels."

Jesse felt a knot in his stomach tighten as his jaw clenched. He still felt on edge, and little angered him more than a man who was insulting or disrespectful to a woman.

He wanted to change the subject before he decided to follow the blood trail like a hungry wolf. "Where're we diving tomorrow?" he asked, though his mind was a long way from it.

"Won't be until afternoon," Rusty said. "Pop also told me there'd be weather in the mornin', so I promised to come over and help him with an outboard."

"We can go there early if you want," Jesse suggested. "I'll help and when we're done, Gina's going to take me to get some new civvies. All the clothes I had at the base were in my seabag and it was only half full."

A soft, burbling sound from out on the water grew steadily louder.

"That'll be Pop," Rusty said, getting to his feet.

Rusty's boat came into view, idling out of the darkness and into the low lights along the two sides of the canal.

The four of them ran over to the dock and spotted Rusty's mom,

Dreama, standing by the bow with a coiled dock line in her hands.

"Hey, Mom," Rusty said. "I didn't know you were coming, too."

She handed the line to Rusty, and he quickly snubbed it to a cleat as Shorty reversed the engine.

Though in her forties, Dreama Thurman was a slim and attractive woman with sparkling green eyes, auburn hair, and a friendly smile.

"We both wanted to talk to you," Dreama said, stepping down lightly onto the dock.

Jesse took a line Shorty handed him and looked over at his friend's mom. "Oh, hey, we can make ourselves—"

"No need," Shorty said with a smile, as Jesse tied the line off. "It's nothing overly personal and your and Gina's insight might help."

Jesse and Rusty grabbed the love seat from the porch in front of his and Juliet's room and made a square seating area around the coffee table.

"Can I get anyone anything?" Jesse asked, looking at Shorty. "Beer? Soda?"

"A couple of beers would be nice," Dreama replied. "Thank you, Jesse."

"Me too," Rusty called out to Jesse as he made his way inside.

Gina followed him, and Jesse pulled a six-pack of beer bottles out of the refrigerator. When he reached for glasses, Gina stopped him.

"Not on her account," she said. "I've known Miss Dreama all my life and never saw her drink beer from a glass. I wonder what they want?"

"Maybe we should wait here," Jesse whispered. "Let them get started on whatever it is."

"I'm thirsty," Rusty called out. "What's takin' so long?"

Jesse shrugged and followed Gina back out to the porch.

Rusty passed the beers around, and once everyone was settled, he looked up at his father. "So, what's this all about, Pop? If it's about us staying at a—"

"Nonsense, James," Dreama said. "You are a grown man and Juliet a grown woman. You're engaged and what you do is none of my and your father's business."

"It's about the bait shop," Shorty said. "I'm thinkin' on sellin'."

"What?" Rusty blurted. "It's been in our family for—"

"I know, son," Shorty said. "But me and your mom, well, we ain't gettin' any younger. Prices what they are, we can retire, enjoy life, and still leave a monster of a nest egg for you and JJ when we're gone."

Rusty looked back and forth at his parents, finally settling on his father. "You sick?"

"We're both perfectly healthy," Dreama said, affectionately patting her son's knee. "We just want to see more of the world."

"Your great-great-grandpa built the place," Rusty said. "Captain Augustus's son was born in the house he built. His son, then your dad, you, and me... we were all born in that house."

Jesse hadn't known Rusty long, but he knew he was very proud of his heritage. He knew his ancestry all the way back to the early whaling days in colonial New England.

"And they all *died* there in that house, son," Shorty replied. "Just stories in dusty old books." He paused and gazed at Rusty. "We were offered over a million, son."

"Is that all?" Jesse asked. "The land alone is worth that much."

Everyone looked at Jesse. He shrugged. "I saw a real estate flyer for vacant property when we checked in. Two-and-a-half acres here on Key Vaca, unimproved, no utilities, $135,000."

"We can't sell it all," Shorty said. "Just the part that's not the wetland. About twenty acres."

"If you divide 135,000 by two-and-a-half..." Jesse said, thinking, "that's over fifty grand an acre. Times twenty acres is one million."

"It's a million bucks," Shorty repeated. "Nobody in my family has ever had that kind of money."

"Sure they have," Jesse said. "They lived on it all their lives."

"Jesse's right, Pop," Rusty said. "You should check with your real estate friend."

Shorty hung his head. "I did," he mumbled. "Sky said the property is worth more if the bait shop and house was gone."

"My grandfather would say the same thing, sir," Jesse said. "It's been happening in Fort Myers for years. They'll bulldoze everything, including the wetland, and build a condo or something. Paying the fine for 'accidentally' destroying the wetland area is nothing compared to the profit. Just think about it for a second. Six floors, and four luxury units a floor, all with a sunrise view of Key Vaca Bight. They'd go for half a million each, easy. The developer's investment in buying your land, leveling it, *and* paying the fine will be covered with the pre-sell of three units. Those will go to investors before they even close on your property. By the time the heavy equipment arrives, they'll have already presold half the units for a profit of four million, and another six just waiting to be sold."

"You sure seem to know a whole lot about real estate, son," Shorty began, surprised.

Jesse shrugged again, feeling a little self-conscious. "I just remember things and am good with numbers. All that's just an estimate, but my grandfather pointed out dozens of places around Fort Myers where developers did the same thing."

"We can buy it," Juliet said, sitting up straight. "We have enough for a down payment at least. We can borrow the rest and we'll match their offer."

Dreama shook her head. "No, no, sweetie, that's your *house* money. You two have been saving it up since the sixth-grade dance."

"It would only have been a temporary home," Juliet said. "Jim's always talked about turning the bait shop into a restaurant one day, and us living there, raising our kids in the same house where he was born."

Shorty placed his beer on the table. "I didn't know it meant that much to you, son. But what we have in mind wouldn't go far if we carry a loan, and besides, you still have three-and-a-half years committed to Uncle Sam."

"I can run it," Juliet declared. "My dad will do the work—he already said so—whenever the time comes. I'll find a good cook and we'll serve breakfast and lunch at the Rusty Anchor."

"No way," Rusty objected. "My wife's not workin' a bar while I'm off in the Corps."

"You've already chosen a name?" Dreama asked, surprised.

"Well, yeah," Rusty replied. "Me and Jewels talked about it when we went to the Bahamas last fall."

"Will it make money?" Jesse asked. "What's the ratio of income between the bar and bait shop?"

"The bar makes more," Shorty replied, looking at Jesse with a puzzled expression. "We've survived."

"He's being humble," Dreama said. "We've never lacked for any *want*, much less need. The bar pays all the bills, and the bait shop is play money."

"I'll cover the difference," Jesse said. "Under one condition."

"You?" Shorty scoffed. Then, when he saw Jesse's serious expression, he gave him another puzzled look. "You have money, son?"

"My dad left a servicemen's group life insurance policy for my mom when he was killed in Vietnam, and when she died, that money, as well as her life insurance and the sale of our house—all they'd saved up, everything—all went into a trust fund in my name." Jesse sat forward in his seat. "It's just been sitting there, growing for ten years,

Mr. Thurman. Pap taught me a lot of things, and one of the biggest was when and how to invest my money wisely."

"You said there's a condition?" Dreama asked.

Jesse looked around the table. "My deal is," he continued, with a half grin, "you have to stay on until Rusty gets out of the Corps. It's only forty-two months. And besides, you have a lot of planning to do, and things to buy, right? You can't just jump on a plane tomorrow. Plus, when you get tired of jet-setting around the world, you'll have a place to come home to and retire."

"You're serious, bro?" Rusty said, leaning forward.

Jesse looked across the table at his friend. "Pap always told me to never invest in any *thing*. He said to only invest in *people*. That money's just been sitting there since I was eight. You can easily repay it before I retire from the Corps in thirty years. Until then, I won't need it."

Shorty sat forward on the edge of his seat and spoke to Rusty. "We can hold off a few years, son, if the place means that much to you. It's been mortgaged several times over the years, but it's always stayed in the family."

Jesse stood and offered his hand to Shorty. "I can call Pap's accountant and have the money sent down on Monday."

Shorty and Rusty both stood, and Shorty shook Jesse's hand, then glanced at Rusty. "I'm in, if he is."

Jesse extended his hand to Rusty. "Monthly payments, thirty years, a third of the going interest rate, and anything extra you want to pay goes to the principal. Pap's accountant will handle everything, and I'll just be a really silent partner who gets to dive and fish for free when I come down for a visit."

"You got a deal!" Rusty said, grinning and gripping Jesse's hand tightly. "But ya better make that Tuesday. Monday's New Year's Day."

Chapter Ten

They talked about Rusty and Juliet's plans for the place for nearly an hour before Dreama announced they needed to get back. So, Rusty and Juliet drove them home.

Jesse sat on the porch, his feet on the table. He couldn't believe what had happened. He was now the co-owner of a bait shop and bar in the Keys, which was about to have the bait shop demolished to expand the business that made more money.

"Here, Daddy Warbucks," Gina said, handing him a beer and settling in beside him.

Jesse chuckled.

"What's funny?"

"I own a bar I can't drink in," he said. "And a girlfriend who brings me a beer."

"Is that what I am?" she asked. "Your girlfriend?"

He smiled in the darkness. "I'd like that," he said softly. "But we won't see each other for long stretches."

"You told me your mom did it," she replied, "and your grandmother."

"Does that mean...?"

She nodded her head, smiling brightly. "We can make it work."

He raised his bottle, and she clinked it with hers.

"There is one thing, though," she said, sitting back for a moment.

"What?"

"When were you going to tell me about the money?"

He smiled again, then put an arm around her and pulled her close.

"I'm glad you didn't ask how much."

"How do you know all that stuff?" Gina asked. "I mean, yeah, you showed me your perfect recall. I checked the tag on the pickup when we pulled in. But an hour ago, you sounded like a financial advisor or something."

"Half my classes in my senior year were college-credited," he replied. "Pap's accountant was the teacher in two of my business class electives."

"You think he's going to be okay with it? Your grandfather?"

Jesse nodded. "I think so. Shorty and Dreama raised Rusty there and they were comfortable. Increasing the size of the part of the business that makes the most money doesn't take a rocket surgeon."

"A rocket...? That's a mixed metaphor."

Jesse grinned. "And you know this because you're a reporter. Words have meaning." Abruptly, he changed the subject. "What else do you know about Scott Ingersoll?"

She lightly pounded a fist on his chest, then flattened her hand and caressed it. "You walked me right into that, didn't you?"

"When people are relaxed and comfortable, they become who they really are. Now... Scott Ingersoll?"

"He's a petty officer something in the Navy," she replied.

"Chief petty officer?" Jesse asked. "Petty officer second class? First Class?"

"First class," she replied, sitting up and looking at him. "Why's that important?"

"That's an E-6, same as a Marine staff sergeant. It means he's probably been in the Navy for at least six years, and likely no more than twelve."

"I don't think he's thirty yet," she said. "So that sounds about right. The Navy sent him to college to get an engineering degree. I know his wife better. They have two boys... about seven and nine. I'm not real sure."

"What's his job in the Navy?" Jesse asked.

"I don't know," she replied, leaning on his shoulder again. "But he has to go away a lot. Not for real long—a day or two—and sometimes like a week or more. Then he's home for a few weeks and gone again."

"Where does he go?"

"I don't know that, either," she replied, "But it can't be far. Most of his trips are just daytrips, and he's back in the evening."

"How do you know all this?" Jesse asked.

BAD BLOOD

She lifted her head and gave him a puzzled look. "The same way half the people on this island know we're here in this motel room. Everyone knows everyone else's business."

Jesse's head came up, eyes scanning the parking lot. "Who knows we're here?"

"I'm sure a few," Gina said, running her hand across his chest. "Maybe not half the island, but we did see a few people we knew already. Word gets around."

It made Jesse a little uncomfortable for Gina, knowing that people he didn't know might be talking about what they were doing there.

She looked up at him. "Does it bother you?"

"Not me, personally," he replied honestly, looking down at her. Gina was beautiful and smart. Anyone who saw him with her would think he was a lucky guy. "I don't know more than ten people in all the Keys and half of those were sitting right here a few minutes ago. I just don't like knowing people might be talking about *you*."

She smiled. "You might not know *them*," she said, "but since your last visit, most everyone around here knows who you are. And quite a few know I went with you for a week in the Bahamas. It's a really small community."

"What about you?" he asked. "I hope what people say... I don't know."

"When anyone asked me," she said, "I told them I spent the week with you in the Bahamas, and it doesn't bother me in the least what they think about it."

She nestled her head against his chest again and Jesse smiled.

"So, Ingersoll's an enlisted man with an engineering degree," Jesse said, steering the conversation back on course. "He's not an officer nor a high-ranking enlisted man. But the Navy paid for his schooling. Do you know how rare that is?"

"You have some college," she replied.

"A few accounting credits," he replied. "All on my own. I know a few enlisted guys with degrees, but they did it on *their* own too, using the GI Bill. But for the military to pay for it meant he must have shown great aptitude. And with a degree, most enlisted Marines would probably be trying to get into officer candidate school."

"So why doesn't Scott?" she asked. "It'd be a raise, right?"

"Maybe," Jesse said. "He'd start as an O-1, and I'd think a staff sergeant with six years of service would make about the same, if not more. But from where he is now, advancement is limited, since there are only three more enlisted ranks above him. As a brand-new officer, there are nine higher ranks. So his remaining an enlisted man was probably not a financial decision for him."

"What else then?"

"The needs of the Corps always come first," Jesse replied. "And I'd guess it's the same in the Navy. He might be in a necessary enlisted MOS and has to serve so many years doing that job to cover his free tuition."

"What's an MOS?"

"Military occupational specialty," he replied. "In the Navy they're called ratings. Basically, it's your job in the military."

"What's your MOS?" she asked.

"Oh-three-eleven, for now. A basic infantryman."

"His... I guess primary workplace... is probably at the Navy base," Gina said. "At least that's where he goes *most* days."

"When he leaves on these day trips," Jesse asked, thinking, "does he drive or fly?"

"He flies," she replied. "A small, twin-engine Navy plane. I know his wife, Carly, but not well. She's a waitress at a place I go to a lot when I'm down there on assignment."

Jesse grinned and hugged her closer. "See? There are news stories in the Keys."

"Key *West*, yeah," she replied. "These days, once you get past Stock Island, it's a different world."

"In what way?" Jesse asked.

"You know," she said. "They're a little... crazier down there."

"No, I don't," Jesse replied. "I've only been there once, and that was when I was a kid."

Gina looked up at him and smiled. "Then that's where we'll go shopping. It's... different down there, but they do have some great stores."

"And your friend, Scott, lives down there?"

"He and Carly live on Stock Island," Gina replied. "Nobody who actually *lives* in Key West works a nine-to-five job."

"We should see him," Jesse said, intrigued to meet a man who'd survived several attempts on his life. "Ask a few questions."

"Like what?"

"You're the reporter," Jesse replied. "The right questions will come to you, but we at least want to know how the attacks were made."

Gina sat up as headlights turned in from the highway. "A knife to the neck, a gun, and poison."

Juliet turned her re-keyed Keys car into a spot, then shut off the engine before she and Rusty climbed out.

"Ya ain't gonna believe what I just heard," Rusty said, a grave look on his face as the two of them approached.

"What happened?" Gina asked, as she and Jesse stood up.

"Somebody tried to kill Scott Ingersoll, again," Jesse said.

Rusty stopped dead in his tracks. "How the hell did you—"

"Just a guess," Jesse replied. "You looked really concerned, and somebody has tried three times and failed. What happened?"

"He's gotta be the luckiest guy in the world," Rusty said. "Somebody put a bomb in his car."

Jesse's eyes widened. "And you call that lucky?"

"They think it had a motion sensor," Juliet said.

"And a drunk in a rental crashed into his car," Rusty added.

"Was anyone hurt?"

Rusty chuckled. "The rental had one of those air bags and it hit the tourist guy in the face. He's got a coupla black eyes, a busted nose, and a whopper of a vacation story to tell."

Juliet yawned and covered her mouth. "Sorry. I've been up since before dawn."

"Me too," Rusty said. "Been a long, hard day."

"We should get some sleep," Gina suggested, squeezing Jesse's hand, then whispered in his ear, "It's going to be a long, hard night, too."

Chapter Eleven

◆◆◆◆

When Jesse opened his eyes, the surroundings didn't seem familiar, but he'd lived out of a seabag in seven different places in the past seven months, so waking up to new surroundings was nothing new.

He sat up slightly in the bed, stuffing another pillow under his shoulders as he listened and took stock.

Outside the window over the bed, he could hear the sound of a soft rain, with heavier drops falling from the edge of the roof.

But the rain didn't dampen the spirits of several birds, all chirping and singing at once.

He felt Gina's warmth beside him under the thin sheet, which covered less than half of her. She stirred.

"Timezit?" she murmured, looking up at him through a tangled mess of sun-streaked blond hair.

"Almost dawn," Jesse whispered, still listening to the sounds outside the window. "Six-thirty."

Gina rolled onto her side, the sheet riding up and exposing her thigh as she propped herself up and looked around.

She was wearing Jesse's T-shirt, which looked like a long-sleeved dress on her small frame, reaching her mid-thigh. He knew she had nothing under it.

"Okay, I give," she said, becoming more alert. "You don't wear a watch, and there isn't a clock in this room."

"Listen," Jesse whispered.

Gina moved closer, nestled against him, and draped an arm over his torso. "It's raining," she said softly.

"Besides that," Jesse whispered.

"Birds chirping."

"Several warblers in the bushes behind us," Jesse replied, turning toward her and pushing a strand of hair from her face. "They start thirty or forty minutes before dawn."

"Tall, handsome, strong, responsible," she said, reaching her arm around him and snuggling closer. "A great lover... photographic memory... college-educated... And now nature boy? The hits just keep coming."

Jesse laughed lightly. "Nature boy?"

"Outdoorsman?"

"That describes my friend, Billy," Jesse said. "He can track an otter through knee-deep marsh. I just remember things that are associated with other things. Warblers and other songbirds are predictable. It's called the 'dawn chorus' and they were my alarm clock growing up."

"What do you associate with me?"

He slowly traced a line with his fingertips up her thigh and over her hip. "When I touch you... here."

She moaned and moved under his hand.

"I want to get a shower before we go over to the Thurmans'," she said, running her leg up his while her hand moved along his ribs. "It's big enough for both of us."

He grinned as he drew her closer. "It's like you were reading my mind."

BAD BLOOD

An hour later, when Jesse stepped outside, the sky was a uniform gray in every direction. He couldn't feel any wind, and the light rain fell straight down.

Jesse knew this kind of weather, since his hometown was only about 140 miles north, just up the southwest coast. Judging by the pools of water in certain places, he guessed it had started raining more than three hours ago, and it didn't look like it was stopping any time soon.

They were socked in. But at least he wasn't crawling through mud in an urban warfare training exercise.

A steady stream of cars passed in both directions on the highway, the swish from tires on wet pavement nearly a constant hiss, rising and falling quickly as each car passed.

Gina came out and joined Jesse on the porch, pulling the door closed behind her. "Think they're up yet?" she asked, looking to the right.

Jesse wore jeans, sneakers, and a yellow T-shirt with the Marine emblem on the back in full color. He'd just bought it from the exchange a week earlier, and it was one of the few shirts he owned that fit well.

By contrast, Gina was dressed like she was going to a beach party or something, wearing a pale-blue, sleeveless blouse and navy shorts that were high-waisted and tight-fitting, which made her legs look longer, even though she was a foot shorter than Jesse's six-three.

The door to Rusty and Juliet's room opened and Rusty stepped out, wearing shorts, flip-flops, and a long-sleeved shirt with the sleeves rolled up. Juliet was dressed similarly to Gina.

Jesse felt he looked like a tourist jarhead on leave. Which... he was.

"I was wonderin' if y'all were awake yet," Rusty grumbled,

sounding like his dad. "I need coffee."

"We might as well head over there now," Juliet said, looking up at the sky. "Your dad was right; it could rain all day."

"We'll follow you over," Gina said, getting her sister's keys from her purse. "Wanna stop at Dion's for some breakfast sandwiches?"

"Good idea," Rusty said, reaching in his pocket and handing Juliet a twenty-dollar bill. "Me and Jesse will take your car and we might even be done before you and Gina get there with breakfast."

Juliet looked up at Jesse as she traded Rusty her keys for the twenty. "I want to thank you again. A year from now, you won't have to stop for breakfast anywhere. As long as Rusty and I live, you have a place to stay in our house, and an open tab at the Rusty Anchor."

Jesse smiled and put his arm around Rusty. "I look forward to eating there one day, JJ."

"Yeah, well, I've seen you eat, bro," Rusty said with a chuckle. "So that part's within limitations."

"See you in about thirty minutes," Gina said, kissing Jesse before she and Juliet dashed through the rain to the Pinto.

"Don't forget the coffee!" Rusty called after them, getting a wave from Juliet.

Jesse opened the passenger door of Juliet's car and again ratcheted the seat all the way to the rear before getting into the small vehicle. His back was already soaked.

Rusty got in and started the engine, then turned to Jesse. "What Jewels said, bro. You ever need it, you got three hots and a cot here with us. Well, a double bed, anyway." Then he grinned. "Or maybe the aft cabin of Rachel and Gina's boat might suit ya better?"

"Drive the car, dumbass," Jesse said, then grinned.

Chapter Twelve

❖━━❖━━❖━━❖

They pulled out several cars behind the Pinto, and then half a mile later, Gina turned off to the right, and Rusty continued ahead.

Through the rain-streaked window, Jesse saw a sign reading, "Dion's Chicken. Best in the Keys."

Rusty slowed just a hundred yards later, then turned into the long, crushed-shell path to his parents' place. The dense canopy over the driveway dripped huge water droplets onto the roof as they drove slowly through the gloom.

"Are all your trips short like this?" Jesse asked. "I mean, when you lived here."

Rusty glanced over at him. "Normally, yeah. Key Vaca's only six miles long. Then seven miles over the bridge to the next island and ten to downtown Big Pine. Then there ain't much of anything for forty miles to Key West. Goin' the other way, there's just a few little towns until you get to Largo, forty miles north. If there's a wreck on any bridge, you're stuck. Except for Key West, Marathon's about the biggest town in the Keys, and we got everything we need right here."

"Even more reason to drive old clunkers," Jesse said, as they came out of the jungle and into the parking area. "The engine barely gets warmed up before you get where you're going."

There, under the old oak tree, parked in the exact spot where it had burned up, sat Jesse's Mustang. It sported stock wheels and tires, and a coat of black primer, with a thick sheet of plastic taped over where the back window had been before Bear blew it out.

The twin, back-swept radio antennas gave it away.

For a second, Jesse felt a pang of sadness, remembering how the deep, candy-maroon paint had reflected the sun. Then he felt a rush of white-hot rage as he remembered how the man who'd torched his car had beat up Gina's sister and brutally murdered another innocent woman just before her wedding.

"I, uh..." Rusty began. "I didn't tell Pop yet that you didn't want to keep it."

Rusty drove around the side of the bar, where Jesse saw Shorty on a ladder, with a large block and tackle rig dangling around his neck. He turned around to face them.

"Don't worry about it," Jesse said, opening the door, then getting out. He waited for his friend to climb out, then added, "It's just a material thing. Like us, it won't last forever. I don't know what to do with it right now."

Jesse strode through the rain, Rusty right beside him. The rain was falling a little harder and they were soon soaked. But the air was warm, as was the rain.

Shorty stepped down off the ladder. Above him was a thick limb from a live oak, and beside the ladder was a large outboard engine, lying on its side. Beyond the motor was a small wooden boat on a trailer.

"I was thinkin' you'd forgot," Shorty said, starting down. "You're a better tree climber'n me, Jim. Can you get that block tied off up there at the Y for me?"

"What's the engine weigh?" Jesse asked.

"More'n one man can lift, son," Shorty said, water streaming down his face and over his bare chest. "Took me and Gifford both to just set it down there out of his truck."

Rusty looked at the outboard, then at Jesse, and grinned.

"Put the block and tackle down, Pop," Rusty said. "Jesse here sometimes works as a forklift."

Jesse stepped over and looked at the engine, then peeled his shirt off. It was already soaked, but there was no sense in getting it dirty, too. He tested the weight at the heavy end.

The cover was off the engine and there was a large eyebolt attached to the upper cylinder head—a place to attach a moving block to, which would then allow one man to lift it easily with a double-pulley standing block tied to the tree limb.

"Do you have a thick piece of rope?" Jesse asked, measuring the height of the wooden boat's transom with his eyes. "At least half an inch thick? Or a nylon tow strap, a couple of inches wide?"

"I think I know what you're lookin' for," Rusty said, then trotted toward a small shed. "Be right back."

"You really think you can lift that by yourself?" Shorty asked. "It's gotta weigh at least two-fifty."

Jesse nodded. "I can lift it, but I won't be able to move with it much, just a few inches. Can you lift the tongue of the trailer, with Rusty standing in the back of the boat?"

"Yeah, easy. Tongue weight's only about a hundred pounds empty. With Jim in back, maybe fifty pounds."

"Here ya go," Rusty said, extending a two-inch tie-down strap with a ratchet.

"Yeah, that'll work," Jesse said.

"Wait till you see this, Pop," Rusty said. "I mean, yeah, he looks strong as a reef donkey, but this guy's... *freak* strong."

Jesse pulled the strap through the ratchet until there was only about three feet between the hooks attached to either end. Then he rolled the engine until it was face down, the mount on the ground.

"Get in the boat, son," Shorty said, as Jesse hiked his pants and did a few deep squats to loosen up. "This boy ain't foolin' around."

As Rusty scrambled aboard, Jesse put the strap around his neck, squatted low over the foot of the outboard, and reached around both sides to grip the mount.

He took a deep breath, then drove his feet into the ground, lifting the outboard to a standing position with its fin buried deep in the grass. The eyebolt was about belt level, so Jesse judged he'd have to lift the engine at least a foot.

Steadying the outboard with one hand, he attached both hooks to the eyebolt, then squatted behind it until the hooks were a few inches below his chin.

Jesse pulled the slack through the ratchet, clicked it a few times to lock the strap in place, then arched his back, ready.

He looked up at Rusty. "You be the guide. Bring the transom to me, okay?"

"Got it," Rusty said, then turned his head. "Lift her as high as ya can and still be able to control her, Pop."

Jesse heard a car pull up behind him as he took a deep breath, dropped his hips lower, and wrapped his long arms around the outboard.

As Jesse stood, lifting the full weight of the engine, Shorty's eyes went wide for a second before he quickly moved to the trailer's tongue.

Like a giant oak tree himself, feet firmly planted in the dirt, and the weight of the engine supported by his arms, shoulders, and neck, Jesse stood there, rain pouring down his body.

"C'mon back, Pop," Rusty said. "Straight back four feet."

Jesse felt sure the outboard was closer to three hundred pounds but set his jaw as the boat slowly rolled back toward him. He'd lifted a log in the same fashion that weighed four hundred pounds.

Out of the corner of his eye, Jesse saw Gina and Juliet step past him, taking cover under a small back porch, but he was focused on Rusty's face getting closer.

"A little right, Pop," Rusty said. "Okay, good. Straight now about two feet. One foot. Easy... easy. Hold it there, Pop!"

The boat stopped moving, and Shorty lowered the tongue's landing leg down.

Rusty braced his feet against both sides of the transom and took the mounting bracket in both hands. "Down easy, bro. I'll guide it. Maybe three inches, then it's over the transom."

With Rusty's hands on the mount, Jesse released his hold and gripped the sides of the lower cowling.

Slowly, he began to bend his knees and hips, his legs starting to shake a little from the strain, but in control.

"Quarter-inch to your right," Rusty said.

Jesse leaned slightly and continued down.

"There! Got it!"

Jesse lowered himself a little more to unhook the strap, but the engine kept going down with him.

"Whoa! Whoa!" Rusty shouted, scrambling backward. "Let me get outta the back first."

Rusty vaulted forward and the outboard came back up. Then he jumped to the ground and Jesse lowered the weight of the engine again. He could tell there was now very little tongue weight—the whole boat and trailer seemed balanced on the wheels like a teeter-totter.

"You might want to hold that down," Jesse said, his breathing labored. "This is a lot of engine for a little boat."

"Go grab a sandbag," Shorty told Rusty, then sat on the tongue to keep it down. "We're gonna have to move the boat up on the trailer some."

"Are you okay?" Gina asked from the porch, as Jesse

straightened himself, arching his back. "That was incredible. How much does that engine weigh?"

"Close to three hundred pounds," Jesse replied, stepping over to her, his breathing a little easier. "And I felt every one of them."

"Now you're all wet," she said, looking him over. "Not that that's a bad thing."

Rusty plopped a large sandbag on the trailer hitch, then he and Shorty came around the boat, water pouring down both their faces.

"Thanks for the help there, son," Shorty said. "If ya ever decide to leave the Marines, I hear Ringling is lookin' for a new strongman."

"Ya probably only need to move that winch post a foot forward," Rusty said to his dad. "That'll give ya back that hundred pound tongue weight."

"Is our shopping trip off now due to rain?" Gina asked.

"Oh, this'll blow out before eleven," Shorty said. "Where were you goin'?"

"Cayo Hueso," Gina replied.

"It's been slow movin'," Shorty offered, "but it *is* movin' a little to the northeast. It'll prolly clear out down there even earlier."

"You think so?" Jesse asked, looking up at the low, gray clouds.

"I know so, boy," Shorty replied with a grin. "But there'll be more later today. Prolly around two or three."

"Well, come on," Gina said, picking up Jesse's wet T-shirt. "Let's get you into some dry clothes."

Jesse chuckled. "I don't need dry clothes on to go buy *new* clothes."

Chapter Thirteen

◆◆◆◆

"This is Stock Island," Gina said, as the little Ford slowed. "Most of the people who work in Key West live over here. I can't believe you're from Fort Myers and have never been down here."

"We docked in Key West once," Jesse said, looking out the window on his side. "With my parents when I was a kid. We sailed down here on Dad's boat for Christmas and New Year's."

"That must have been fun," Gina said, slowing to make a right. "Now we're on Cayo Hueso—Bone Island, or as locals call it, The Rock."

"It *was* fun," Jesse continued. "Christmas morning, we were anchored off Cape Sable. Dad had snuck ashore during the night and set up a little fake Christmas tree on the beach."

The road curved to the left and suddenly, the rain stopped.

"Perfect timing, Sears is just ahead," she announced, then looked over at him. "How old were you then?"

"Seven," Jesse replied, looking out over a small, shallow bay. "Dad left for Vietnam the next month, in late January, and he was killed a few months after that."

"Does coming here bring back bad memories?"

Jesse looked over and smiled. "Naw... only good ones. I didn't see my dad a lot, sometimes not for long periods. But when he was home, he took me everywhere he went."

They spent an hour roaming through the men's clothing section of the large department store, and with Gina's "local's fashion" sense guiding him, Jesse picked out four pairs of rugged shorts with large cargo pockets—grenade pockets, they were called in the utility uniform.

They also found a few new T-shirts that fit perfectly, as well as what Gina called "fisherman" shirts, like Rusty had had on that morning. They had long sleeves and back panels with vent openings to keep the sun off and allow heat to escape.

"This doesn't seem so weird," Jesse said, as they made their way to the checkout. "Seems like a regular department store in any town."

"This is *New* Town," she replied, getting in line behind a large woman with dreadlocks and skin the color of light coffee. "We'll go to Old Town for a bit if you want. What time did Jim say we were going diving?"

"Thirteen hund... I mean one o'clock."

"That gives us two hours," she replied, as the dreadlocked woman gathered her bags and left.

Jesse stepped up to the counter and started placing his things on it.

"Did you find everything okay?" the cashier asked.

Jesse looked up, nodding his head.

The guy behind the counter had tattoos all over his neck and face, with at least a dozen piercings.

"Uh... yeah," Jesse said, pulling his wallet out.

Gina stood beside him, looking up with a smile, waiting.

Jesse said nothing as the guy rang up his order. Then he handed him three twenties from his wallet. He'd brought two hundred with him from the seabag. The guy gave him his change, then Jesse picked up the bags and followed Gina to the door.

Outside, they crossed the parking lot to the Pinto, and Gina continued to smile, waiting.

"I think that guy must be a real die-hard fisherman," Jesse said, straight-faced, as he put his bags in the back.

"A fisherman?" Gina asked dubiously, as she closed the trunk.

Jesse opened the door on his side and looked over the roof with a crooked grin. "Imagine falling face first into a tackle box and leaving all that metal in your face. A real diehard, I tell ya."

Gina burst out laughing as Jesse lowered himself into the car. She got in the driver's seat beside him, and he took her hand.

"I love the sound of your laugh," he said, grinning. "Don't ever stop."

"And now we add a wicked sense of humor," she said. "I was wondering if you had one."

"Okay," Jesse said. "That was a *little* weird."

She turned the key and started the engine. "Not on The Rock. He's actually pretty normal. His name's Kris, with a K, and he and my dad used to work together. It's short for Kristian, also with a K. His wife ran off and left him and their two kids a few years ago."

A part of Jesse could understand why, but his mind moved straight to the two motherless kids. "She left her children?"

"Drugs make people do crazy things," Gina said, pulling up to the light. "It's almost noon. Are you hungry?"

"I could eat," Jesse replied, still thinking about the kids. More than anyone, he knew the heartache of losing a parent.

The light turned green, and Gina turned left, drove two blocks, and turned left again, into a neighborhood. A couple of blocks later, she made a right onto Flagler.

There were a few people on the sidewalks and the roads were crowded with cars, mopeds, and even golf carts.

"Where are we going?" Jesse asked after a couple of blocks.

"You'll see," was all she said, then continued several more

blocks.

Finally, she made another right, then an immediate left onto Waddell Avenue, where she pulled to the curb.

"This is where Jimmy Buffett wrote 'Trying to Reason with Hurricane Season' a few years back."

Jesse opened the door and stepped out onto the curb. "Who's he?"

"Who's Jim..." She came around the front of the car and joined him on the sidewalk. "You've never heard of Jimmy Buffett?"

Jesse shook his head as they began to walk. "Rock and roll?"

Gina took his hand in hers, clinging to his arm with the other. "Do we have to dive this afternoon?"

Jesse thought about it for a moment. They had a whole week, even if they took the two-day local Greyhound back to the base, and hit every Podunk town in Florida, Georgia, and the Carolinas.

"We have all week for that," he replied. "But I should call Rusty and let him know. He'd probably like some time with Juliet anyway."

"Across the street," Gina indicated, turning Jesse toward the crosswalk.

Reaching the other side, they went up the steps of a place called Louie's Backyard, which had a view of the ocean.

Jesse looked out over the water and smiled, feeling more relaxed than he had in days.

Loud voices came from the sand off to the side, and Jesse turned toward it. Two men, sunburned and apparently drunk, were arguing.

"Wait here," Jesse said, then went down the steps and around the side, walking straight toward the two men.

He stopped ten feet away and stood loosely, hands at his sides. One man turned toward him, then the other. Both were older, probably in their thirties, and dressed in gaudy tropical shirts like a pair of idiot bookends.

"Whatta you want, punk?" the older-looking of the two slurred.

Jesse said nothing and just stared at the man. Even if they were sober, he knew both of them together were no threat, so he felt no rush of adrenaline, no immediacy of the fight or flight impulse, just a calm assuredness born of the fact that he was six inches taller than either man, younger, and in *far* better physical condition.

And he knew *how* to fight.

The other guy took a step toward Jesse. "You got a problem, kid?"

The first man laughed nervously. "Yeah, maybe he can't hear."

There was nothing threatening in Jesse's posture. He stood relaxed, his head up and alert for anything, though his face was inscrutable.

For a long moment, neither man said anything. But Jesse knew it was already over.

"Hey, look," the first man said, taking a slow step back. "We don't want any trouble."

Jesse remained motionless.

"We'll just... uh... get back to the wives," the younger of the two stammered. "Sorry to bother you."

Jesse watched as the two men started toward the beach, stumbling a little, but supporting one another.

There were fast footsteps behind him, but Jesse expected her. She was a reporter, so curious.

Gina was suddenly there, holding his hand. "What did you say to those guys? I could only hear them."

"Nothing," Jesse replied. "They just realized they were making a scene, and everyone was looking at them."

Gina glanced around. "*You* were the only one looking at them, Jesse."

Chapter Fourteen

They sat outside on the deck behind the main part of the restaurant, at a small, umbrella-covered table close to the handrail. Jesse positioned himself with his back partially to the rail, but with a fantastic view of the ocean and the steps leading down to the beach.

"This place looks incredible," he said, gazing around at the palms scattered across the sandy yard, all the flowering plants around the deck, and at the white sand and turquoise water.

"One of the best-kept secrets of Key West," Gina said, as a waitress approached with menus. Gina turned and smiled. "Hi, Carly."

The woman smiled back, recognizing her.

It didn't escape Jesse's attention that the two of them could almost be sisters. Carly was a little taller than Gina, maybe five-four, slim, with short blond hair and blue eyes. Jesse guessed she might be a little older, but not by much.

"Hi, Gina," Carly said, placing the menus between them, then pulling a chair out to sit down. "I wasn't expecting to see you this weekend. You always come for lunch every other Friday, like clockwork."

"I'm not here on assignment," Gina said.

Carly's eyes shifted to Jesse. "Obviously."

"This is my boyfriend, Jesse," Gina said, as Jesse stood and offered his hand. "Jesse, this is Carly Ingersoll."

He shook her hand, then sat back down. "I'm here on leave and Gina's showing me around."

"You're in the Navy?"

He shook his head. "Marines. I'm stationed in North Carolina."

"We heard about the bomb in Scott's car," Gina said. "I hope the cops and the Navy will take it seriously now."

Carly rolled her eyes. "The cops say it's a military problem, and the Navy says it's on the local police."

Gina's face showed alarm. "So nobody's doing anything?"

"The Navy flew him to Andros. He's staying at the Acoustics Range."

"We heard the bomb had a motion sensor switch," Jesse said. "Have the police or the Navy said anything else about how it was built?"

Carly studied Jesse's face for a moment. "No. They didn't even release the part about the motion sensor, but one look at his car and you knew that's what it had to be."

"How come?" Jesse asked.

"The location was obvious," Carly replied. "It was on the floor behind the driver's seat. Scott wouldn't have seen it getting in the car and it would go off as soon as he started driving. The drunk rear-ended our car instead and thankfully nobody was hurt. The floor where it was is dented downward, and the driver's seat and door of our car were completely blown out. Are you some kind of military police or something?"

Jesse grinned. "Nothing like that," he said. "I just know a little about car bombings and don't like to see innocent people hurt. I understand you have kids."

"Two," Carly replied, her tired expression giving way to the smile again. "Seven and eight, both boys. Thank God they were at school."

"Mind if I ask what Scott does in the Navy?"

She glanced at Gina for a second, then back at Jesse. "He's an acoustics engineer," Carly replied. "He works back and forth between here and Andros Island, in the Bahamas."

"AUTEC?" Jesse asked, remembering a friend of his grandfather's who had once worked there.

She nodded. "Yes, he's one of the lead engineers there."

"So, why aren't you and he both living there?" Jesse asked. "In Androstown or San Andros?"

"You're in the Marines, huh?" Carly asked, giving Jesse a suspicious look.

"Just an infantryman," Jesse said. "Someone blew up my car a few months ago. I thought maybe Gina being a reporter and all…"

"I don't know anything at all about acoustics or whatever AUTEC us," Gina said. "You can trust Jesse. He's one of the good guys,"

"What's being a reporter got to do with it?" Carly asked.

"The press has been able to get a lot of things done," Jesse said, "when the government isn't doing its job."

Carly looked back to Jesse. "The Navy has a daily flight there," she said. "I guess it's cheaper to house families here than build new quarters there. Locals charge high rent to the government. And besides, there's not enough work there to keep him busy. He works here most days."

"Do you think all this has to do with his job?" Gina asked.

"Are you asking as a friend or a reporter?"

"Both, I guess," Gina replied. "If the police and the Navy aren't doing anything, maybe a little press will push them to take action."

"You can do that?" Carly asked.

Gina smiled. "All I can do is submit the story," she replied. "If my editor likes it, he'll run it."

"Actually, I don't think it has *anything* to do with his work for the

Navy," Carly said. "I don't think a foreign assassin would be so inept."

"The first attack..." Jesse began. "That was a stabbing?"

"We took a walk on the beach," Carly replied, nodding. "It was late on a weeknight, and we'd left the boys with a sitter after they went to bed." She looked over at Gina. "You know how pretty it is with a full moon over on Smathers. Anyway, it was late and a weeknight, like I said, so there weren't many people around. We sat down on the sand for a bit, then some guy snuck up behind us out of nowhere, and stabbed Scott in the back of the neck."

"The back of his neck?" Jesse asked, thinking.

"He bled a lot," Carly said, shuddering. "But thankfully, the knife didn't hit any arteries or anything. It did hit one of his vertebrae, though, and the tip of the knife was lodged in his spine."

"And the second attempt?" Gina asked.

"Let me get your orders in," Carly said. "Then I can talk for a bit."

Jesse started to reach for a menu, but Gina stopped him.

"Two blackened hogfish sandwiches with fries and Cokes," Gina said, then smiled at Jesse. "Trust me on this."

"Two specials, coming up," Carly said, then hurried away.

"Really sloppy," Jesse said, taking a bread fork and holding it low at his side, his arm fully extended. "With Scott seated, an attacker doesn't have a lot of power behind the knife in a low-handed position like this." He thrust his hand forward awkwardly.

"And you know how a foreign hitman would use a knife?"

He grinned. "No kind of 'hitman' would be that incompetent."

"So, what would a competent assassin have done?"

Jesse reached across the bread plate with his left hand, curling his fingers over the far side, then, in one fluid motion, pulled it toward him and thrust the bread knife into the wooden table with great force.

Gina shuddered. "Um... What's that tell you?"

"A couple of things," Jesse replied, rocking the knife, then pulling it out and setting it back on the plate. "I'm six-three and the way I was just holding that knife down low like that, it would be above a sitting person's head, so I'd have to bend over. But I still wouldn't have much power behind it. That tells me the attacker was a good deal smaller than me, to even make the movement comfortable. And second, the whole idea of a knife attack on a public beach, uncrowded or not, is very unprofessional."

"A short rooky murderer?"

Jesse shrugged. "Just my knee-jerk reaction to what she said."

Carly returned a moment later and sat down again. "It'll be up in ten minutes."

"The second attack was a shooting?" Jesse asked.

"We think so," Carly replied. "It was three days later, as he was leaving the house. I heard the shot but couldn't tell where it came from, or even if it was a gun. It might just have been a car backfiring or maybe a firecracker. But Scott said he could hear the bullet go past his ear and the police *did* pull a bullet out of a tree in the neighbor's yard. But they said it could've been there for years."

Jesse had already learned there was a big difference between the sound of a gun being fired, and one being fired at you. "Where do you live?"

"We have a little house on Ninth Avenue over on Stock Island," Carly replied. "It isn't much, but it's all the off-base housing allowance would allow."

"I'm not familiar with the area," Jesse said. "Can you describe your street?"

"Our house is about in the middle of our block, which is in the middle of the subdivision. All the houses are small—the biggest in the whole neighborhood is only a thousand square feet. They're close together and sit too near to the street with a tiny backyard."

"Parking?"

"On the street," Carly replied. "Sometimes in front of your own house. Why's that important?"

"A lot of people around," Jesse replied. "Confined area. The shooter probably wasn't far away, within a block. Did anyone see the shooter?"

"Ha!" Carly exclaimed. "They didn't even ask anyone. Just swept it under the rug so the tourists wouldn't find out."

Tactically, Jesse would never have chosen a neighborhood for an ambush. At least not in the middle of the block. A shooter could wait at a stop sign and take the shot when the target stopped.

"And the third attempt?" Gina asked. "We heard it was poison."

"Scott was violently sick one day last week," Carly said. "He was taken to the hospital and almost died. The lab found high levels of... poly... something... glycerin."

"Polyethylene glycol?" Jesse asked.

"Yeah! That's it. His levels were high, but not enough to kill him."

"Antifreeze," Jesse said, looking out over the water as he considered the first three attempts.

"And now a bomb?" he asked rhetorically. "Whoever it is, they're very sloppy."

Two couples came out onto the deck and sat at a table on the opposite side.

"I have to get back to work," Carly said. "Your order should be up in a minute."

She hurried to her station, gathered up some menus, and went to the newcomers.

"I think she's right," Gina said. "I don't think any of this has anything to do with his work. What's AUTEC, anyway?"

"The Atlantic Undersea Test and Evaluation Center," Jesse replied. "They do a lot of certification on the Navy's submarine captains and crews in action and measure the accuracy of underwater weapons systems."

Gina rolled her eyes. "I'm dating Captain America. And you know this how?"

Jesse grinned. "A friend of my grandfather worked there. He's retired now, but still lives on Andros Island. You met him while we were there—Henry Patterson."

Gina's eyes widened. "I thought he was some kind of old ex-pat hippy."

Jesse shook his head. "Nautical engineer. He and Pap went to school together after the war in the Pacific. He used to do a lot of AUTEC's shallow-water recoveries, freediving to a hundred feet to clip a lift bag to a spent torpedo."

"A hundred feet isn't shallow."

"Compared to the Tongue of the Ocean, just offshore, it is," Jesse replied. "Remember how it dropped off just past the reef? The TOTO drops to a mile deep."

"Never judge a book," Gina said, shaking her head in wonder. "I just thought he was one of those burn-outs from the sixties."

"You and Carly could pass for sisters," Jesse said, changing the subject.

Gina glanced over at her friend for a moment, then squashed her face up at Jesse. "You think so?"

"Not so much in the face," he replied. "Almost the same height, both pretty, blond, slim, and blue eyes."

Gina smiled. "I'll take that as a compliment then. Besides waiting tables, she used to be a fitness trainer." She paused and looked over at Carly again. "So, if it's not some foreign spy or whatever, then who *is* trying to kill Scott? And why?"

Jesse looked over at Carly, chatting with the two couples.

"If you ask me," he replied, "I'd say it was personal."

Chapter Fifteen

◆━━◆━━◆━━◆

As they were leaving, Jesse spotted Carly talking to a very beautiful woman with long, raven hair. Gina steered him that way and as they approached, the two women turned to face them.

Carly smiled, but the other woman seemed almost put off, as if the interruption was keeping her from something important.

"We're heading out," Gina said. "It's been good to see you again. I hope they find out what's going on. Can I call you tonight to get some more information for the story?"

"Yeah, sure," Carly said. "This is my friend, Amber. We knew each other back home in New York, and she's been helping with the boys while she's in town for the holidays."

Jesse and Gina both shook hands with the woman, and again, Jesse got a negative vibe from her touch. He could see something in Gina's eyes too but hadn't known her long enough to read any more than that.

They left the restaurant and when they reached the sidewalk, Jesse looked up and down the street before they strolled to the crosswalk.

"You don't think it was Carly, do you?" Gina asked.

Jesse knew that the spouse was always the first suspect, and was sure she'd been exonerated by the police, even if their investigation didn't go very far.

"No, I don't," he replied. "She seemed genuinely pissed about the police inaction. Can you really help with a news story?"

"I hate to say it," Gina began, "but the police here tend to look the other way a lot. Never underestimate the power of the press, though."

"You were right," Jesse said, putting an arm around Gina's shoulders and pulling her close as they walked. "That sandwich was great."

They crossed the street and Jesse looked up and down the block again before getting into the car. On the other side, about a hundred yards down the street, a car idled with a man sitting at the wheel.

It'd been sitting there when they'd come out of the restaurant several minutes earlier.

"There was something about that woman, Amber," Gina said, standing in the street and looking at Jesse over the car. "The way she looked at Carly. And I guess at me, too. But not you."

"I don't get it," Jesse replied, keeping an eye on the idling car without turning his head that way.

"I think she's gay," Gina said, then opened the door and got in.

Jesse climbed in on his side. "Gay?"

"I think so," Gina said, starting the Pinto and putting it in gear.

She checked her mirror, then pulled away from the curb. "You'll see a lot of that here. Key West is very socially liberal."

The guy in the car just beyond the intersection seemed to be waiting for something or someone.

"Not that I have anything against it," she continued, as she stopped at the corner, then began to turn right. "I think everyone should be free to do whatever they want."

She quickly turned right again, onto South Street.

"How others choose to live their lives is none of my business," Jesse agreed, turning his head and looking back. "As long as they keep their nose out of mine."

Gina continued a few blocks, then made a right on White, then left, back onto Flagler.

"We need to find a phone booth," Jesse said, rolling his window down and adjusting the mirror on that side so he could see behind them.

Gina looked over. "I need that to drive."

Jesse watched closely behind them. "Just let me know if you need to make a lane change."

"We're on a two-lane road, Jesse. What's going on?"

"Then you won't need it for a while," he replied, as the same car he'd seen idling turned onto Flagler, two cars behind them.

It wasn't the first time Jesse had seen it, either.

"Someone's following us."

"Where?"

"Not the car behind us," he replied. "But the white Chrysler two cars behind it. The same car was parked down the street when we left the restaurant and I saw it at Sears when we were there earlier. Do you recognize it?"

Gina glanced in the rearview mirror. "No, I don't think so. Are you sure it's the same... Never mind."

Jesse grinned. "There was a phone booth at Sears," he said. "Pull in there and I'll call Rusty. We'll see if the car's following us."

A few blocks later, Gina turned into the shopping center and drove toward a payphone mounted on the wall.

"Go slower," Jesse said, as he looked in the mirror.

The Chrysler continued past the light.

When they reached the curb next to the payphone, Jesse got out and made the call to the bait shop.

It only rang once. "Shorty's Bait Shop. Shorty speakin'."

"It's me, Jesse."

"Oh, hey," Shorty said. "Jim just left a few minutes ago. He's makin' a delivery for me."

"You deliver bait?"

Shorty laughed. "No, but we deliver booze."

"Could you let him know that Gina and I are going to hang out down here a while? We were going to go diving, but I thought he and Juliet might want some time to themselves. Besides, you said it was going to rain again."

"I'll be sure to let him know," Shorty said. "He told me ya don't want the car anymore."

"Do you think you can sell it for what you've put into it?" Jesse asked, his voice becoming detached.

"I tell ya what," Shorty said. "Come Tuesday, when you bring the money for the bar and bait shop, I'll give you a grand for it. All that was left was the shell. I shipped the engine, tranny, and wheels back to your friend in LaBelle."

"That's a deal," Jesse agreed. "That'll allow me to pay Pap back for what he didn't get from insurance without dipping any more into my savings."

He hung up the phone and got back in the car.

"I saw the car go by," Gina said. "Just a coincidence, I guess. What did Rusty say?"

"He wasn't there," Jesse replied. "Shorty sent him on a bottle delivery."

Gina started the car and headed for the exit.

"Where are we going?" Jesse asked.

"Well, I wanted to take you to Mallory Square for the Sunset Celebration. But I don't know. That car spooked me."

"And this evening is the celebration?"

She laughed. "No, they do it every day."

"We can go," Jesse said. "Whoever it was, they were probably just waiting for something, or maybe making a delivery, like Rusty with the bottle of liquor."

She looked over at him and smiled, then took his hand. "We can see the sunset anytime. How about if we just play hooky from everyone and go back to the motel?"

Jesse leaned over and kissed her. "You don't have to twist my arm."

Gina made a right out of the shopping center, went around the curve, and got into the turn lane for the light. It changed to green before they stopped and she turned onto Overseas Highway, crossing the bridge to Stock Island.

As she accelerated, Jesse glanced in the mirror on his side. Nothing.

"She looked like a model or something," Gina said.

Jesse kept his eyes on the mirror. "Who?"

"Carly's friend, Amber," she replied. "She said she was here for the holidays, and I know there's a bit photo shoot going on this week."

The woman had seemed distant to Jesse, almost aloof. He knew he possessed many physical traits girls and even older women liked. He was tall, had broad shoulders, and was in peak condition. He often caught women looking at him, but his tendency toward shyness always got in the way.

A professional model could have her choice of men, so maybe that was why she'd seemed distant.

The four-lane changed to a two-lane, and they were soon caught behind a line of slower cars.

"The traffic's the worst part about coming down here," Gina said, settling in behind a Lincoln with Minnesota tags. "One lane in, and one lane out. And of course, some tourist has to slow down to look at the water."

"Everyone seems so negative toward tourists," Jesse said. "But it seems like they bring a lot of money to the Keys."

"It's a love-hate relationship," Gina replied. "Yeah, we really count on tourist dollars, but every now and then one of them will do or say something stupid. It's hard not to stereotype, it happens so often."

A few minutes later, they crossed another bridge onto a long causeway with water and hundreds of small islands and sandbars on both sides.

Jesse glanced in his mirror again. There were two cars behind them, one blue and one green, but no sign of the white Chrysler.

"This is the Saddlebunch Keys," Gina said. "It was one of the hardest parts of the early railroad and bridges to build because of the mosquitos. They nearly drove the workers insane."

Jesse caught a flash of white out of the corner of his eye as they passed a sideroad. He looked in the mirror again, just in time to see the same Chrysler pull out three cars behind them.

"He's back," Jesse said, his tone sounding ominous. "It's no coincidence."

Chapter Sixteen

Jesse looked over at Gina as her eyes, usually bright and happy, cut to the rearview mirror with a very worried look.

"Behind the blue and green cars," he advised.

Gina glanced over, nervous. "What do you want me to do?"

If he were alone, Jesse knew what he'd do. He'd stop the car and ask the guy why he was following him. But he wasn't alone.

"It still might be just a coincidence," Gina said. "Maybe he *is* making deliveries."

Jesse looked in the mirror again. "Or he might be following us."

"Why would anyone be following *us*?"

"I don't know," Jesse replied, but was very curious to find out.

The two cars behind the slow-moving vehicle ahead pulled out to pass at the same time.

"I know one way to find out," Gina said, reaching for the shifter.

Jesse looked over at her. "How much juice does this little car have?"

She downshifted and floored the accelerator as a line of cars went by in the opposite direction.

The little Ford passed the three cars that were in front of them, quickly gaining on the other two passing cars.

Gina didn't let up, but shifted to high gear and floored it again, passing the large opening vacated by the other two cars and gaining on the slow one.

Another long line of traffic loomed in the distance, half a mile up the highway.

Gina cut over in front of the slow car with room to spare as the oncoming traffic flew by. Then she had to brake hard to keep from rear-ending the car ahead.

She looked over at Jesse, eyes wide with an adrenaline rush, something Jesse knew well.

"Rach's car isn't a real Keys car," she said, looking ahead again, waiting for another opening in the oncoming traffic. "It only has fifty thousand miles on it, and she takes really good care of it."

After the next line of cars went by, Gina performed the same maneuver, dropping to third gear and passing two cars, with nothing ahead in their lane for at least a mile and plenty of oncoming traffic to keep the Chrysler pinned in.

"Go for it!" Jesse said.

A moment later, he glanced over at the instrument panel. The little Pinto was pushing ninety miles per hour and Jesse could tell by the sound of the engine that it was a six-cylinder, instead of what he assumed would be a four.

Jesse glanced at the mirror and noticed the Chrysler pull out to pass, far behind them. Then it quickly had to swerve back in, got stuck behind the slow-moving station wagon, and dropped back even more. He leaned over and looked at the speedometer.

The Pinto was once more up to just over ninety, and still had a little pedal left. With every minute, Gina was gaining more distance from the following car.

She kept the little car at high speed, passing other cars when traffic was clear, and soon the Chrysler was out of sight.

"There'll probably be a cop as soon as we reach Big Pine," Gina said. "They always work the bridges on either end. Should we stop and ask for help?"

Jesse looked back. They were at least a mile ahead of whoever was following them.

"I don't think a cop could do anything," Jesse replied. "Not unless they see a crime taking place. It'd be our word against his."

She slowed as they neared Big Pine Key, large signs warning of Key deer. Just as she'd predicted, a sheriff's patrol car sat just off the bridge, hiding in plain sight. But by the time a speeder would see him, it was too late.

Hopefully, the guy in the Chrysler was still being impatient.

Jesse looked down a sideroad to the left, then another one. They were long and straight.

"What's to the north of here?" he asked.

"Mostly residential streets; some just dirt."

A line of cars was coming at them.

"As soon as these cars get past," Jesse said, looking in the mirror again, "take the next left, but don't signal. Then start turning at every intersection you come to."

"Good idea," she replied, still fairly calm after a fifteen-mile car chase. "He won't see us turn for the other cars."

A moment later, Gina downshifted and made a hard left between two packs of cars without even braking.

The Pinto's tires protested, and when she gassed it again, the car fishtailed slightly before she got it straight on the sideroad.

At the first intersection, Gina turned right onto a dirt road, driving slowly, until she came to another dirt road on the left.

"There's a trail just ahead," she said. "It cuts over to Sandy Circle."

A moment later, she turned right, following a double-rutted trail under low-hanging tree branches.

"You know the area really well," Jesse said, turning and looking back.

"I was born and raised here," she replied. "I know every footpath on half these islands."

Jesse looked back again. "I think we lost him."

"Why was he following us?" Gina asked again, pulling up to another paved road, where the trail they were on ended.

"I have no idea," Jesse said, checking the mirror before Gina turned left. "But that car was leaving Sears when we got there. And later, it was parked and idling, just down the street from where we ate lunch."

"I hope he slowed down when he reached Big Pine," she said, continuing straight and now driving slowly, alert for anything. "There's only about five hundred Key deer left, but they're coming back. Ten years ago, there were fewer than half that."

As if on cue, an antlered buck stepped out into the road, and Gina stopped a hundred feet away.

There were no houses nearby, just the natural landscape and partially cleared lots.

The buck was no bigger than a large dog but had a rack with at least eight or ten prongs.

"A little over fifty years ago," Gina said softly, looking at the tiny buck, "they'd been hunted almost to extinction. There were only about twenty of them in existence."

"He's so small," Jesse said, as the buck took a few more steps out to the middle of the road.

Suddenly, two does came out of the woods, bounding across the road, as if their tiny legs were made of springs.

When they'd disappeared on the other side, the buck sprang across the road and was gone in two leaps.

"Road guard," Jesse said, grinning.

Gina let the clutch out and slowly started forward. "Huh?"

"When we march in formation," Jesse explained, peering into

the woods where the deer had disappeared, "anytime we come to a road, two road guards with reflective vests run from the back of the platoon and out into the street to stop traffic."

"The bucks are very protective," Gina said. "Especially this time of year."

"Oh?"

"Both of those does were pregnant," Gina replied, as she pulled up to a stop sign and turned toward him for a second. "Of those three adults, and their two offspring, the odds are that one of them will be hit by a car and die before this year is over. The mortality rate by car is over ten percent every year."

"Ten percent?" he asked, as Gina turned right, headed east. "That'd be more than twenty million people, just in this country."

Gina glanced over again. "Key deer are one hundred times more likely to be killed by a car here on this one island than a person is, anywhere in the county."

About a mile later, they crossed a bridge to an even less populated island.

"This is No Name Key," Gina said, continuing straight. "They don't have electricity or water out here."

But there were a few houses, Jesse noticed. Large lots with moderate-sized homes, all with solar panels on the roofs.

They reached the end of the road and Gina turned off to the right, following another double-rut trail. "This goes out to the old ferry dock ruins."

"Ferry?"

"There were roads on most of the bigger islands before the railroad came," she replied, as they pulled out into a small clearing. "But nothing connecting them for cars until after the Labor Day Hurricane of 1935, when the railroad was so badly destroyed, they decided to rebuild the bridges for car traffic."

"Where did the ferry come from?" Jesse asked, as Gina parked the car and shut off the engine.

It was very quiet outside the car.

"They had daily service to Lower Matecumbe Key, and a supply barge that came once a week from the mainland."

They got out and Gina grabbed a large canvas bag from the trunk, then they walked to the end of the double ruts.

"What's in the bag?" Jesse asked.

"A great big blanket. We can sit on the beach down there if you want." She pointed ahead to the remains of old wooden dock pilings, reaching way out into the water. "It made regular stops at Grassy Key and the old Eleventh Street pier on Key Vaca. Then it stopped right here. That bridge we crossed used to be an old wooden bridge that cars from the ferry could use to reach Big Pine."

They could see the highway from the old pier's beachhead and Jesse pointed. "Look."

Though it was a good three miles away, Jesse could make out a white car passing a truck on the bridge.

A light rain began to fall, and Gina turned toward him. "Do you really think he was following us?"

"I'm sure of it," Jesse replied. "But I don't know why. Seeing the same car twice could be a coincidence, maybe even three times, since it's a small island. But four? I don't think so. And he was aggressively chasing someone."

"I've never been in a car chase before."

"You could've fooled me," Jesse replied, grinning.

She turned to face him, then put her arms around his neck, standing up on her toes as she pulled him down closer.

They kissed deeply for a moment, oblivious to the rain, which was starting to come down harder and making it obvious that Gina wasn't wearing anything under her cotton blouse.

"I feel totally comfortable with you," she whispered, wrapping her arms tightly around his neck and hugging him close. "Even the rain feels good."

Jesse reached lower and grabbed her thighs, easily hoisting her up as she wrapped her legs around his midsection, and they kissed passionately.

Still holding onto him, Gina lifted her body higher, to look down at Jesse's face. "I think you did that outboard 'motorboat' thing all wrong," she said and pulled his face into her breasts, wiggling her upper body from side to side while she lifted her head and laughed up at the rain.

Chapter Seventeen

"Dammit!" Chuck shouted in frustration, pounding the wheel. He slowed the Cordoba to the speed limit before crossing over the bridge to Big Pine Key, where he knew there'd be a cop.

And sure enough, there he was, sitting at the foot of the bridge, where he wouldn't be seen until too late. Chuck passed the cruiser going exactly the speed limit and waved, even though he couldn't see the guy through the tinted windows.

As soon as he was past him, Chuck held a middle finger up.

He'd chosen the Cordoba for a reason. It didn't look like a car someone doing what he did would drive. And it had a large trunk.

In the last ten minutes, he'd made up some of the distance he'd lost early on, but Gina and the jarhead had gotten so far ahead in the sparser section of the Lower Keys, he knew he'd lost them by the time he'd reached Big Pine.

Just the same, he looked down each road he passed.

Chuck was tired, still had a hangover, and was now pissed and grumpy.

He hadn't rolled out of bed until almost noon, after partying with the two dancers until way late. He did learn the other dancer's name was Kiki, though. Probably another stage name, but what did he care? He'd call them whatever they asked.

When they'd reached his apartment at La Concha the night before, Chuck had broken out a small stash of coke, which, along with the weed, booze, and the right music, hadn't taken long to get things moving.

Then, miracle of miracles, the little minx Amber Henderson had shown up. In no time at all, the four of them were naked in his huge Jacuzzi tub.

He vaguely remembered they'd snorted the last of the coke off each other's bellies while they were all stretched out on the floor in a circle, naked.

Only in Key West.

The porn star had left after the coke was gone, and after Kiki and Crystal told her they weren't interested in what she had to offer. She'd been particularly interested in the small blonde.

He'd dropped the dancers off around noon, one at the house they shared on Stock Island and the other at her day job at the Sears store in New Town. Then he'd headed back over to The Rock, and Louie's Backyard for breakfast and a Bloody Mary.

Amber had been there when he arrived. She'd been working on the wife of a Navy guy who was a waitress there, or so she'd told him. And the more he thought about it, she too had been a petite blonde.

Chuck knew which way Amber leaned; it'd been obvious the night before. Either the producer guy she scouted for was looking for girls for lesbian scenes, or more likely, Amber was after this one for her own pleasure.

He'd first met the tiny, hard-bodied porn star at a club meeting up island, just over two years earlier. Bear had heard she was in town and invited her and the film crew to a private party at the clubhouse. When she'd arrived, she just walked in and announced there wasn't a man in the bar who could satisfy her.

After that, the Sun Devils and Playtime Productions, who she contracted with, entered into a business arrangement. The guys in the club never had any trouble finding girls who needed the cash and would do anything. And one in ten was good-looking enough to put on film.

As he'd sat there, eating his breakfast, Chuck had seen Gina Albert with the tall jarhead come up the steps. Before entering, the guy had confronted two men on the side of the restaurant and faced them down over something before he and Gina walked right past his table to sit outside.

He'd been looking at a menu and she didn't even notice him. But he'd noticed her, and a light bulb came on in his head.

Just that morning, the new leader of the Sun Devils had let the word out that Playtime was looking for a particular kind of girl. Chuck suddenly realized that Gina Albert fit the description perfectly for the scene they wanted to shoot.

He'd quickly finished eating, paid his tab, and went out to the Cordoba. He'd parked inconspicuously in the next block to wait and see where they were going.

Less than an hour later, they'd come out, and Chuck had followed them to the Sears store, where they'd stopped. He'd continued past, knowing there was only one way off Key West and eventually they'd head up island. All he had to do was find a shady spot and wait.

He hadn't waited long, and when he'd seen them go by a few minutes later, he'd pulled out to follow them again.

The crazy bitch had driven like a maniac, passing cars with little room and waiting to do it when he'd have even less.

They could be anywhere, he thought.

It didn't matter; Blue Waters Motel was just on the other side of a few more bridges.

First, he intended to make sure they were there, then he'd get Gary King to bring some muscle over. He could let Bear know he'd fixed things for him within the day of the two jarheads' return. And maybe as a bonus, take Gina Albert up to the club's "studio" in Key Largo.

But when Chuck arrived at the motel, the Pinto wasn't there. He pulled back out, heading north, and considered going to Thurman's old man's place. But there was only one way in and out of there. He'd have to go in and buy something.

Bait would be quicker, he thought.

If you bought a beer in a bar, you were expected to stick around and drink it. That's what a bar was for. But nobody would hang around after buying bait.

He just wanted to see if the car was there.

"Fuck it," he said, and turned the Cordoba luxury car into the gloomy driveway.

The low-hanging plants made Chuck cringe behind the wheel as he idled down the narrow driveway. Finally, he pulled into the clear area in front of the bar and parked the car.

The Pinto wasn't there, either.

But he was committed; backing out and leaving would look suspicious and draw attention. So, he got out and went into the bait shop side of the business.

"Sorry, we're closed," a guy in back said.

It was Jim Thurman, the other jarhead.

"Closed?" Chuck asked, drawing unwanted attention.

Chuck Bering was an average-looking guy, dressed nicely, but not flashily, and was also average in height and weight. He wore his hair collar-length, combed, and he had no facial hair.

Not memorable. Invisible. People forgot him.

He kept a low profile most of the time and knew a lot of people, remembering names and faces easily. He'd only met Jim Thurman once, several years ago, and only for a few seconds.

"Yeah," Thurman replied. "Shuttin' down the bait shop to make room for a restaurant. Sold all the bait we had this morning to Phillips, down on Ramrod. Ya might try there."

"Okay," Chuck said, thinking quickly. "I was headed that way anyway. Have a good day, and good luck with the restaurant."

Relieved the guy hadn't recognized him, he went back outside, got in his car, started the engine and let it idle a moment as he considered the day's events.

McDermitt! he thought. That was the other guy's name. And now he'd completely lost them.

But sooner or later, that McDermitt guy was going to head back to that motel bed with that nosy reporter, Gina Albert.

And *that* would be where he'd get his payback.

He backed out and drove through the jungle once more. Five minutes later, he slowed as he passed the motel and looked in. Not seeing the Pinto, he pulled into Hall's Dive Center and parked next to a phone booth where he could see the motel entrance.

As he walked to the well-lit booth, Chuck looked back on his pager's log and found the number from the night before.

He opened the folding door and left it open as he dropped a coin in the slot and then dialed the number.

"Hello?"

"It's Chuck," he said. "How'd you like to make it a whole O-Z. I need a couple of guys. Big guys who ain't afraid to get their hands dirty for a buck."

"That'd be more than an ounce, man," Gary King replied.

"I'll take care of paying them," Chuck replied. "The O-Z is your finder's fee if you can get someone to Marathon fast."

"Sideshift and a couple others just rode in," King said.

That's perfect timing, Chuck thought.

Monte Brisco, who went by the name Sideshift because of the antique Harley he rode, had been tight with Chuck's cousin who was the leader of the Sun Devils before he got locked up. They'd done time together, and Bear had made him the new leader until he got out. Which, barring an escape, wouldn't be for twenty years.

Having the gang leader in town meant Chuck wouldn't have to rely on deadbeats like Gary. After all, he was Bear's cousin; he could be trusted.

It also meant he wouldn't need to go through Amber to get Gina Albert in front of a camera. Cutting out the middleman was what had made his and Bear's pot-growing business so lucrative.

"See if you can reach him," Chuck said, looking toward the motel, a malicious grin on his face. "I think he'll be very interested in the proposition I have for him."

Chapter Eighteen

The rain continued to beat down on the corrugated metal over their heads in an almost mesmerizing way. The lean-to, or wrecked building, or whatever it was, canted down toward Jesse and Gina's feet, and was blocked off on two sides by rubble.

Under it, nothing grew, and Jesse could tell by the sand that it was underwater during the highest high tides. The floor was barren sand.

When they'd spotted the makeshift lean-to, Gina headed there instead of going back to the car.

By the time they got under the lean-to, they were both drenched. But the blanket in Gina's canvas bag was large enough to spread out, folded in half, for them to lie on, as well as under.

Gina lay back, resting her head against Jesse's shoulder as he wrapped an arm around her and pulled her closer. She turned on her side, putting her right arm across his belly and intertwining her right leg with his.

Jesse took a deep breath and let it out very slowly.

"Still thinking about it?" Gina asked, gently stroking Jesse's belly under the cover.

"I was just thinking I was the luckiest guy alive," Jesse replied.

Gina was quiet for a moment, then asked, "That car started following us right from the restaurant, didn't it?"

"What if he was following us because we were talking to Carly?"

he asked, more to himself. "If that was why he followed us, wouldn't everyone she served have been targets?"

Gina's hand moved lower. "I bet I can make you forget it."

He smiled. "I know you can."

When her fingers touched him, their lips met, and they kissed each other very slowly at first.

Suddenly, Gina jumped and wiggled her body against his. "Oh! There's a leak! A cold drop just landed on my back."

Jesse grinned. "I should punch more holes in it."

"Do you think this rain will ever—"

The pelting on the metal suddenly ceased and they both started laughing as the sun came out.

"If you don't like the weather here..." Gina began.

"Just wait a little bit," Jesse finished.

Gina's blouse and Jesse's new fisherman's shirt were hanging on nails sticking out of a board that seemed to be holding the corrugated sheets together. The rest of their clothes and shoes were lying on the sand beside them.

"It's still early," Gina said, leaning forward and letting the blanket fall away.

As she twisted her body around to look out toward the southwest, Jesse admired the taut muscles of her lower back and the deep tan of her skin.

"Looks like about three o'clock," she said, turning back to face him, exposed to the waist. "We could probably find Jim and JJ and get a couple of dives in."

Jesse smiled, nodding. "We might," he replied, drawing the word out.

Gina shook her hair over the front of her shoulders, lowered her head a little to one side, and looking at him seductively. "Or not?"

"This side's dry," he said, lifting the blanket in invitation.

Just then, the sound of motorcycles could be heard out on the bridge.

Jesse looked toward the highway and saw two bikes passing a truck. Then he looked back up at Gina.

She moved in close, sliding under him as she lay back on the blanket. Jesse slowly began to lower himself on top of her.

The sound of a car's brakes squealing caused them both to freeze.

"That's close," he said.

The creak of two car doors could be heard swinging open on noisy hinges, then they both closed, one after the other.

"Get dressed," Jesse whispered urgently, as he pulled on his skivvies and cargo shorts. He peeked around the side. "It's the police."

They hurriedly got dressed, but there was nowhere to go. The rubble they were hiding under was in the open.

"Follow my lead," Gina whispered. "Sit back and look comfortable, but then startled when they find us."

"Okay," Jesse replied, as Gina pulled her purse closer and got a small pad and pencil out.

In seconds, she'd drawn a very realistic-looking pier and the outline of a double-decked ferry.

She started sketching the rough shape of an antique car's grill on the lower deck as she laughed loudly, then spoke in a normal, conversational tone. "The ferry looked something like this. It could carry up to five cars and forty people, I think. And they—"

"Can I ask what you're doing here?" a voice asked from behind Jesse.

He jumped and turned suddenly, and it wasn't all an act.

"Oh!" Gina shouted, jumping away from the officer. "Oh, my

God!"

"Relax," the man said, and Jesse noted he was a deputy sheriff with three stripes on his sleeve—a sergeant.

"We... we were looking at... the ruins," Gina explained. "My boyfriend is on leave from the military, and he's never been here."

"You're not *supposed* to be here," a second deputy said, joining the first. "We could detain and search you both."

"Feel free, Deputy," Jesse said. "We don't have anything to hide."

"Is that your white Ford parked by the entrance?" the sergeant asked.

"Yes it is," Gina said. "I didn't know it was posted. We just got under here out of the rain a few minutes ago, and I was telling him about the old ferry, and—"

"The ferry doesn't run anymore," the second deputy said.

He was younger, a lot younger. Probably not much older than Jesse.

The sergeant glanced back at him as if he were an imbecile, then turned back to Jesse and Gina under the lean-to. "I'm going to need to see some ID."

"Yes, sir," Jesse said, moving his hand with exaggerated slowness toward his hip and pulling his wallet out.

He noticed that the older deputy watched him closely as he did so.

Taking his Florida driver's license and military ID out, Jesse handed them over. "Lance Corporal Jesse McDermitt, USMC."

Gina handed hers to the deputy as well, along with her newspaper ID. "Gina Albert, *Key West Citizen*."

The look the sergeant had given the younger deputy was unusual for two cops, even in a small town.

The sergeant looked at their IDs briefly, then handed them

back. "The posted sign is just on the other side of where you parked your car, miss. I'm afraid you'll have to leave."

Jesse put his IDs away, shuffled out from under the lean-to, and stood, looking down on the two deputies. They both had the same name on their right chest—Johnson.

That explains the look, Jesse thought. They're not just co-workers.

"I'm afraid the rain was so hard, Sergeant Johnson," he said, "we must have missed the sign."

"No harm, no foul," the older Johnson said. "Kids come out here to smoke grass and drink beer."

Jesse cocked his head slightly, giving him a curious look. "Is that a big problem here? Marijuana?"

Gina crawled out and stood beside Jesse, gathering up the blanket.

Jesse noticed the younger deputy looking her over.

"It was until recently," the sergeant said. "Then we busted the local supplier."

Gina smiled. "With the help of a couple of Marines."

It was like the proverbial lightbulb turned on behind the sergeant's dull eyes. "McDermitt! That was you!"

"I just reported what I saw," Jesse replied. "Your guys brought him in to face trial."

When they started walking toward the cars, the younger Johnson lagged behind them.

As he walked next to the sergeant, Jesse spoke to him without looking over or breaking stride. "If your son doesn't get his eyes off my girlfriend's ass, deputy or not, I'm going to remove them."

The sergeant glanced back quickly, then stopped, and wheeled around. "Get in the damned car, boy."

The younger Johnson walked quickly past them and did as his father said.

"I apologize," the sergeant said to Jesse. "There's no excuse sometimes."

Jesse grinned. "No harm, no foul."

"You kids have a nice day," he said, then strode toward the cruiser.

Jesse and Gina got in the Pinto and Gina started the engine.

"Good thing their brakes were squeaky," Gina said. "Another two minutes...."

"Quick thinking with the tour guide stuff," Jesse said, pulling out the notepad and looking again at the sketch Gina had drawn. "And really quick drawing. This is good."

"You may keep it," Gina said with a smile. "That was some... uh, really bad timing."

"Think they're back at the motel yet?"

"Jim and JJ?"

Jesse nodded.

"Only one way to find out," she replied, then reached over and raked her fingernails up Jesse's thigh. "Besides, I need to get you somewhere warm and dry, like, right now."

Twenty minutes later, as they were approaching the swing bridge at Pigeon Key, a motorcycle passed them, probably going eighty.

"Those things are dangerous," Gina said, cringing at the roar.

"It's not the motorcycle," Jesse said. "It's the rider."

Even though he was moving away at a high rate of speed, Jesse could tell the guy was big. He made the Harley look small.

They passed the turnoff to Pigeon Key and a moment later, Gina slowed as they came off the bridge, then turned into the motel parking lot.

During the drive from No Name Key, they'd caught up to the weather and a light rain was falling again.

BAD BLOOD

"Nope, not here yet," Gina said, parking the car, then looking over at Jesse. "Oh, what *will* we do to pass the time?"

"I can think of a thing or two," Jesse replied. "But let me call Rusty first."

"He thinks we're in Key West."

"Oh, yeah."

"When they *do* return," she said, opening the door as the rain stopped, "we can say we just got back, too."

Jesse followed her into their room, and they embraced, peeling off one another's damp shirts as they kissed.

"Let's get in the shower," Gina suggested. "I feel cold and there's no rush now."

He chased her, squealing, into the bathroom, both wearing only their shorts. Gina turned on the hot water as Jesse grabbed two big, fluffy towels from the closet and hung them on a hook beside the shower door.

Gina began pulling her shorts down, wiggling until they were over her hips, when suddenly, they heard the sound of several motorcycles outside.

Gina's shorts dropped to the floor around her feet as she froze, looking up at Jesse. "What's that?"

"Harleys," he replied. "Wait here a second."

He went back out into the large room and was headed toward the front window when he heard voices outside the door.

Suddenly, there was a crash, and the door flew in, smashing a picture mounted on the wall.

Gina screamed as a huge, bearded man stepped into the room dressed in leather and denim. There were two more bikers just outside the mangled door.

Chapter Nineteen

◆ ◆ ◆ ◆

The tension was palpable. The man glared at Jesse, then his eyes cut quickly over his shoulder and Jesse knew that Gina had stepped out of the bathroom wearing nothing but her panties.

"Well, well," the biker said, taking another step forward. "Just what Amber said to keep an eye out for. Looks like we might have a little fun in the studio after the job's done, boys."

"I don't think you're going to enjoy this," Jesse said coldly.

The biker was already unbuckling his belt, ignoring Jesse, his lust-filled eyes looking past him at Gina.

As he'd done earlier in the day, Jesse simply stood there, hands loose at his sides. He was wearing only his new cargo shorts, and his feet were bare. He had no weapon within reach.

The man shifted his gaze to Jesse. "What'd you say, you scrawny-assed gym rat?" the man growled.

His hair was long and wild from the wind. He wore a thick beard, going gray on either side of his chin. He was well over two hundred pounds—probably closer to three.

Time seemed to slow as Jesse faced the three men, his eyes missing nothing. The room he stood in was massive. He had eight feet of space between the side of the bed and the wall—the perfect place to store dive gear. The wall behind him was six feet away from where he stood by the foot of the bed, and it was a good ten feet to the exterior wall and door in front of him. And the room was twenty feet wide, with nothing but a TV on a stand in the corner—enough room for a dance floor.

In that two hundred square feet of open space at the front of the room stood only the big biker and Jesse. The others were outside and would be of no help to the big man.

"You're in my room, fat-ass," Jesse stated flatly, intentionally goading the bigger man. "And I didn't invite you in. That means I don't have to wait for you to make the first move."

"Ha-ha, that'd be funny if it wasn't pathetic. They's three of us!"

"Good," Jesse said. "Your friends can carry your fat carcass out when I'm finished."

He took a slow step toward the bigger man. "I think I'll start with your eyes, fat man," Jesse growled, slowly lifting his right foot to take another step. "That way you won't have to look at what I do to the rest of you."

The man lunged, and Jesse's right leg, the foot already off the floor, snapped forward, driving his toes into the man's groin.

As the biker buckled over in pain, Jesse slammed a hard right fist into the side of his jaw, following him down and delivering a second blow before pouncing on the bigger man and lifting his body off the floor. He slammed his face repeatedly into the bed's heavy mahogany footboard until the man stopped moving.

Then Jesse flung the biker backward onto the hardwood floor. The man's head hit with a thud, bouncing up, his face a bloody mask.

Jesse's hands came up, his feet planted, ready for the next adversary.

It had all happened so quickly, the other two bikers hadn't even moved, and were just standing there, slack-jawed.

"Choose now!" Jesse roared, fully enraged and pointing a finger at the nearer man, a bald guy with a mustache. Both men were smaller than Jesse and he considered them no threat, even if armed.

"You can carry your fat friend out or join him and *be* carried out."

The two looked at one another and the bald guy shrugged. "We been paid, and Chuck's an asshole, anyway."

Jesse stepped back slightly, ready for anything, as the two men approached the inert body on the floor and grabbed him by either side of his leather vest. Then they dragged him out through the busted door and Jesse followed.

The bald one looked back. "Whatta we do with him now?"

"He's your problem, not mine," Jesse said. "Drape him over the back of one of your motorcycles."

"What about *his* bike?"

Jesse heard Gina behind him at the door and turned to look back at her. She had a towel wrapped around her body, under her arms.

"You ever ride a motorcycle?" he asked her, then turned back to the two men.

"No way, dude," the bald guy said, taking a step toward Jesse. "You ain't stealin'—"

He stopped mid-sentence, staring past Jesse's shoulder.

Gina stepped up beside Jesse, pointing a small handgun at the man.

"We're going for a ride," she said. "Do you have a problem with that, Baldy?"

"C'mon," the other guy said, pulling Baldy's arm. "Let's get the fuck outta here."

"Get rid of him yourself," Baldy said, then headed toward his bike.

"You might want to rethink that," Gina said.

He stopped and wheeled around. "I don't need no advice from some split—"

"He's going to wake up soon," Gina said, still pointing the gun at the man's chest. "He'll either be with you two, recuperating somewhere from quite a severe beating, or in a jail cell, knowing you two ran out on him, crying like little girls at the first sign of trouble. Because that's exactly what I'll be telling the police when they come to get him. Crying like little schoolgirls. He'll be awake by then, I'd think."

The two men looked at one another again. "He ain't gonna stay on my backseat," Baldy said. "Yours is bigger."

Jesse glanced at the three motorcycles. One was slung low, with a rigid frame and no rear shock. It had a tiny pad mounted on the rear fender, barely the size of a slice of bread. Another bike was an older Harley with a hand shifter on the right side of the seat, and no backseat at all. Jesse guessed it belonged to the guy they called Chuck. The other was a Sportster, with a full backseat and sissy bar behind it.

"But your hardtail has a bigger *front* seat," Jesse said. "And foot boards. Carry him over your lap so he doesn't fall off. I imagine someone's already called the cops by now."

The two men struggled to get Chuck upright, then the other guy held him while Baldy got on his bike, started it, and pulled up next to him.

A moment later, the two bikes roared away, turning right and heading toward the bridge.

The manager came out of the office, trotting toward Jesse as the man with the little girl came out of a room across the pool.

"Get packed!" Jesse whispered urgently to Gina. "We're getting out of here, right now!"

He followed her inside and went straight to his seabag, digging the sock out. Then he carried the seabag to the door and plopped it down, just as the manager appeared.

"What in the world is going on here?" he shouted.

BAD BLOOD

Gina came out of the bathroom, fully dressed, and began stuffing things in her overnight bag.

"It was a misunderstanding, Craig," Jesse said, glancing at the damaged door. "We've never seen those guys before."

"I have everything," Gina said, hurrying past as Jesse peeled five bills from his roll.

"You're going to have to leave," Craig said. "The police are on the way. We can't have—"

"This should cover the door," Jesse said, stuffing the bills into Craig's shirt pocket.

He picked up his seabag, feeling bad for the guy.

"We paid for five nights," Jesse said, stepping past him. "You can keep the balance for the trouble, until you get the door fixed."

Gina already had the engine running and the tiny trunk open when Jesse got to the car. He tossed his seabag in, slammed the trunk lid, and got in the passenger side.

Gina stabbed the shifter into reverse and backed out.

"I thought you were going to move Chuck's motorcycle," she said, putting it in first and scratching off.

"It's a side shift," Jesse said, looking down US-1 in the direction the bikers had gone as Gina pulled out, going the opposite way.

"A what?"

Jesse tapped her hand as she shifted to second. "It has a shifter on the right side, like a car, instead of a foot-shifter. I'd probably wreck it. Head for Rusty's. I'll call the police from there and we can try to figure this all out."

She snapped her head around toward him, hair flying wild in the wind. "You're going to get a reputation as a troublemaker."

"You know I didn't *make* trouble," Jesse replied, as Gina turned her attention back to the road. "I have no idea why those guys came to our room. Did you recognize them?"

She shook her head. "Not the two outside." She turned toward him again as she slowed for the turn. "I didn't get much of a look at Chuck's face before you changed his appearance, though."

She turned into the opening next to the leaning mailbox, and it became suddenly darker as they were swallowed up by the dense canopy of trees.

"Six-five," Jesse said. "Almost three hundred pounds. Long black hair, brown eyes, full beard with some gray on either side of his chin, and he had a small scar on the left side his face, near his temple."

Gina turned to look at him as she pulled into the parking area at Shorty's Bar and Bait Shop. Jesse just shrugged.

The Mustang was there, but in a different spot.

It now had a glass back window instead of the plastic sheet, and all the side glass had been replaced.

Rusty and Juliet were sitting on the seawall out in back and they came running when Jesse and Gina got out of the car.

"I thought y'all were gonna be down in Key West all—"

"Something happened," Jesse said, cutting him off. "I don't know why, but someone followed us all through Key West, and all the way to Big Pine."

With sudden clarity, Jesse's conscious mind caught up with his subconscious, linking the two events.

He looked back toward the opening in the treeline. "And just a few minutes ago, three bikers broke down our door at the motel."

Chapter Twenty

◆━━━◆━━━◆━━━◆

Saturday would've been a good day on Mallory Square. A cruise ship was due in, full of happy tourists looking to score. If Chuck had been there, it would've been. But as usual, his supplier had been nowhere to be found.

Instead, he'd spent most of the day trying to locate and take out the two troublemakers who'd landed Bear in prison.

That'll soon be over, he thought. And Sideshift would have the reporter—fresh meat for the whole gang.

A few minutes after the three bikes roared into the motel, two of them pulled out, headed south in a hurry.

Chuck pulled out to follow them, figuring they were headed back to their clubhouse on Big Pine Key. But where was the third?

It should've been an easy payback hit—three bikers against one guy and a girl—but Sideshift wasn't with the other two.

Chuck had heard stories about what a sadistic animal Sideshift was, and he'd seen it firsthand the night Amber Henderson had come to the clubhouse. But she'd enjoyed it.

Had he remained behind to "audition" the reporter woman after smashing her boyfriend all to pieces? As leader, he'd get to go first anyway. Whether that was here or the clubhouse, or both, nobody would argue.

It'd be just like him, Chuck thought. *Right in front of the beaten and bloody boyfriend.*

And Sideshift wouldn't worry about spectators either. He was that crazy and he'd served time for the same reason. He just didn't give a shit.

Only when the two bikes slowed and turned did Chuck see that the guy called Cueball had Sideshift across his lap.

"What the hell?" Chuck muttered, as he slowed to let the motorcycles get farther ahead of him.

Several miles and three turns later, Chuck pulled into the bar's parking lot, as two other men were helping Grinder and Cueball get the bigger man inside.

Sideshift's face wasn't pretty, and they nearly had to drag him through the door. Not that he was a GQ model before, but it looked like somebody had used his face for batting practice with a Louisville Slugger.

Sideshift was as big as they came, bigger than most NFL linemen, and he had a cruel streak that was equally immense.

What the hell happened? he wondered, as he got out of the Cordoba.

Grinder and Cueball gave him extremely hostile looks when Chuck entered the clubhouse, a rundown bar on a canal on the north side of Big Pine Key.

Besides them and Sideshift, there were two other bikers who went back to shooting pool. Chuck didn't recognize either of them. The bartender, an attractive and very large and intimidating local woman named Donna Jennings—who preferred to be called Karma—was hovering over Sideshift.

"You got *some* balls comin' in here," Cueball said, approaching Chuck at the door. "Who the fuck *was* that guy?" He pointed at Sideshift, sprawled in a chair. "He did *that* in all of two *seconds*, man!"

Sideshift was semi-conscious and moaning as Karma wiped some of the blood from his face with a bar towel.

"What happened?" Chuck asked. "They should've been there alone."

Grinder slid off his barstool and approached Chuck. "It *was* only the two of 'em, man. The tall guy put Sideshift down before either of us could even move. Never seen anyone in a maniacal rage like that. And the chick had a gun."

Karma stood and turned around. "His nose is broke. Again. When this man wakes up, he's gonna be all kinds of pissed. So help me, Chuck, if you had anything to do with this, you'd best be gone."

"Tell me what happened," Chuck said. "How did one guy get the drop on all of you?"

"He didn't," Sideshift grunted, coughing up blood as he struggled to sit up. "Fucker kicked me in the balls and sucker-punched me."

"Easy there, Side," Karma said, pushing the big man back down in the chair. "I gave you a shot for the pain. Grinder said there was a lot more happened after that punch, but you were probably already knocked out."

The giant man slumped back in the chair, all eyes on him as he looked around at them, trying to focus.

"What?" Sideshift croaked, shaking his head to try to get rid of the double vision.

Karma knelt instantly and took his head in her hands. "Don't do that, Side! Don't shake your head."

"You're pretty fucked up, man," one of the other bikers said, standing by the pool table, a cue stick in hand.

Sideshift turned his head to look at the man. "Whatta ya mean?"

Cueball stepped closer to Sideshift, but not too close. "The guy smashed your face to a pulp on the bed rail, man. Your left eye's barely sittin' in your skull."

Flashing blue lights outside got everyone's attention.

"Oh, great," Karma said. "That's all we need. The cops."

Sideshift planted his feet and pushed himself up in the chair. "None of y'all know nothin'," he growled. "I got drunk and fell down out back."

Cueball turned to Karma. "I been tellin' you those big ass rocks were dangerous."

"Keep the cops outta this," Sideshift growled, then spat a glob of blood on the floor. "I want another shot at that little shit and next time, I ain't gonna get distracted."

The door opened and two deputies came in, spreading out at the door as a second police car pulled in, lights flashing.

The older cop looked around the room, pausing on Sideshift for a second. "Monte Brisco... I think. You look like somebody beat you with a *big* ole ugly stick."

Chuck knew him. His nametag read "Johnson" and he wore sergeant's stripes on his uniform. He'd only met the man once, and it'd been a cordial meeting, years ago. It was unlikely he'd remember.

Deputy Sergeant Bart Johnson turned and gave a friendly nod to the bartender. "Donna."

"He fell down out back," Grinder blurted. "Hit his head on a—"

Johnson's head turned toward him.

"A rock," Grinder muttered, looking down at the floor.

The sergeant turned back to Karma and smiled. "There was a disturbance up island a few minutes ago, Donna." His eyes moved to Cueball and Grinder, then he nodded toward Sideshift. "Witnesses described those two as being there with Brisco."

"Wasn't them," one of the pool players said, stepping around the table. "They been here all afternoon."

The door opened and two more deputies came in, each holding a pump-action shotgun at the ready.

Johnson looked at Chuck for a moment. Then he glanced over at the stricken biker, and finally back to Chuck once more. "I think I'm beginning to understand what might have happened."

Johnson turned toward Sideshift as the other three deputies spread out. "Bear's *cousin* and his former *cellmate* together in one room? How convenient."

"He fell down outside," Grinder persisted.

"You know I can't take the word of anyone here," he said, as he moved toward the big man, taking out a set of handcuffs. "You'll have your chance to explain it to the judge."

Johnson paused and turned back toward Chuck. "I'd suggest a quick retreat back to your rock, Mr. Bering."

Then he stepped in front of Sideshift. "Can you stand on your own?"

Chapter Twenty-One

Rusty and Juliet listened intently as Jesse and Gina explained what had happened in Key West, about being chased all the way from the Saddlebunch Keys to Big Pine where they lost the car, and then what happened at the motel.

They left out the events at the old ferry dock on No Name Key.

"You'll stay here," Rusty said. "We got plenty of—"

"Whatever these guys were after me for," Jesse said, "I'd rather not bring them here while I'm sleeping in your mom and dad's house."

"What'd they look like?" Juliet asked.

"One, the guy Jesse knocked out, was as big as a mountain," Gina replied. "Long hair and a beard, same as one of the smaller guys, and the third one was bald and had a mustache."

"Baldy rode a hardtail," Jesse added. "The other guy rode a Sporty, and the guy they called Chuck rode an antique side-shifter."

"Sideshift?" Rusty asked, looking quickly toward the parking lot entrance. "A guy taller'n you, and half again as heavy?"

"You know him?" Jesse asked.

"They call him Sideshift," Juliet replied. "He was close with Bear Bering, years ago."

"His real name ain't Chuck, though," Rusty said. "It's Monte Brisco. He did time upstate with Bear."

"Oh, great," Jesse said. "That's just perfect. So, who's Chuck?"

"Somebody spotted you in Key West, bro," Rusty said. "And they called Sideshift to let him know. This guy's even more dangerous than Bear."

"Not anymore," Gina said. "We can stay on the boat, even take it out and anchor somewhere."

Shorty came walking toward them from the bar. "Hey, kids," he said, and waved. "Goin' divin'?"

"We have to tell your dad either way," Jesse whispered.

"Hey, Pop," Rusty called. "Got a second?"

Jesse gave Shorty a Reader's Digest version of what happened, including the name of the biker.

He nodded, one arm crossed, and the other hand stroking his chin in thought. "Did you get a look at the car?"

"A white, 1979 Chrysler Cordoba," Jesse replied. "Never saw the tag, though."

"Chuck *Bering*," Shorty said. "This just keeps gettin' deeper. He's a cousin of Bear's. They been in the pot-sellin' business for years. It was his equipment you boys burned, up there in the Contents last fall."

The squeak of worn-out suspension and brakes could be heard from the entrance, and as they all turned toward the sound, a police car pulled into the parking area.

Not just any police car, Jesse realized, noting the number 12 on the fender.

"Let me do the talkin'," Shorty said.

"I don't think that's going to be an option," Jesse said, stepping up onto the seawall, ready to be arrested.

"Hey, Bart," Shorty said, as the sergeant and his son came toward them. "What's brought you out here?"

Sergeant Johnson strode straight toward Jesse, his eyes locked on him like lasers. "I think this one here knows."

"Brisco kicked in our door," Jesse said. "He entered my and Gina's room uninvited. I stopped him and decided it was better to leave in case the other two came back. I was just about to call you."

"Were you now?" Sergeant Johnson glared up at Jesse for a moment, then turned toward Gina. "Witnesses said there was some gun play."

"Registered and licensed, Deputy Johnson," Gina said. "And I don't *play* with guns."

Jesse grinned.

"I'll need to see the gun, your registration, and permit."

"In my purse," she said, nodding her head toward where they'd been sitting. "It's loaded and the safety is on."

The younger Johnson went over and picked up the purse, then carried it to the sergeant.

"If you'll remove my gun for me," Gina said, obviously knowing he wouldn't let her, "I can find the license and registration for you."

The sergeant pulled the gun out, which Jesse noticed was a compact semi-auto, and removed the magazine. Then he racked the slide and his son picked up the ejected round that'd been in the chamber.

Gina found her paperwork and handed it over. "By the time I came out of our room, the other two had dragged Brisco out to where their motorcycles were parked. A few words were exchanged, and Baldy started toward Jesse. I stopped him and told them to leave. They took Brisco with them, leaving his motorcycle."

"They headed south, toward the bridge, Jesse added. "Baldy's license number was 54781 and the other guy's was 27843, both Florida."

Johnson looked up at him. "You had time to write them down?"

Gina smiled at the sergeant. "He has a photographic memory." Then she glared over at the younger deputy. "He never forgets *anything.*"

The sergeant handed Gina her paperwork, then reluctantly, her weapon and the magazine.

Gina held her hand out to the younger cop. "Give me back my bullet."

He dropped it into her open hand.

Gina dropped the round in the chamber, released the slide, then inserted the magazine before putting the gun back into her purse.

"How long are you here for, McDermitt?" Sergeant Johnson asked.

"We were planning to head back next Friday," Jesse replied, then grinned down at the man. "But we don't *have* to be back until a week from Monday."

"I'm not gonna waste my and the court's time arresting you for what happened at Blue Waters," Johnson said. "And a couple with a little girl in another room saw Brisco kick the door in. I saw the damage, and Brisco will be charged with B and E, at least. He was transported to Mount Sinai in Key West for treatment, then he'll be booked. It's New Year's weekend, so he won't see a judge until Tuesday. But you probably don't want to be around here when he makes bail."

The sergeant turned to leave, but Jesse caught up to him in two strides. "There is one thing I think you should know, Sergeant. It's about when he gets out."

Johnson stopped and turned to face Jesse. "What's that, kid?"

"I don't have a reverse gear," Jesse replied in a low tone, so only the sergeant could hear. "I don't back up, back down, let up, or quit. Ever. So when you let him out, you might want to tell him that."

"Brisco's a good-for-nothing thug and a rapist," Sergeant Johnson said, his tone also even. "In my *opinion*, you did the world a favor making him uglier. But you listen to me, you wet-behind-the-ears—"

"If I see Brisco again," Jesse interrupted, softening his voice, but his eyes remained as sharp as glacial ice, "I'll consider him an immediate threat, and only one of us will survive the meeting. *Next* time I won't stop with just a beating. So, you tell him, or you don't tell him. It makes no difference to me."

"Don't go starting trouble, here, son," Johnson said. "Soldier or not, I'll put you down in a flat second, boy."

"Marine," Jesse corrected him, snapping his jaw. "Soldiers clean up the mess we leave in our wake."

The two scowled at one another for a few seconds, then the sergeant turned, and he and the junior Johnson got in the cruiser and turned around.

Shorty and the others came up behind Jesse as the police car disappeared down the driveway.

"What in the world was that all about?" Shorty asked. "How is it you know Bart Johnson?"

"We met on No Name Key," Gina replied. "That's where we hid out to get away from Chuck Bering."

"Don't piss Bart off, Jesse," Shorty warned. "He's a good man, a good cop, and he's raisin' a good kid, all on his own."

"I wouldn't call that guy a good kid," Jesse retorted. "He's a pervert at best, masquerading as a cop."

"Not Tony," Shorty said. "That boy's a lost cause. Bart's got a little girl about ten, and his wife run off on 'em, just a year ago. That's why Tony wears a uniform. They need the money. But he ain't got any bullets in that gun he carries."

Shorty turned toward Rusty. "Jim, you and JJ go on over and get your stuff. Y'all'll stay here tonight."

"Actually," Juliet said, "I kind of like the idea of Gina and Rachel's boat. When's she coming back?"

"Not until Saturday," Gina said. "Two cabins, kitchen, bathroom... we just need to get our stuff from the kitchen at Blue Waters."

"We'll take care of that," Rusty said, then turned to his dad. "She's right, Pop. It'd be better all the way around if we stayed on the boat. We came down here to be with the girls, anyway. No offense."

Shorty glanced at Juliet and grinned. "None taken, son."

"It's settled then," Juliet said, blushing as she turned to Gina. "Jim and I will go get our stuff and meet you at the dock, while you go get the boat ready to sail. We still have a couple of hours of daylight."

"Where will you take it?" Shorty asked.

Jesse turned toward them. "Key West Bight."

Chapter Twenty-Two

◆――◆――◆――◆

Although he was still months from being a legal adult, physically and mentally, Jesse was a grown man. He'd never backed down from a fight or altercation, but always tried to negotiate first. He'd never gone looking for trouble, but due to his stature, he was often the target of those who thought they could build their "street cred" by besting him.

So far, they'd all come out holding the short end of the stick.

"What are you thinking?" Gina asked, as she turned off the highway toward the marina.

"Just wondering when or if it will end," he replied.

She glanced over quickly. "What do you mean?"

"Have you ever been picked on?" he asked, turning toward her.

"Well, yeah, I guess. Everyone has at some point, probably."

He looked back through the windshield. "I was picked on when I was little. Kids made fun because my dad wasn't there most of the time. At thirteen, I hit a growth spurt, my grandmother says. I went from five-nine to six feet, almost over the span of the summer. Since then, bigger guys have always singled me out. And there's always someone bigger."

"Is that what you think this is? Some kind of macho thing?"

He glanced over at her once more as they pulled into the marina parking lot. "Maybe from their point of view, I don't have anything to prove to anyone."

"Don't lose that, Jesse. Humility is a gift, and it was one of the first things I liked about you when we met."

She parked in the same spot, and they got out of the car.

"But I won't let someone walk on me," Jesse said. "The fuse is very long, but the explosion is massive."

She opened the trunk and looked up at him. "I know. I saw it."

"I'm sorry," he said, hanging his head. "You shouldn't have had to see all that."

"It's not the first time," Gina said, searching his eyes. "And I could tell you tried to control it as long as possible. That guy got what he deserved, just like the two by the pool."

Jesse lifted their bags out and followed her to the docks.

"I didn't know you had a gun," he said.

She smiled. "It wouldn't be concealed if you did."

"You carry it all the time?"

"I'm five-foot-three, Jesse, and less than half your weight. That's called an easy victim in some places." She wrapped an arm around him. "I doubt I'd ever need it with you around. Did they teach you to fight like that in the Marines?"

"Some," Jesse replied. "The Corps teaches a style of hand-to-hand combat utilizing many martial arts strikes. I've studied several forms of martial arts since I was ten, so I picked it up pretty quick, and even taught our instructor a couple of moves."

They climbed aboard and Jesse waited for her to unlock the companionway hatch, as he looked all around. Not seeing anyone, he followed her down into the cabin.

"What do you need me to do?" Jesse asked, putting both their bags on the couch.

"Do you sail?"

He grinned. "My dad and grandfather were boat builders."

She went to the electrical panel and started flipping switches.

"Go topside and disconnect the shore power and water from the pedestal. I'll be up in a sec to help get the spring lines untied. We'll just leave one line on the bow and another on the stern until we're ready to leave."

"Aye, aye, Captain," Jesse said, then went up the steps and out into the cockpit.

He paused for a moment, taking another quick look around, then headed to the side, jumped down to the dock, and walked over to the pedestal.

After shutting off the water and electrical breaker, he disconnected the hose and power cord. Unsure of where Gina and Rachel stored things, he simply coiled them and placed the coils on the aft deck.

He heard the small diesel engine start and water began chugging out of the through-hull fitting as he began untying and coiling the spring lines.

"The engine's running normally," Gina said, climbing up into the cockpit. "It only takes a few minutes to warm up."

"Raw water's flowing good," Jesse said. "I didn't know where you kept the shore power cord and hose."

"I'll get them," she said, stepping up onto the small aft deck.

As Jesse finished untying and coiling the spring lines, Juliet's car pulled in. She parked next to Rachel's Pinto, and she and Rusty started toward the dock, each carrying bags.

Jesse trotted toward them.

"There's more in the car," Rusty said, gesturing over his shoulder, so Jesse continued past them.

In just a few minutes, they had everything aboard and were casting off the two remaining lines.

"We goin' straight through to Key Weird?" Rusty asked, as Gina nudged the throttle forward and steered toward the mouth of Sister

Creek.

"It's a downwind run," Gina said. "We could get there just after sunrise."

"And why are we going there, of all places?" he asked.

"Because that's where all this started," Jesse replied. "Chuck Bering."

"I heard someone say once that he was an *asshole*," Gina said, grinning over at Jesse as she turned into the creek. "Besides, we still have a mystery to solve and a story to write."

"A mystery story?" Juliet asked.

As Gina guided the boat through the creek, she and Jesse told them about their meeting with Carly Ingersoll, and the straight scoop she'd given them on the four attempts on her husband's life.

"Or maybe it's just been three," Gina said. "Nobody saw anyone shoot a gun."

"But they did find a bullet," Jesse added. "Whether it's four or three, the guy survived at least a stabbing, a poisoning, and a bombing."

"Sound like he's in the wrong branch of service," Rusty said with a chuckle.

"The Navy's got him hidden over on Andros," Jesse said. "I don't think any of this has anything to do with the Navy, but if it does, they might go after his wife and kids."

The three of them stood in the center cockpit as Gina guided the boat around the last turn, and the ocean spread out before them.

Jesse felt a pull from seaward. Whether it was the ocean calling him or just an outgoing current, he had to admit, this could be nice. He moved over beside Gina at the helm and took a long breath, releasing it slowly.

"You feel it, don't you?" Gina whispered, as Rusty and Juliet moved forward along both side decks, pulling in the fenders.

BAD BLOOD

"Something," he said with a nod. "I've felt it a few times in the past when heading out. What's your boat's name? I didn't see one on the stern."

"It was removed by the previous owner," she replied. "But her name's *Pleiades*. She's a Morgan Out Island 41, and a pig upwind, but tonight will be comfortable."

"Aren't you missing five sisters?" Jesse asked.

The constellation Pleiades, also called the Seven Sisters, was an easily recognizable star cluster, with seven bright stars.

"The boat came with the name," she said. "We just never got around to changing it. Can you hoist the mainsail?"

"On it," Jesse said, then turned to Rusty. "I'll get up on the mast and you take up the slack on the winch."

Rusty nodded, and Jesse climbed quickly onto the roof, went over to the side of the mast, and located the main halyard and its clutch.

"I got three turns on the drum," Rusty said, indicating he had the slack wrapped around the winch and was ready.

Jesse released the clutch and looked back at Gina, waiting.

She turned the boat into the wind, watching the vane on the top of the mast through a clear plastic window in the bimini. Jesse looked up at it too.

When the arrow pointed forward, Gina shouted, "Hoist the main!"

Jesse reached up high and pulled out and down on the halyard as Rusty pulled on the bitter end, wrapped around the winch.

Over and over, up, down, up, down, until the sail reached the top.

Gina turned to Rusty at the winch. "Give it another half turn with the handle."

When he did, she called up to Jesse, "Lock it in."

Jesse locked the halyard clutch in place and Rusty did the same with the winch clutch. The mainsail snapped, filling with wind, as Gina began a slow turn to the right. Juliet was on the main sheet, letting it out as the boat turned downwind.

Looking ahead, Jesse saw that they were sailing straight toward the setting sun, which was still an hour or more above the horizon.

The chug of the engine stopped, and they were moving under wind power alone.

"Engine's off," Gina said, needlessly. "The spinnaker pole is on the other side of the mast, Jesse. We'll use it with a back haul and put a line on the boom up to the bow to prevent an accidental jibe."

It took a few minutes, but they got the furled foresail rigged on the port side with a line to a stern cleat, and ran another line from the boom to a cleat on the foredeck to sail wing-and-wing.

When he got back to the cockpit, *Pleiades* was sailing at six knots.

"The wind will drop a little after dark," Gina said. "But we should be able to maintain four or five knots."

The suddenness of everything hit Jesse. Just a couple of hours ago, they were enjoying lunch in Key West, and not even one hour later, he and Gina were naked under a metal lean-to. And just thirty minutes ago, he'd beaten up a guy.

"We can trade off during the night," Juliet suggested. "Two on at all times, sunset to sunrise. That'll be three hours on and three off, two shifts, right?"

Jesse had done a lot of day sailing, but he'd only been a passenger on the few night crossings he'd done.

"Works for me, JJ," Gina said, nodding at her. "Your math's always been better than mine. You and Jim... er, Rusty, have sailed with us plenty enough, so you know the boat. You guys take the second and fourth watch and wake us up at sunrise when we get close."

She smiled up at Jesse. "I'll keep the rookie as my cabana boy."

"Can I rub some suntan lotion on your back?" he asked jokingly.

She gave him a quizzical look. "Are you sure you don't know Jimmy Buffett?"

"He listens to jazz," Rusty said. "Mostly instrumental stuff. Not *too* hard on the ears."

Gina was right; the ride was quite comfortable, with a following sea gently lifting the stern a couple of feet as the rollers passed beneath the hull. Each time it did, about every fifteen to twenty seconds, the boat's speed would increase slightly as it rode down the face of the wave for a moment.

Sailing downwind, the boat didn't heel over, but it did roll slightly from side to side as the waves passed under.

"C'mon, Rusty," Juliet said. "You can help me with dinner."

"What're we havin'?" he asked, following her toward the companionway.

"Something simple," Gina suggested. "I'll make a big breakfast in the morning."

Gina took a long, thick, rubber cord with hooks on both ends and secured one end to a small eyebolt on one side of the helm. Then she wrapped the thick bungee twice around the topmost handle on the wheel and hooked the other end to another eyebolt to the left.

"Now all we have to do is watch for anything in the way," Gina said, pushing Jesse down onto the cushioned seat on the starboard side and then sitting beside him. She took his right hand in hers, turning it over to look at his knuckles. "You're bleeding a little."

"It's fine," Jesse said, trying to pull his hand away.

"No, it isn't," Gina replied, not letting go. "Do you know how much bacteria you might've picked up from that animal?"

Chapter Twenty-Three

♦──♦──♦──♦──♦

As Gina moved to the other side of the cockpit, Jesse looked around the minimal helm. On one side was a small depth-sounder showing the bottom was a little shy of a hundred feet below. Beneath it was a knot meter, and in the middle was a compass, which indicated their course was 255 degrees, roughly west-southwest, following the island chain.

On the right side was the engine control at the top, with a tachometer and oil pressure gauge below it.

Gina returned and kissed Jesse on the cheek, then sat down beside him and opened a small first-aid kit. In minutes, she'd cleaned, disinfected, and dressed a small cut on his middle knuckle.

"Thanks," he said, when she'd put the kit away and sat back down beside him.

"Do you really plan to go after him?" she asked.

"He sent those guys," Jesse said. "Remember? Baldy said they'd already been paid, and Chuck was an asshole. But we thought they were talking about the guy they call Sideshift."

"The giant you beat up."

He looked over at her. "Yeah, he was big. I couldn't let him make the first move."

"What will you do? In Key West, I mean."

"I haven't thought it all the way through yet."

She looked over at him. "You'll let me know when you do?"

"If and when I do," Jesse replied. "You'll be the first to know."

Rusty appeared with a tray of sandwiches, and right behind him, Juliet came up with a large bag of potato chips.

"Ya said keep it simple," Rusty said, placing the tray on the small table in the middle.

Juliet sat down, then grabbed a sandwich. "We made more for the night watches, too."

Rusty sat next to her and grinned at Jesse. "I didn't get a chance to tell ya," he said. "It's about the Mustang."

"What's that?" Jesse asked, reaching for one of the sandwiches.

"Pop knows outboards, but he don't know squat about cars. And I reckon he ain't the only one."

"What do you mean?"

"Whoever he bought that 289 from didn't know what he had," Rusty replied. "I looked under the hood. It's a K-code motor."

Jesse took a bite. "K-code?"

"There was over 600,000 Mustangs built in 1964 and '65," Rusty said. "And thirteen thousand K-code 289s were built those years. But only about half of 'em went into Mustangs. About one out of a hundred built has a K-code motor."

Jesse chewed, then swallowed. "That doesn't tell me what it is."

"It's a *high-performance* 289, bro," Rusty replied. "I drove it on a bottle run this mornin', and it's still got some pep."

"Think it'll make the thousand-mile trip back to Lejeune?"

"Wait," Gina said. "I always thought it was pronounced la-june."

Jesse grinned and nodded. "It probably *should* be, but it's named after General John A. Lejeune, and he was a Louisiana man. My grandfather served under him and said that was how he pronounced his name—la-zhurn."

"I think it could make the trip," Rusty replied. "Oil looked clean, and I didn't see no sign of leaks. You should hang onto it."

Jesse grinned. "It's yours."

"Wait... what?" Juliet blurted out.

"That car was built from the fantasy ideas of a kid," Jesse said, shaking his head. "Don't get me wrong. I thought it was a great gift and my friend and grandfather put a lot of work into making that fantasy a reality." He paused and looked at his friends. "But the current reality is, I don't need a car. You do. What if you suddenly had to get home in a hurry?"

"For what?" Juliet said. "We already planned things with us being mostly apart for four years."

"You're getting married," Jesse replied. "You two might have a baby one day and Rusty would have to..."

The two of them were looking at Jesse with odd expressions, somewhat shocked.

"A baby ain't in our plan until after I get out, bro," Rusty said.

"Still... I don't need a car. And you do." Then he grinned. "Besides, it's kind of a Keys car now, anyway. I want you to have it. Billy would too."

"I don't know what to say," Rusty said, looking across the small table at Jesse. "Thanks, bro."

"You'll have to explain it to your dad," Jesse added. "I told him to sell it for what he's put into it."

It was Rusty's turn to give a sly grin. "I know. I told him if he couldn't find a quick buyer, I'd buy it from him on time."

Jesse laughed and reached across the table. "Deal?"

Rusty shook his hand. "Done deal, bro. I'll just pay off what Pop's put into it, then. Hot damn! A hot rod Mustang with a Hi-Po 289 for under a grand!"

Gina got up and went to the wheel, then looked at the compass.

Jesse joined her as she forced the wheel slightly to the left, against the bungee cord, and held it there for a few seconds.

"It's not the greatest auto-steering," she said, checking their course again. "It needs an adjustment every now and then. One day, we want to get a mechanical wind vane for long crossings."

"You've done a lot of those?" Jesse asked.

She turned toward him, smiling. "A few. Over to the Bahamas and back a couple of times, and we sailed to New Orleans for Mardi Gras last year."

"I'd like to do something like that one day."

"You're doing it now," Gina said. "Sailing to Cayo Hueso, one time home port of Blackbeard, Black Caesar, and my favorite, Stede Bonnet, known as the 'The Gentleman Pirate.'"

"I mean like you and Rachel," he replied. "When I was a kid, I watched a lot of reruns of *Adventures in Paradise* and dreamed of owning a charter boat in some tropical place."

"The *Tiki* was a pretty big boat," she said, looking up at him.

"Eighty-five feet," he replied. "An Alden-designed schooner, but *Tiki's* real name was—"

"*Pilgrim!*" she exclaimed. "Loved that show. But I see you more as a dive charter captain, running a custom live-aboard dive boat from the flybridge, heading out to the next dive site with a bunch of drunk bubbas from Ohio."

"That'd work too," Jesse said. "But it'll have to wait until I retire."

She looked up at him. "It's a long time until retirement."

"Not in the military," Jesse replied. "I could take a partial pension when I'm thirty-seven, but I'm planning to go the full thirty years. I'll only be forty-seven when I retire."

Gina looked back at Rusty and Juliet. "You're more like them," she said. "Lives all planned out. Rach and I haven't planned beyond the next summer since we were sixteen and eighteen."

"You've been on your own since you were sixteen?"

"Not completely," she replied. "But when Rach moved out, I did too. Our parents' boat was too small even for just the two of them. Rach and I slept in the salon."

"What about your brother?"

"Gregor dropped out of school and moved before we did, but at least we both finished school. Now, the only thing we plan is where we're going in the summer to have fun. We work hard from September to April, whatever work we can find—waiting tables, slinging drinks, or yacht deliveries, then we relax during the off season."

"Yacht deliveries?"

"Pays better than behind a bar," she replied. "Usually it's just me and Rachel, and sometimes we bring a friend or two, but now and then, like on our last one, the new owners come along to learn the ropes."

"And this summer?" Jesse asked.

"Well, we *were* planning to sail over to Bimini, then to the Out Islands, but lately I've been thinking about visiting the OBX. Do you know it?"

Jesse grinned. "I have a friend... well, my squad leader, actually. He has sort of a second home in the Outer Banks. Rusty and I are diving for treasure with him this spring. But I wasn't supposed to say that."

"I've heard there were a lot of shipwrecks there," she said. "Diving for treasure sounds like fun. And speaking of fun first things.... Is this your first night sail?"

"First in a long time," he replied. "That one time I told you about was when I was little. And I went out with Pap and a couple of his friends on two overnight sails. But I was just ballast, according to Pap."

Gina glanced back at the others, then whispered, "You know

what else is going to be a lot of fun?"

"What's that?" he whispered back.

She stood on her toes and whispered, "I'll be your first."

Jesse cocked his head and arched an eyebrow. "Are you forgetting our week in the Bahamas? Or last night?"

"First time under sail? Up in the pulpit?"

Jesse felt his face flush and he turned toward the others.

"During the second watch, of course," Gina whispered, rising up on her toes again to kiss him. "They'll sleep hard after the first mid-watch."

Chapter Twenty-Four

◆◆◆◆

A tapping on the overhead woke Jesse. He opened his eyes, which took way more effort than it should have, and he could see that it was still dark. But he knew immediately where he was.

Gina's cabin, aboard *Pleiades*.

For a moment, his mind drifted to their second watch, making love while standing in the very front of the boat, dolphins playing in the bow wave below them.

"They must have the lights of Key West in sight," Gina said, sitting up and tapping three times on the ceiling. "We'll be docking in an hour."

"You don't wear a watch either, and the sun isn't even up. How do *you* know what time it is?"

"Ocean warblers," she said with a smile, crawling naked across him. "C'mon, rise and shine."

She went to a drawer and pulled a bikini out, along with a pair of cutoff jeans that'd seen better days.

Moving stiffly, Jesse pulled a clean pair of skivvies and cargo shorts from his seabag. Their escapade on the bow wasn't the only one of the night, yet Gina was bouncing around, full of energy.

A few minutes later, they were both dressed and heading up the companionway ladder.

"Good morning," Juliet greeted them, a bit over the top. "It's about an hour before sunrise and we're a mile south of Smather's

Beach."

"You seem awfully chipper," Jesse said, looking forward.

The nearly full moon was on the horizon, appearing much larger than it actually was.

"Chipper? Me? No," Juliet replied nervously. "To tell you the truth, I'm pretty tired."

"Ain't seen a thing," Rusty added, looking like the proverbial cat next to an empty birdcage.

Did they do it, too? Jesse wondered.

"We'll swing around to the anchorage off Wisteria Island," Gina said. "You'll want to see if there's a slip available in the marina, right?"

"Yeah," Jesse replied. "We need to be close."

"That could get expensive, bro," Rusty said. "And that's only if there's even a slip available. And you're already out the motel money."

"I'll cover it," Jesse said.

"Okay, then," Gina agreed. "We can get anchored, eat, rest up a little, and take the dinghy to see about a slip when the dockmaster gets in at eight."

Before reaching the main ship channel, Gina started the engine, and they turned windward to lower the sails before motoring north on the west side of the island.

Jesse went up to the bow to watch for any boats that might not be lit, and as they approached Wisteria Island, he saw a few.

Finally, Gina picked out a clear spot, with no boats nearby, and they dropped the anchor. She reversed the engine to make sure the anchor would hold, then shut off the diesel.

"The hot water tank is only twenty gallons," Gina said, and motoring in probably got it nice and warm." She turned to Juliet. "You guys go ahead, but save us some."

BAD BLOOD

Rusty and Juliet went below, and Gina moved to follow them.

"Can you get the dinghy in the water?" she asked. "I'll get things ready for breakfast. There's a clip on the safety cables where you can put it over the side."

"Where's the engine for it?" Jesse asked.

"Your arms and back," she replied with a smile, before heading toward the hatch. "We row."

Gina disappeared below, and Jesse went up onto the foredeck, finding the cables with the clips on the starboard side. He unhooked them and moved the cables out of the way, then turned to the small fiberglass sailing dinghy.

It was inverted and secured to the deck with a single strap, which he undid, then moved around to the little boat's transom.

It was lighter than he anticipated, and he easily swung the stern around, so the transom was hanging over the side.

He continued to work it out farther, until it was just about balanced. Then he went to the front, tied the painter off to a nearby deck cleat, then heaved the bow of the dinghy as high and fast as he could, flipping it away from him.

The stern hit the water and the little boat teetered for a second, then went on over, splashing upright into the water.

Below where the dinghy had been secured were two oars with oarlocks, which Jesse lowered into the small boat, along with a small rudder and tiller assembly.

He rose and stood for a moment on the foredeck, looking around at all the different boats anchored there. Many looked like they were on the verge of sinking any minute, but there were a couple of newer-looking yachts moored along with the derelicts.

Key West, he thought.

The place where Hemingway wrote, where President Truman had once had a private retreat, and where "wreckers" had lured ships onto the reef to "salvage" them.

And it was the island he'd come to with his mother and father, the last time they were all together.

Like they were doing now, his father had also anchored and taken his dinghy to the marina to see if there was room. They managed to get a slip but could only stay two nights.

Just across the channel, Jesse could see Key West Bight and the marina where they'd docked when he was a kid. The waterfront beyond was lit up much like he remembered it.

The soft sound of their halyard moving against the mast was also familiar to him. And looking off to the south, the channel markers even looked the same.

When they'd returned to Fort Myers, his dad had to go back to Camp Lejeune the following month, to ship out to Vietnam again. That was the last time he'd seen him.

"I see you didn't have any trouble," Gina said, walking up behind him. "You looked like you were lost in thought."

"I was," Jesse replied, turning toward her. "We anchored near here, and the town looks the same."

"You mean the time you came here with your parents?"

"Yeah. We could only get a slip for two days, then we came back out here for two more. I remember walking down the streets in town, looking at all these big, tall houses. Dad wanted one, but Mom would never have gone for it."

"Your mom didn't like the people here?" Gina asked, slipping an arm around his waist and looking toward shore.

"It wasn't that," Jesse replied. "I remember everyone was really friendly. But there's what? Twenty, or twenty-five thousand people living here?"

"That's close today," she replied. "Ten years ago, there were more than thirty thousand."

"On an island that's only seven square miles," Jesse said, looking toward shore again. "She thought it was too crowded."

And somewhere in that throng of people, Jesse thought, remembering the large crowds on Duval Street, *there's a man named Chuck who sent others to hurt me and Gina.*

Chapter Twenty-Five

◆━━━◆━━━◆━━━◆

After they'd all showered and had breakfast, it was still more than an hour before the marina office opened, but the sun was up, and the sky was clear of clouds.

"We can walk around town," Rusty suggested. "Any idea where this guy lives?"

Jesse turned his head and looked across the channel. "I only saw him from a distance—across the street. He was dressed nice. Clean-cut. And the car. It wasn't a typical Keys car, so he's got more money than brains. He wants to make a good appearance, without being too flamboyant."

"And you got all that from a quick glance?" Juliet asked.

Jesse shrugged. "He could've been sitting in his underwear for all I know. But I'm guessing neatly pressed pants and Italian loafers."

"So, he might live right here in town," Juliet said. "Rather than over on Stock Island."

"Makes it easier," Rusty agreed. "But it's still a big-ass island."

"We find the car," Jesse said, "we find the snake who sent that sideshow freak after us."

"If he's got a lot of money," Gina said, "then he probably lives in Old Town." She stepped over beside Jesse. "Those big, tall houses you remembered."

Jesse shrugged. "Nothing to lose walking around, I guess. But I remember those houses going on for blocks and blocks."

The four of them got in the dinghy, and Gina quickly mounted the tiller as Rusty and Juliet settled in front. Jesse put the oarlocks in place and pushed away from the boat, quickly turning the bow toward Key West Bight with the oars.

It only took Jesse a few minutes to row across the channel, where they tied the dinghy up with several others at a small dock.

"These mostly belong to liveaboards," Gina said. "A lot of people who work the bars at night live on their boats out there where we're anchored. They won't be up for hours."

As they walked out to the street, Jesse could see that the town was already starting to wake up, and the scent of fresh bread and pastries filled the air.

"We should split up," Rusty suggested. "Me and Jewels will take Caroline Street, and y'all take Eaton. Probably only have time to walk a single street each."

"Meet up back here in an hour," Jesse added. "I think he's a night-owl, too. So, finding him later might be easier."

"This way," Gina said, taking Jesse's arm and turning right.

They walked a block, then crossed the street and continued on Eaton, strolling slowly.

"The odds of finding him this way are really slim," Jesse said, looking over a fence at a driveway. "But this street seems familiar."

"Then the morning's not all lost," she said. "You get to revisit memories from childhood."

"Where's that place we had lunch yesterday?"

"Louie's Backyard?" she asked. "About ten or twelve blocks from here. This end of town is probably the most affluent neighborhood. At least once we get across Duval Street."

Jesse could see a busier cross street ahead as they approached the corner of Whitehead Street. On the opposite corner, a tall fence surrounded what appeared to be a vacant area.

BAD BLOOD

When they stepped up onto the sidewalk on the other side, Jesse paused to look over the fence.

"What is it?" Gina asked.

"A big parking lot," Jesse replied, turning right and following the wall.

"La Concha Hotel," Gina replied. "The oldest hotel in Key West."

Jesse stopped and peered through a gap in the foliage. Halfway down the second row was a white Cordoba.

"We found him," Jesse said, without looking away.

"No way!"

"Five spots in. Second row."

"Uh, yeah.... You might be able to stand flat-footed and look over a six-foot privacy fence, but I can't."

Jesse squatted and scooped her up, holding her easily at his level as he looked around. "Where's the entrance?"

"It looks like the same car," she said. "I think. The entrance is around on Duval. Now put me down."

He grinned as he gently placed her back on her feet. "I thought you liked to climb."

A middle-aged couple walked past, hurrying somewhere.

"Not in public," Gina admonished.

"How can we find Rusty and Juliet?"

"This way," she said, taking his hand. "If they're being thorough, there's a little neighborhood off Caroline they would probably check, and we can catch them at the corner of Duval."

They walked quickly to the next block and turned left on the famous Duval Street, where they passed a real estate office, then several small boutique shops and a bar before reaching the corner at Caroline Street.

Rusty and Juliet were just approaching the corner too.

167

"We found him," Gina said. "Or Jesse did. I couldn't see over the wall. He's staying at La Concha."

"Ya don't say," Rusty said. "That actually makes more sense, now I think about it. More transient."

"So, what do we do now?" Juliet asked.

"Let's go back to the marina," Jesse suggested. "Maybe the office will open early."

When they reached the marina office, it was still closed, but it was only fifteen minutes until they were supposed to open. Jesse turned and looked back toward Eaton Street.

"We need to find a way to get him outside," Gina said. "The hotel won't just give us his room number."

"He was in business with Bear, right?" Jesse asked. "Selling pot?"

"That's what Pop said," Rusty agreed.

"Until he was sent upstate for twenty years," Gina replied. "I'm sure he's got a new supplier now, though."

Turning, Jesse noticed the large bumpers set out away from the seawall. There was another one a hundred yards to the left, with a fence around a big, open area. "Is that where cruise ships dock?" he asked.

"Yes, it is," Gina replied, then pointed to the fenced area. "The passengers disembark through those gates."

"Then this is where we set up surveillance," Jesse said. "He sells pot to tourists."

"Of course!" Gina exclaimed. "They can't bring it with them on the ship, so anyone selling it here could charge double or triple."

"Especially if they're the only game in town," Rusty added. "That operation of Bear's was huge. We're talkin' a quarter million street value."

"Chuck's got the muscle to enforce it, too," Jesse said, thinking out loud. "Big and dumb, but probably enough to keep other dealers out. How often do ships stop here?"

"Just about every day," Gina replied. "They kick up a lot of silt, killing nearby reefs."

"S'cuse me," Rusty said, turning toward a man who was reaching for the door. "Are you the dockmaster?"

"Yeah," the man replied. "Fuel dock don't open till nine."

Gina stepped toward him. "We'd like a slip if there's one available."

"On New Year's Eve?" the gray-haired man replied with a light chuckle. "Good luck with that. But c'mon in, let me check the boards."

"New Year's is big here?" Jesse whispered to Gina, as they followed the others in.

"Always has been," Gina replied. "They had a huge blowout of a party here last Halloween, and if they do it again, it could be bigger than tonight's celebration."

"Lemme see what happened last night," the dockmaster said, reaching for a phone that had a flashing light on it. "Where y'all comin' from?"

"Up island," Rusty replied. "Marathon."

The dockmaster picked up the receiver and held it to his ear as he pressed the red button. After listening for a few seconds, he scribbled something on a notepad, then paused and listened again. Once more, he wrote something down, then listened for a moment longer.

Finally, he made another note, then hung up the phone and turned toward the group. "You're in luck," he said. "That last message was a cancellation. Folks won't be arriving for two more days."

"We'll take it," Jesse said.

"There's just one thing, though," the dockmaster replied,

looking up at Jesse. "That's a sixty-foot, premium slip on the end of the dock. Two hundred bucks, in advance, for the two nights."

Jesse knew when he was being ripped off. The man had written something down after listening to the last message. If it was a cancellation and he had paying customers standing right in front of him, why would he need to write *anything* down?

And what were the odds that someone else was going to come sailing in, willing to pay double?

"One hundred for two nights," Jesse countered. "Including water and shore power."

The man's eyes narrowed and hardened for a moment, then the realization came over him. A bird in hand....

"One-fifty's as low as I can go," he offered.

"Deal," Jesse said, extending his hand to the man.

Ten minutes later, they were walking back to the dinghy dock, and far to the south, a large cruise ship could be seen.

"Think we can get in before that thing gets here?" Jesse asked, nodding toward the south.

"Oh, shit," Gina said, grabbing Jesse's hand. "We'll have to hurry."

They raced to the end of the seawall, then out onto the dock where their dinghy was tied, and got in.

Rusty untied the line, and Jesse started pushing on the oars, backing the little boat out as Gina held the tiller over.

Once clear, Jesse turned the dinghy the rest of the way around, and said, "Hang on."

His strokes weren't fast, but the oars dipped deep, and with his long arms and powerful body, the boat jumped forward with every long stroke.

Gina sat facing Jesse in the back, one hand on the tiller, smiling as he rowed hard.

When they got to *Pleiades*, they hurried up onto the deck and Juliet started to take the dinghy's line aft.

"No, we have to get it up on deck," Gina said, going to the helm. "We can't maneuver if we're pulling it."

"I got it," Jesse said, taking the line and moving up along the side deck. "Don't wait on me."

"Rusty, get the anchor," Gina directed, as she started the engine.

With Rusty and Juliet both heaving on the anchor line, which was looped around a drum, the boat started inching forward as Jesse unclipped the side safety cables.

Reaching down, he got the oars out of the dinghy and placed them up on the cabin top, then sat down on the edge and, using his feet and the dinghy's bow line, moved the boat so the stern was against the hull, a couple feet forward of the center of the opening.

Jesse rose, and as the sailboat inched forward, he took the line in both hands, reaching as far out as he could, then heaved.

He kept pulling hand-over-hand, until the dinghy was standing upright, almost centered on the opening. Then he reached up and grabbed the loop at the end of the line and pulled down with all his weight. The dinghy flipped onto the deck, upside down, and halfway through the opening.

In minutes, they were moving toward the marina, as fast as the sailboat could go, which was only slightly faster than the speed of mud.

"We'll make it easy," Rusty said, flopping down on the other side of the cockpit with Juliet.

Gina turned toward Jesse, an amused look on her face. "Is that how you got the dinghy in the water earlier? Just *muscled* it in?"

Jesse looked up, breathing hard from the exertion. "Yeah. Why?"

"I usually use the spare halyard."

"Spare halyard?"

Chapter Twenty-Six

◆━━◆━━◆━━◆━━◆

Gina maneuvered her boat to the dock with a soft hand on both the wheel and throttle control, making the whole thing seem effortless. The dockmaster and a young boy who was maybe twelve or thirteen came out and met *Pleiades* at the slip to help with the lines and they had her tied up in a matter of minutes.

Jesse retrieved the water hose and shore power cable from where he'd seen Gina put them, and as he stepped over to the dock, he noticed the cruise ship was still a quarter mile out.

He connected the hose and cable, then stood and looked around the marina. As boat slips went, it was okay, but in Jesse's opinion, it was way too close to the fuel pumps. If there were a fire or something, it could be dangerous, and he figured it'd probably be a loud and busy place throughout the day—hardly a "premium" slip.

Jesse guessed it was more likely that it was overflow parking for the fuel dock, and the dockmaster was pocketing the cash. It was doubtful the owner even lived in the area, and there was little chance of them finding out the guy was skimming.

But it suited their needs perfectly.

Since it was located on the outside of the T-dock, they could throw off the lines and get moving pretty quickly. And it had a good view of the fenced area where the cruise ship passengers would disembark before descending on the T-shirt shops and bars.

He could even see the upper floors of La Concha.

"I'll take those," Gina said, and Jesse turned to find her reaching over the safety cables.

"Oh, sorry," he said, handing her the coiled hose first. "I think we have a good spot here."

"And for two nights," she said, attaching the hose. "Just like when you came here with your mom and dad. That's a sign."

"We should make a point of going to see your friend, Carly," Jesse said. "See if anything more has developed. You have a good story there."

"You think?" she asked, taking the power cable.

"Headline! Bungling Psychopath Still on the Loose!"

Gina laughed, then looked at him with a serious expression. "That might not be far off the truth. The psychopath part."

"What do you mean?"

Gina stepped back down into the cockpit and plugged the cable into the receptacle before turning around. "The level of violence is escalating. Whoever it is, they're coming unglued."

"You're right," Jesse said, thinking back. "A knife, poison, a gun, and then a bomb. Thankfully, no innocent person has been hurt."

"Scott's innocent," Gina replied.

He looked over at her, standing on the aft deck. "Not in the killer's mind. To them, he's an obstacle."

"In the way of what?" she asked.

"I don't know," Jesse replied. "Which is why we need to talk to Carly again."

"Then let's do it," she said. "Let me go down and switch the breakers off before you flip the main on."

He nodded and she went down into the boat as Rusty and Juliet went back aboard.

"All the lines are snugged," Rusty shouted down into the cabin.

"Thanks," Gina called up. "Tell Jesse he can turn on the main breaker now."

Hearing her, Jesse bent over and flipped the breaker to the on position, then stood at the stern, waiting. After a few seconds, water started pumping out of one of the through-hull fittings, and he could hear the hum of the boat's air conditioning.

Rusty pointed toward the large, open area behind them, beyond the small marina. "Good spot. We can see most of Mallory Square." He turned back toward Jesse. "Ya think one of us should go to La Concha and watch for him to leave?"

"And do what?" Jesse asked. "If he drives off in the car, we don't have one to follow him with. And we don't have any way of communicating if he leaves on foot."

"Sure we do," Rusty said, then disappeared down into the salon.

A moment later, he returned, Gina right behind him, both carrying handheld radios. Jesse recognized the one Rusty had. He'd used it to talk to Shorty, just before he blew up Bear's boat.

"We have two handheld VHFs," Gina said. "But they're bulky. Plus we have the radio here on the boat."

"How far will they reach?" Jesse asked.

"From one handheld to another, in town," Rusty said, "maybe a mile apart—here to Southernmost Point. The east end of the island'll be out of range, but the boat's radio can reach these all the way to Stock Island, maybe farther."

"And talk back?" Jesse asked, picking up Gina's radio.

It was heavy and the size and shape of a brick, but it'd fit in the big cargo pockets of his shorts.

"The boat will probably be able to pick the handhelds up farther than a mile," Gina replied. "The antenna's on top of the mast. Except maybe way over by Smathers Beach."

"Okay, we have communication," Jesse said. "Gina and I want to go see Carly again. So, will one of you go watch La Concha, while the other stays here to relay messages?"

"I'll stay," Juliet said. "Channel sixty-eight?"

Rusty shook his head. "Let's pick another channel. Sixty-eight and sixty-nine can get busy. Try seventy-two; it's a noncommercial working frequency, but a whole lot less used."

"Works for me," Jesse agreed, then switched on the battery-operated radio and turned the channel selector to 72. "Check that his car's still there first, Rusty. There's a gap in the back fence on Whitehead. If the Cordoba's still there, go around to the next corner north of Eaton. You should be able to see the parking lot entrance from there, and if there's a side door, you can see it too. I didn't see a gate or door on the other two sides of the lot."

"Got it," he replied. "And Jewels can watch the square. She knows what the guy looks like."

"You do?" Jesse asked.

"One of the advantages of being a bartender," Juliet replied. "You see everyone and hear everything they say. A lot of times, things they shouldn't be saying in public."

"That's the truth," Gina agreed. "Behind the bar, we're invisible."

Rusty kissed Juliet and jumped down to the dock.

"Do you think Carly would be at work now?" Jesse asked, watching the cruise ship move up alongside the dock ahead of them.

"Maybe," Gina replied. "She doesn't work nights, but usually tries to get a shift whenever a cruise ship comes in."

Jesse stepped over to the dock, then lifted Gina down. "So, she would've left her kids with the lesbian babysitter."

"So you think she's gay, too?"

"How would I know?" Jesse replied. "I'm just going off your intuition."

"Only one way to find out if she's there," Gina said, taking his hand and leading the way. Then she stopped and looked back toward the sailboat. "Yell if you need anything, JJ."

Juliet waved, and they continued out to the street.

As they walked down Duval, Jesse got that feeling of familiarity again, but he didn't remember there being so many T-shirt shops and places to drink.

"How many bars do you think there are in this town?" he asked.

"Almost three hundred," Gina replied. "More than forty just here on Duval Street."

They took a few more steps before Jesse responded. "That seems like an unusually high number for a small town."

"It's a drinking town with a fishing problem."

Jesse laughed as they passed La Concha, and he spotted Rusty on the other side of the street. He was leaning against a signpost, where he could see all the entrances, a Coke in hand.

They nodded at each other, then Jesse and Gina continued across Fleming Street.

"Most of the bars are for tourists," Gina said. "On any given day, there are thousands in town."

"You talk like it's your hometown," Jesse said.

"I don't know," she replied, looking up at him. "I think it is sometimes. Maybe in another life."

They walked half a block in silence, holding hands.

"What will you do to this guy?" Gina asked. "Chuck Bering, I mean."

"I don't know," Jesse admitted. "First contact has already been made. My squad leader says that any plan goes out the window as soon as first contact is made with the enemy. Then everything falls into reactionary chaos."

"Reactionary chaos?" she asked. "So you *chose* to start at that level when those guys broke into our room?"

Jesse looked down and nodded. "His kicking the door in was the first contact. My reaction would be the same any time someone did that. He didn't have a plan B for when he met someone tougher."

"You went on the attack before he did something to hurt you, right?"

"Not exactly," Jesse replied. "Guys like that intimidate people with their size and they hardly ever have to back it up. I never felt that I was in any danger—they didn't come in with guns or anything—but you might've been hurt. I saw the way he looked at you."

"I had a gun," Gina reminded him. "Still do."

He looked at her and grinned. "Would have been nice to know that at the time."

Chapter Twenty-Seven

⬥⬥⬥⬥⬥

As they walked, Jesse wondered how he could get all the players involved in one place at the same time. Johnson had said that Brisco had needed a visit to the hospital before being taken to jail and it being a Sunday and New Year's Eve meant that he wouldn't get out until Tuesday.

"Do you know anyone here with a car?" Jesse asked suddenly.

"Well, yeah," Gina replied. "But it's only about a mile."

"I need to go over to Stock Island before we go see Carly."

"What's on Stock..." She paused and looked up at him. "Are you scheming something?"

"I think so," Jesse replied.

"I know a guy who drives a cab," she said. "His wife dispatches him using CB radio. There's a phone booth on the next corner where I can call her from."

Five minutes later, a blue Chevy pulled to the curb and honked. It had a yellow "Taxi" light on the roof and the word Thum on the passenger door.

Jesse thought the name was pretty clever.

"Hiya, Gina," the driver said through the open passenger window.

"Hey, Nick," she replied, as Jesse opened the back door for her.

They both got in, and Gina leaned over the seat. "Jesse, meet my friend, Nick Thacker. Nick, this is my boyfriend, Jesse McDermitt."

He reached across the back of the seat and extended a hand. "Any friend of Gina's... Where to?"

Jesse told him, and Gina looked surprised. "The sheriff's office?"

"I'll tell you when we get there," Jesse replied.

Gina leaned forward again. "Hey, Nick. Do you know Amber Henderson?"

"The smarmy brunette who likes to party with girls?"

"I didn't know that about her," Gina lied. "About my height—"

"Know her name and a lot of her habits," Nick replied. "Picked her up yesterday morning after an all-nighter at La Concha." He pressed a finger against the side of his nostril and sniffed. "She had a little happy dust on her nose."

Jesse and Gina glanced at one another, exchanging surprised looks.

Gina grabbed his headrest and pulled herself closer. "Do you know whose room at La Concha?"

"Chuck Bering's?" Jesse asked.

Nick glanced in the rearview mirror at him. "You didn't hear that from me. But word gets around. Chuck had a couple of dancers over when Amber got there. She called me and had me deliver three veggie pizzas to his room." He shook his head. "No meat... damned shame."

It'd taken a little longer to get to Louie's Backyard after the stop on Stock Island, but when they arrived, they found only a handful of people on the back deck. A couple in their thirties sat at the table Jesse and Gina had eaten lunch the previous day, and there were two guys sitting at different tables, both eating breakfast.

Jesse's stomach rumbled.

Carly was sitting with the couple, taking their order, so Jesse led Gina to another table that was close to the exit stairs to the beach and pulled out a chair for her.

"I hope you know what you're doing," Gina said, sitting down.

"We'll just have to wait and see," Jesse replied with a shrug, taking a seat with his back to the corner of the deck. "How many people do you think are on that cruise ship?"

"That's why we have so many bars here," Gina said. "Some cruise ships carry over a thousand passengers, and it's getting to be like two or three times a week. Plus all the people on the mainland who drive down."

Jesse rose as Carly approached them.

"Back again?" Carly asked, as she slid onto a chair at their table.

Jesse could sense that she was stressed as he sat back down.

"We're going to be staying in town for a few days," Gina replied.

Jesse nodded. "We wanted to check with you and see if the police were doing anything, or if there was anything... odd going on?"

"Anything odd?" Carly asked.

"Any suspicious people hanging around?" he replied. "That kind of thing."

"Ha! You guys are about twenty minutes ahead of them. A cruise ship docked less than an hour ago."

"We barely got to the marina ahead of it," Gina said, nodding. "But Jesse didn't mean the tourists. Has anyone suspicious been hanging around your house, maybe?"

"Or even here at the restaurant?" Jesse added.

Her expression turned to one of frustration. "There's no shortage of suspicious looking people around this town. But no, nothing out of the ordinary that I've noticed."

"I don't mean to be blunt," Jesse said. "But how well do you pay attention?"

She locked eyes with him. "Since all this started, I've been keeping a very sharp eye out. I have kids to worry about."

"I didn't mean to criticize," Jesse said. "It's good that you're vigilant."

"Vigilant?" she asked, then looked over at Gina. "Where did you find this guy?"

Gina smiled and patted Jesse's hand. "He's kind of an *old soul*. I'd bet he's been around since the dawn of time."

"I'm sorry," Jesse said, giving Carly a crooked grin. "I was raised by my grandparents." He grinned at Gina. "Were the sixties considered the dawn of time?"

"Some would say that," Carly joked. "You're on a boat?"

Just then, Jesse saw the babysitter friend, Amber, coming down the steps to the deck and looking around. She wasn't dressed like any babysitter Jesse'd known. The dress she wore was more suited to a nightclub than brunch on the beach.

Behind his sunglasses, Jesse noted her expression change when she spotted Carly sitting with them.

"We're in Key West Bight," Gina replied. "We're also here looking for someone else."

"Who?" Carly asked, as Amber turned and strutted toward them as if she were on a fashion runway.

Her attitude reminded him of Cathy, a girl he'd gone out with several times when he'd returned home from boot camp.

"Being aware of *how* you look to others," Mam had often told him, "and *striving* to show others how you look, are two different things. One is neatness, and the other, vanity."

"His name's Chuck Bering," Gina said.

Jesse caught the flicker of recognition in Carly's eyes when Gina said the name. As Carly slowly shook her head, he rose from his seat.

"How would Carly know anyone like that?" Amber asked, stepping up beside her friend and putting an arm around her shoulders. "Just because we live in the party destination of America doesn't mean we do drugs too."

Except you don't live here, Jesse thought. *And you do do drugs.*

Jesse pulled a chair out for the woman. "Um, nobody said anything about drugs. Gina and I were attacked last night, and this Chuck Bering guy was the one who sent the thugs."

Amber looked up at Jesse for a moment, a defiant set to her jaw, then her face changed instantly, and she smiled as she sat down. "Thank you."

"My sister was partly responsible for Chuck Bering's cousin being sent to prison, and last night he sent some of his biker friends to get revenge."

Jesse sat back down and looked at Amber. "What's all this about drugs?"

"He's the local pot dealer," Amber said to Gina, as if it'd been she who'd asked the question. "He sells mostly to the cruise ship tourists. We don't have anything to do with that ilk."

Ilk? Jesse thought, noticing that Carly's body language said something different. Not to mention the "happy dust" Nick Thacker had told them he'd seen on Amber's nose. She was throwing her own drug dealer under the bus. But she didn't live here, so probably didn't care.

But Carly had tensed at Amber's words.

Also, Amber had used the word "we" twice already. Was she just being protective of her friend? Or was Gina right, and there was more to her interest than just being old friends?

He decided to push it.

"All the more reason for me to bounce his head off a curb," he said, watching both women for a reaction. "I don't like being attacked in my own motel room, and Chuck Bering has some payback coming."

The dark-haired Amber's cool façade changed only slightly, and

Jesse sensed a vindictive or cruel side to her, almost as if she relished the chance to see harm done.

What happened in Bering's apartment? he wondered.

Carly's reaction was also barely noticeable, but very different. Her eyes showed concern. Not like the kind of concern a person might feel when told that a friend was sick or in danger, but more like the kind of slow-growing panic people exhibited before a hurricane when they found the bread aisle empty.

Though both women denied it, Jesse knew that Amber and Carly were *both* Chuck Bering's customers. Or had been.

Chapter Twenty-Eight

◆━━━◆━━━◆━━━◆━━━◆

Carly had taken their order and Amber had gone with her to the kitchen to put it in, then the two women had hovered near the front of the restaurant, talking.

While Jesse and Gina waited, he watched the two of them chatting at the hostess station, and wondered if Amber also worked there, since she was hanging around so much. He decided not.

Amber didn't return to the table with Carly when she brought their order. She sat down for a moment and told them that with Scott safe over on Andros Island in The Bahamas, there hadn't been any more attempts on his life, but it was hard for them, personally. He'd tried to find lodging so he could bring his family over, but the assignment was temporary, and the Navy had said no.

It was obvious to Jesse that Carly cared a great deal for her husband. She hadn't been able to add anything more than she'd already told them, so after a quick meal, Jesse and Gina decided to head back to the boat.

As they were saying goodbye, Gina gave her friend a hug and Jesse noticed Amber looking Gina over.

He pretended *not* to notice.

"Do you think Carly's gay, too?" Jesse asked when they reached the sidewalk. "Because Amber seemed like more than just a concerned friend."

"You caught that, huh?" Gina replied. "No, I don't think Carly has any idea that Amber might be. But then again, I could be completely wrong and my gaydar is on the fritz."

"She was definitely checking *you* out," he said, glancing down at Gina as they walked along the sidewalk.

"When?"

"When you were hugging Carly," Jesse said. "She was looking at your butt."

"And how did that make you feel, Jesse?" she asked, taking his hand.

"Not good," he replied. "A guy wouldn't do that in front of me. I'd knock his block off."

She smiled at him. "You passed the test."

He glanced down at her puzzled, but let it go. "What's this photo shoot you mentioned?"

"It's for one of those big fashion magazines," she replied, as they sidestepped several folks, obviously tourists, gathered around a sidewalk fortune teller.

"Don't ask me which one," Gina continued, glancing back. "If it's fashion you're looking for, I'm not your girl."

Jesse laughed, putting an arm around her and pulling her closer to him. "That's not why I asked. When did they get here?"

"The day after Christmas, I think; some of the top models, photographers, and designers from all over the world."

"And you think Amber's a model?"

"Well, she's pretty enough," Gina replied. "And she arrived that day, too. If she's not, she's probably a part of it somehow, maybe an assistant or something."

"You're prettier," Jesse said as they stepped off a curb. "I think you're right. I think it's more likely that she works for a modeling agency or something. Most models are taller."

Gina took his hand and gushed, "Oh, Jesse! You think I'm

prettier."

He laughed, comfortable in knowing when she was joking. "Just stating a fact."

There was a crackle, then muffled words and a click.

Jesse pointed to a narrow alley, reached into his cargo pocket, and took the bulky two-way out. When they were far enough from the busy street not to be heard, he turned up the volume a little and keyed the mic.

"Repeat your last," he said.

"Our guy left the hotel a coupla minutes ago," Rusty replied over the radio. "He's headin' toward the square."

A young couple paused on the sidewalk, looking down the alley toward them. Jesse faced them, locking eyes with the man, then jerked his head sideways, giving the universal "get lost" signal. They immediately continued on their way.

"Make sure he doesn't see you," Jesse said into the radio. "And keep that walkie out of sight. We're on our way. Meet you at the boat."

"You can't just beat him up in the middle of Mallory Square," Gina said, as they hurried along Duval Street again. "There are cops there, and always at least one tourist with a movie camera going."

"You can if you do it right," Jesse replied, picking up the pace to the point that Gina was almost running to keep up.

When they reached the marina, they went straight to the boat and found Rusty and Juliet sitting in the cockpit under the bimini top, looking toward Mallory Square. There was a large crowd of people there.

"Those passengers just disembarked," Rusty said, as Jesse stepped over. "That's Bering in the lime green shirt near the seawall 'bout halfway down."

Jesse scanned the square and easily spotted the man.

"Whatta ya think we should do?" Rusty asked.

Jesse's eyes moved along the seawall, the walkway, and the small pedestrian bridge, then on to the marina and docks. Everything they took in, he processed, discarding the distractions and seeing opportunities to exploit.

"You girls stay here," Jesse said. "Keep a lookout for the police, and if you see any, click the mic button three times. Rusty and I are going to have a talk with Mr. Bering."

"What are you going to do?" Juliet asked.

"Take him for a walk," Jesse said. "And explain how we settle disputes in the squadbay."

"Be careful," Gina said, as Jesse and Rusty stepped over to the dock.

"Nothin' to worry 'bout," Rusty said. "This won't take long."

After they'd moved away from the boat far enough so that the girls couldn't hear him, Rusty asked, "What's the plan? I don't wanna get busted for fightin' in public."

"We split up on the other side of the bridge," Jesse said. "You circle around the right side of the square. There's a two-wheeled cart just past the midpoint of the seawall. I'll wait for you to grab it and come up behind him."

"Then what?"

Jesse grinned over at his friend and spoke with a drawl. "Good ole Chuck's been a drinkin' all mornin'."

Rusty laughed. "I knew there was somethin' I liked 'bout you, right when ya sat down next to me at that diner up in Jacksonville. Yup, ole Chuck done fell off the wagon."

After they crossed the bridge, Rusty went one way, and Jesse waited a minute before slowly going the other. He moved slowly through the crowd, stopping occasionally to give Rusty time to get into position. He kept his face down, glancing up only on occasion.

At six-three, Jesse had no trouble looking over the heads of most of the people in the crowd, but it also made him easy to spot.

The lime green shirt was easy to keep track of, but tall as he was, Jesse couldn't see Rusty anywhere. But he could see people making a wide path, then a hand reached up and waved.

Rusty was just beyond Bering, slowly moving into position.

From the boat, Jesse had noticed a small outdoor bar on wheels. He angled toward it, fished a ten from his pocket and asked for a shot of rum in a plastic cup.

Then he turned and strode toward Chuck Bering, holding the drink in his left hand.

Bering was talking to two men in their late twenties or so. Jesse waited, keeping other people between them. He saw Bering take a bill from one of the men and then hand him two joints.

When the two men turned to walk away, Jesse immediately sidestepped a large woman in a muumuu, and was suddenly right in front of Bering, who was looking down.

When the pot dealer's face came up, his jaw fell open.

"I can find you this easily any time I want," Jesse hissed, as Rusty moved the cart up behind Bering. "It's what Recon Marines are trained to do."

Just as the front of Rusty's cart hit the back of Bering's knees, Jesse's left hand shot out, throwing the cup of rum in the man's face, then grabbing him by the shirt collar.

His right hand moved in a blur, delivering a hatchet blow to the side of Bering's head, then grabbing his other lapel.

The drug dealer's body went limp.

Chapter Twenty-Nine

◆━━◆━━◆━━◆

Bering was out cold and reeked of cheap alcohol as Jesse lowered him down into the cart, pretending to be drunk and off-balance and making a scene.

"Whoa, buddy! I think you had enough," Jesse slurred, winking at Rusty.

"I b'lieve you're right," Rusty said, laughing loudly and matching Jesse's pretended drunkenness. "We better get you home."

People around them were watching, but nobody was moving to help the man who, if they'd noticed Jesse's blow, was an apparent mugging victim.

All they saw was what Jesse wanted them to see. And smell. A couple of drunk guys helping a passed-out friend. He was sure it happened a lot on cruise ships.

"Lead the way," Jesse whispered. "Anywhere out of sight."

Jesse took the handle of the cart as Rusty pushed his way through the crowd, shouting, "Gangway! Got a passed out drunk here."

A drinking town with a fishing problem, Gina'd told him.

The crowd parted, some laughing and pointing, as if seeing a drunk being carted away was a normal occurrence. One person stepped closer and took a picture of the "drunk" man in the cart, laughing to his buddies.

In a matter of minutes, they reached the far end of the square, and Rusty led Jesse onto a walkway that circled around two large cisterns.

"This is good," Jesse said, as Bering began to stir.

Jesse tipped the cart up, sliding its inert load unceremoniously onto the concrete walkway.

Bering let out an oomph.

Jesse grabbed his lime green shirt and hauled him up to a sitting position, his back against the brick wall of one of the cisterns.

His eyes were partly open but unfocused.

Jesse lightly smacked his cheek several times trying to wake him up, then looked up at Rusty. "See if you can find a piece of rope or something."

Rusty turned to start scrounging around as Bering began to regain consciousness.

Quickly, Jesse went through the man's pockets. In one, he found a wad of $1 bills, and in another a bunch of fives. He rolled him over to check his back pockets for a wallet but found a few $10 bills in one back pocket and a large wad of twenties in the other.

Jesse pocketed all the cash and then checked Bering's shirt pockets, where he found five joints, already rolled. He placed those on the sidewalk out of Bering's reach.

The man started to struggle, pushing to get away.

Once more, Jesse grabbed his lapels and jerked him forward, their faces inches apart.

"Don't move," he growled. "If you do, you'll feel pain like you've never felt before."

"Here," Rusty said, handing Jesse a part of a stream of pennants.

Jesse tied the man's hands and feet tightly, then squatted down in front of him.

"You can yell if you want to," Jesse said quietly, staring into the man's eyes. "But your scream will only last about half a heartbeat before I knock you right out of your pants. Nod if you understand."

Bering slowly nodded, terror in his eyes.

"I'm going to ask you some questions," Jesse said, taking the slack line and lifting Bering's bound hands. "Some I already know the answers to. If you lie to me, even once, I'll start breaking fingers." He glanced down at the joints lying on the ground. "You kinda need your fingers to roll those, I'm guessing."

"What do you want from me, man?" Bering asked, trying to sound tough, but his voice was cracking too much to pull it off.

Having met Marines from just about every state east of the Mississippi already, Jesse had learned the many different regional accents, and though Bering's was slight, Jesse pegged him as being from western Pennsylvania, Pittsburgh, maybe.

"You sent those bikers after me and Gina, didn't you?" Jesse said, stating it as fact.

"I don't know what you're— Aarrgghh!"

Jesse bent the man's left pinkie back until he heard a satisfying snap, like a dry twig under a layer of pine needles.

"He ain't foolin' with ya, dumbass," Rusty snarled. "Your cousin, and now you, done fucked with the wrong folks. You was smart, you'd keep an honest tongue in your pie-hole."

"Okay, okay!" Bering said, nearly sobbing. "Whatever you want, man! Yeah, I sent them."

"Why?" Jesse hissed, taking the man's left ring finger in his hand and wrapping his fist tightly around it.

The color drained from Bering's face and beads of perspiration rolled down his forehead.

The man was a drug dealer. Jesse felt no pity or remorse.

"Why?" Bering croaked. "Because you got Bear locked up, man."

"He killed a woman!" Jesse spat. "And he beat up another! He got *himself* locked up."

"That ain't the way the Sun Demons see it," Bering said. "Now they got *two* reasons to come after you. You put a past leader in prison and the current one in the hospital."

"A whole biker gang?" Rusty asked.

"Go see if you can grab one of those chickens," Jesse told Rusty.

"A chicken?"

He'd seen them all over Key West when he'd come there as a boy and seeing them again as they walked around had ignited another happy memory.

Jesse looked up and winked as Gina and Juliet came around the cistern and stopped behind him. "A rooster if you can catch one. They peck the eyes out first, right?"

Rusty grinned and sprinted past him as Jesse turned his attention back to the pot dealer.

"I want you to do something for me," he said, patting the man's cheek hard where his side fist had landed, causing him to wince. "When you wake up, you probably won't be here where we are right now. But as soon as you can, I want you to call Sideshift and tell him to come to Smather's Beach alone tonight at midnight, and he and I can end this, man to man." He paused and grinned. "Or whoever's next in charge since Sideshift's face is pretty messed up."

Gina stepped forward. "Do you know Amber Henderson?"

Bering looked up at her, as if seeing her for the first time, a look of hope in his eyes. Jesse also saw recognition at the mention of Amber's name, but Bering started to shake his head.

He tightened his grip and pushed back on the man's ring finger just a little, as if getting ready to speed-shift up to third gear.

"Yeah, yeah! I know the bitch!"

Gina took another step forward. "What happened in your apartment between her and the two dancers?"

BAD BLOOD

His eyes showed fear, darting between Gina's and Jesse's.

Slowly, Jesse began to apply more pressure.

"She's an agent!" he replied, trying unsuccessfully to pull his hand away or reduce the strain. "Or she's some kind of a uh...talent scout, or something."

"A talent scout?" Jesse asked, continuing to hold the pressure.

"For that porn mag, man! Playtime! She lures new models into porn, man! She tried to hire the two dancers, Crystal and Kiki. They're neighbors of the waitress chick and work at Key West Bar. But word's already out about her. She offers big money, but the producer don't deliver." He looked up at Gina. "Please don't let him hurt me anymore."

"Got the chick—" Rusty stopped in his tracks when he saw the girls, a white hen tucked in the crook of his arm.

"Now say goodnight to the ladies," Jesse said.

Bering looked at him with a puzzled expression, then in a flash, the side of Jesse's fist met the crown of Bering's head, and once more, his lights went out.

"Neighbors of the waitress chick?" Gina asked. "Did he mean Carly?"

"I think so," Jesse replied. "I think all this is tied together somehow."

"Whatta ya want with the chicken," Rusty asked, one hand over the bird's eyes to keep it calm.

"Hold her for a second," Jesse replied, as he picked up the joints and put them partly back in Bering's shirt pocket but sticking out in plain sight. Then he thought better of it and took one out and placed it behind the man's ear.

Quickly, he untied Bering's hands and feet, then wrapped the line around the palm of his right hand several times, leaving a couple of feet dangling.

Rising, Jesse took the short end of the banner line and tied it around one of the chicken's feet, tight enough so it wouldn't come off, but not so tight as to hurt the bird.

"Let's get out of here," he said, as Rusty put the hen down and uncovered her eyes.

As they hurried away, the hen began clucking and squawking, louder and louder. They went around the small museum next to the cisterns and back out onto Mallory Square, hurrying along the side, toward the bridge and the marina beyond.

People started to point toward the noise coming from the north end of the square and two police officers on foot started hurrying that way.

Rusty chuckled as they crossed the pedestrian bridge. "Reckon what those cops are gonna think he was doin' with that chicken?"

Chapter Thirty

◆━━━◆━━━◆━━━◆━━━◆

In a hospital room in Key West, Sideshift struggled to get the T-shirt Cueball brought him over his head. He had a patch covering his left eye, as well as most of his forehead and cheek. The shirt he'd had on when they brought him in was blood-soaked, and the idiots in the ER had cut it off, thinking he'd been shot.

The doctor had just left, after telling Sideshift that his left orbital socket was fractured, and he wouldn't be able to see with his left eye for a while.

He finally got the shirt over his head and was pulling it over his huge shoulders when the door opened and a nurse no more than five feet tall walked in, pushing a wheelchair.

She had long, dark hair, and though his mind was drug-addled, he thought she looked a lot like the porn star, Amber Henderson, except just the opposite—innocent and wholesome.

"I ain't ridin' in that thing," he slurred, struggling to his feet with Cueball's help.

She gave him a shy, almost apologetic smile, craning her neck to look up at him. "It's hospital rules," she said. "Patients never walk out on their own."

Cueball laughed nervously, watching the gang leader. "I know some bars like that," he joked.

Though his mind was still confused, Sideshift remembered the description the guy named Neil Downe had given him. He was the producer for Playtime Productions and offered a bonus for the right chick. The tiny nurse was almost perfect for the role, except he wanted a blonde.

Nothing a dye job couldn't fix.

"It's okay, Mr. Brisco," she said, still smiling brightly. "Your friend can push you, so we won't need an orderly."

Sideshift's mind flashed to the scene in the motel room, just before the guy kicked him in the nuts. He'd been distracted by a naked blonde, who was exactly the same size as the nurse, *and* the porn star, Amber.

Exactly what the producer wanted, and now they had *three* possible choices. Except he was in the hospital because of the boyfriend of one of those candidates.

In Sideshift's twisted mind, that made a huge difference.

With his brain wandering unfettered, he wasn't paying any attention to the nurse's words as she rattled off instructions. His one good eye was fixed on the tiny pendant between her tits—a silver cross.

He smiled at her, but it was a cruel, sadistic smile, brought on by dark thoughts of lust and pain.

She smiled back.

Then he turned and slowly sat down in the wheelchair, so as not to crush his nuts, and let Cueball push him as they followed the little brunette out of the room.

Even if the producer didn't want her, she could be a lot of fun for all the guys at the clubhouse.

The bright lights in the hospital hallway glared off brightly painted walls, burning into Sideshift's eye. He wanted nothing more than to close them, but he was mesmerized by the piston-like motion, just three feet in front of his face—almost close enough to bite.

BAD BLOOD

He remembered wanting to grab the blonde girl at the motel, just before the guy kicked him. Normally, a woman wouldn't be a distraction when Sideshift was squaring off to hurt a man. Not even a naked woman.

But she *had* distracted him. She was exactly what the shoot needed—blonde, very small, and with a wholesome, girl-next-door look.

And they could tie the boyfriend's broken body to the stripper pole and force him to watch while they filmed.

Sideshift sat in the chair, his mind drifting between maniacal lust, fuming rage, the drowsiness of the drugs they'd given him, and the pain they were meant to mask.

The pain was just on the edge of his consciousness, kept at bay by the drugs, which also allowed his thoughts to lose all inhibition and drift into a dark world where there were no rules, where a man just grabbed what he wanted. By force, if needed.

His mouth slowly pulled back, revealing stained teeth as Cueball kept the wheelchair right behind the cute nurse, those perfect little ass-cheeks bouncing enticingly.

She stopped at an elevator and held the door open so Cueball could wheel him in. Then she stepped in right in front of Sideshift and bent to push the button.

The big biker's mind went completely off the chain as drool dripped into his beard, and he licked his lips.

The elevator lurched as it began to descend, rocking slightly.

Sideshift felt certain that the occasional twitch of the little hardbody's butt muscles were an invitation to him. He became uncomfortable and tried to shift in the chair, which sent a jolt of pain to his nuts, swollen as big as oranges, making sitting very uncomfortable, and sitting with a hard-on, excruciating.

The elevator doors opened, and the nurse stepped out, the

wheelchair-bound biker right behind her.

But man, what an ass... Sideshift thought, forgetting his balls as the the haze of the drugs washed over him again.

Slowly, Sideshift leaned forward, reaching out to grab those little alternating pistons.

The doors ahead whisked open, and the big biker saw the cop standing outside waiting for him in the mid-afternoon sun.

The fog began to lift as he slumped back in the chair.

He remembered being transported from the clubhouse to Mount Sinai in Key West so he could be treated before they took him to the jail to be booked.

The reality of what lay ahead pushed the fog from his brain and his hands fell onto his thick legs.

He was headed back to the state pen.

Leaning against the patrol car's fender with his arms crossed, Deputy Sergeant Bart Johnson grinned down at Sideshift as the nurse turned to face him.

"You'll need to change that dressing daily, Mr. Brisco," the raven-haired nurse explained, as Sideshift glared up at the cop with his one good eye. "You can reuse the plastic shield—just be sure to clean it. And be very careful not to pull at the stitches."

The deputy lurched away from his car. "You look a *little* better than the last time I saw you, Brisco," Johnson said. "Now you just look like a pile of loose shit."

Slowly, Sideshift pushed himself up out of the chair, lifting himself to his full height of six-five, then stared down at the cop. "You here to take me to jail or fuckin' bore me to death?" he growled. "Cuz right now, I ain't in no mood."

"Your bail was posted while the doctors were putting your ugly face back together," Johnson said, his voice belying the fact that he would probably rather cuff him and beat him with a tire iron than deliver *that* news.

Sideshift grinned and took a slow step toward the deputy. "Then why are you here, standin' in my fuckin' way?"

"Because I'm a cop, *freak* show," Johnson hissed. "It's what I do. I keep degenerates like you two off the streets."

"Mr. Brisco," the nurse interrupted nervously, pulling at Sideshift's sleeve. "Try not to get too excited. You'll probably be a little woozy still from the anesthesia and meds." She pressed a small pill bottle into his hand. "These are for later. For when it starts to hurt."

He turned to face the tiny nurse, leering openly at her cleavage, then grabbed his crotch and shook it, ignoring the pain. "You wanna know what *real* hurt is, little girl?" he asked, his voice dripping with unbridled lust. "I'm talkin' about a real *good* hurt? Cuz this'll split you open, baby doll. Come on by the clubhouse some time and I'll show ya."

Her hand flew to her mouth as her face drained of color. Then she turned, ran toward the door, pausing before it opened, and disappeared inside.

"You're a lunatic, Brisco!" Johnson snarled, stepping toward him, his right hand on the grip of his holstered .38. "I should arrest you right now for that."

"What charge?" Sideshift replied, turning toward him. "I was just askin' a pretty girl out on a date. So, I'm a little crude; they gave me drugs. That ain't a crime."

"Just so you know," Johnson said in a threatening tone, "if you see a police car behind you, it's because we're *following* you. Give me *any* excuse to have the judge revoke your bail, which I *know* you're going to do if you stick around here, and I'll put a stick up your ass, plant it in a cell, and make sure you never see daylight again."

"C'mon, man," Cueball said. "Your bail's paid. Let's get outta here."

Slowly, Sideshift turned and started to walk away from the cop, curious to get out of earshot and find out from Cueball who'd posted the bail money.

"We gotta find that chick with the soldier boy at the motel," he growled so only Cueball could hear. "Her and Amber in the same scene with the whole gang. I gotta call her and that Neil Downe guy. Who put up the bail?"

"One thing I should tell you, Brisco," Johnson called out.

The big biker stopped and slowly turned around. "What?"

"Remember that kid? The one who... rearranged your face?" Johnson began. "He told me to tell you that he doesn't back down. I think it's best if you just head on back up to the mainland."

Sideshift grinned maliciously, feeling the rage forcing the rest of the fog from his brain. "Is that right?" he sneered. "Might wanna keep those words handy. For his *tomb*stone. 'Here lays a guy who wouldn't back down.'"

When Sideshift laughed and turned to walk away, the cop called after him again. "It was McDermitt who paid your bail."

Chapter Thirty-One

♦―――♦―――♦―――♦

"What in the hell was all that Smather's Beach at midnight stuff?" Rusty asked, as all four of them climbed onto *Pleiades's* side deck.

They ducked under the bimini, and Jesse stepped down into the cockpit, falling back onto the port bench with a grin. "You trust me?"

"Well, yeah," Rusty replied. "What you got in mind?"

Gina tucked a leg under herself and sat next to Jesse, curling her other leg up and leaning on his shoulder. "The cruise ship will leave before sunset," she replied.

"We're going to leave here right after it," Jesse said, "and anchor off the beach tonight."

"And then what? You and that cyclops gonna dance a two-step on the sand?"

"Something like that... combat swimmer," Jesse replied, grinning.

A slow smile came to Rusty's face. "You know I ain't no CS yet, bro. But I reckon me and you are about as close to one as you'd find around here,"

"Don't worry," Jesse said. "We'll have backup."

"Backup?" Rusty asked. "From where?"

"I'm still working on that," Jesse replied. "Should know something shortly, though."

"So, what do we do until the ship leaves?" Juliet asked.

Gina rose and went to the companionway hatch. "The AC's on," she replied. "Rest when you can, I always say."

Rusty chuckled, getting to his feet. "Our squad leader says the same thing, right, Jesse? That guy can sleep through an artillery barrage."

They all went below, then split up, Gina pulling Jesse through the narrow passageway to the aft cabin, while Rusty and Juliet headed forward.

Gina sat on the edge of the small bunk, then sighed and rolled back, moving as close to the hull as she could get. She patted the spot next to her. "Do you think he'll find us?"

Jesse sat down, then lay back and stretched out. "He should. Enough people could describe us. I mean, how often do you see two drunk guys, one real tall and the other real short, wheeling away another drunk? One guy even got a picture."

Gina wrapped an arm across his chest and placed her head on his shoulder. They both lay still like that for several minutes as cool air from the vents blew across them.

"What are we doing after this?" she asked, not looking up at him.

"I guess we could go back to the motel," Jesse said. "Or find another one; finish our vacation."

She sighed again. "Will it always be like this? You, coming down on vacation and me, taking time off work to be with you?"

"You're not taking time off," he replied. "You're a reporter... on assignment."

"You're dodging the question."

Jesse looked down at her face and she turned her eyes up to meet his.

"Right now," he said, measuring his words carefully, "my work is in North Carolina. In the coming year? Who knows? I could be transferred to Japan, or deployed to the Middle East, or who-knows-where."

"Can't you take me with you?"

Jesse wasn't ready for that question. He liked Gina a lot and could easily feel himself falling in love with her. But his commitment to the Corps superseded everything else, at least until he made rank and could afford to live off base with a family. Or maybe buy a house, like his dad had done.

"We couldn't survive on what I make," he replied. "And there would be constant moving."

"You sound like a guy trying to talk his way out of a relationship," Gina said, then looked away. "You don't even need the income."

Jesse tipped her chin up with one finger. "Yes... I do. Most of my inheritance is tied up and will be needed in the future. A house, a family, and maybe a charter boat, like you said."

Gina lifted her head, propping herself on an elbow. "A charter boat? Your dream is to take tourists out fishing?"

He shrugged and kissed her. "Or scuba diving." He grinned. "Look, I'd love to have you be with me on a more permanent basis, and if you become part of that future life, all the more reason to save up until I make rank. But right now, I live in a dorm room with two other guys."

There was a knock on the hull right behind Gina, causing her to jump suddenly and roll on top of Jesse.

He held her in his arms, letting his hands move lower. "While I appreciate the idea," he said with a lecherous grin, "I think he found us."

Jesse held onto her as he rolled and got his feet under him, standing almost fully erect while still holding her to him with her legs locked around his hips.

"Tonight for sure," he said, bouncing her a little.

Gina arched her back, kissing him deeply and grinding her pelvis against him as she'd done in the rain. Squeezing him with powerful thigh muscles, she lifted her head, bumping it on a ceiling beam, then laughed, and let herself down to her feet.

"That's the third interruption in a day's time," she said, smiling, as she slipped past him in the confined space. "I'm going to hold you to that."

He followed her into the galley, where Rusty and Juliet were looking out through one of the portholes.

"It's that cop who came to the bait shop," Rusty whispered in an urgent tone. "Sergeant Johnson. Somebody musta saw us."

Jesse went up the companionway steps first, with Gina following. He stepped up into the cockpit to find Sergeant Johnson standing beside the boat with a small group of spectators on the dock thirty or forty feet behind him. The junior deputy Johnson was keeping them back.

"There was an incident on the north end of Mallory Square," the deputy announced, somewhat loudly. "Witnesses said they saw you four leaving the scene and going aboard this boat."

"We just left the square a little while ago," Gina admitted, also speaking loudly enough for the onlookers to hear. She looked around at the others with a bewildered expression, then added, "We didn't see any commotion. What happened?"

"Who owns this boat?" Johnson asked.

"I do. Oh, I'm sorry. Would you like to come aboard?"

"Thank you," he replied, then stepped up onto the side deck.

Jesse noted that he didn't wear leather-soled uniform shoes but had on a pair of rubber-soled deck shoes.

"Have a seat," Johnson said, quietly. "Act natural and look

helpful."

"Would somebody tell me what's goin' on?" Rusty asked, sitting down beside Juliet.

Johnson sat on the coaming on the port side, as Jesse and Gina sat opposite him on the bench.

"Did somebody really see us?" Gina asked.

"No," he replied, then looked at Jesse. "But the guy you beat up identified you and your girlfriend by name. You were supposed to avoid that."

Rusty's mouth fell open. "Wait... *what?* Y'all are in cahoots!"

Chapter Thirty-Two

After Johnson had shared with the others the plan he and Jesse had cooked up, he glanced around at the four of them and spoke quietly.

"You're sure you can do what you say? A boat like this will have to be anchored a good two hundred yards from shore. The sheriff'll have my ass if I get a civilian hurt, and make no mistake, son—here, you're civilians."

"We can do it," Jesse assured him. "And happy to assist."

"We'll look for your signal about midnight, then," Johnson said, then rose to leave.

Having not witnessed an immediate arrest or shoot-out, most of the onlookers had drifted away by the time Deputy Johnson stepped down off *Pleiades*, and the last two turned away as soon as they realized there wouldn't even be an arrest.

"Sergeant Johnson?" Jesse called down.

The deputy stopped and turned back to look at him.

"Happy New Year."

Johnson stared at Jesse for a moment, then he tipped a finger to his hat. "Good luck."

"You, too," Gina added.

The younger deputy began talking as soon as they turned to walk toward shore with his father. He looked back several times and was obviously asking questions.

But he didn't seem to be getting many answers.

"What did he mean by you being a civilian?" Gina asked.

"It was called the Posse Comitatus Act," Jesse replied, sitting down next to her. "It bars federal troops from participating in civilian law enforcement. In this case, it wouldn't apply anyway. We're not under orders to assist. I wonder why he made his son stay back?"

"That boy's about useless," Rusty said, sitting back on the bench.

"You know him?" Jesse asked.

"Know *of* him," Rusty replied.

"He was expelled from school," Gina said. "Two years ago, up in Key Largo."

"I heard he attacked a girl in the bathroom," Juliet added. "But no charges were ever filed."

Jesse's eyes went wide in amazement. "And now he's a deputy?"

"Not exactly," Rusty said. "From what Pop says, the department has sort of a 'slush fund' for hirin' temporary manpower. Like in case of a hurricane."

"A single dad raising two kids on a cop's salary?" Juliet said, shaking her head sadly. "And one a delinquent? So, he's padding his income with county funds. He's keeping Tony out of trouble and a roof over their heads."

"So, he's not really a deputy?" Jesse asked.

Rusty shook his head. "No more'n I'm the pope. He rides along with his dad on twelve-hour shifts."

"What time does the ship leave?" Jesse asked, changing the subject back to the task at hand.

"An hour before sunset," Gina replied. "City ordinance."

Jesse leaned back to check the sun. It was past noon, probably close to 1400.

"It's one-thirty," Gina said, glancing at a small clock on the dash.

"Three hours, then," Jesse said. "We should be ready to leave when the ship does."

"You prepaid this slip for two nights," Gina reminded him.

He took her hand. "We'll be back before the sun comes up. Then we can see what else we can find out about Amber Henderson."

Juliet looked over at Jesse. "You say that as if it's a foregone conclusion. What you and Deputy Johnson talked about doing sounds dangerous."

Rusty patted her knee. "It'll go down just like they planned. We got the sheriff and the city cops backing us. All me and Jesse gotta do is swim ashore and take out a coupla lookouts, if they have any."

"And then what?" Juliet asked. "The cops swarm in and arrest everyone for being on the beach in leather jackets and boots?"

Rusty's expression became grave, and he looked to Jesse for backup.

"They're coming for just one thing—to *kill* me," Jesse said, in as even a tone as he could. "Sideshift won't come alone and every biker on that beach will be armed, and guns aren't allowed on public beaches. Says it on the signs at both ends."

"That's it?" Juliet asked. "If they have a gun they'll be arrested?"

"I don't imagine this'd be the first run-in with the law these guys've had," Rusty said. "We know Sideshift served time with Bear, and convicted felons can never own or carry a gun. That'll violate his parole and put him away for a long time. If it's his third strike, life."

"We won't get hurt," Jesse reassured her. "We're both trained to avoid detection and do exactly this sort of thing."

"Tell me somethin'," Rusty said, leaning forward. "Why'd he tell Sideshift you posted bail? It's New Year's weekend and the clerk's office ain't even open."

Jesse shrugged. "He had to tell him something. And if he told him the charges were dropped, Sideshift would take that to mean I was afraid."

"He's really dangerous, Jesse," Gina reminded him. "And you're not afraid? Not even a little?"

"I respect his size," Jesse said, looking off toward the cruise ship terminal gates. "I know he'll have backup. But fear?" He shook his head slowly, then looked down at her. "With him thinking I paid his bail, along with what Chuck's going to tell him, Sideshift will have no doubt it's an open invitation to a fight. He won't back down. He can't. At least he can't and remain the gang leader. And he won't come alone. In their minds, I crossed a line, and for that, they have to kill me. They'll all be armed, alright."

Chapter Thirty-Three

◆――◆――◆――◆――◆

Though Gina and her sister, Rachel, had masks and fins aboard, none of the fins fit Jesse's size thirteen foot, so Jesse and Gina headed to the nearest dive shop—there was no shortage of them.

"I think the deputy was a little off," Gina said. "Anchoring in open water, we'll need at least five feet under the keel for wave action and will probably be closer to three or four hundred yards from the beach. Do you really think you can make that swim in open water?"

He took her hand and kissed the back of it. "We've already done a two-mile ocean swim."

"Really?" she asked skeptically.

"Our whole squad jumped out of a perfectly good helicopter two miles off Onslow Beach, and we had to swim to shore. It took the whole day."

"The whole day to swim two miles?"

He looked down at her and grinned. "We were wearing boots, packs, and carrying rifles."

She looked up, surprised. "You never mentioned anything like that in your letters."

"We usually train six days a week," he replied with a shrug. "In the air, on land, and sea. You'd get bored hearing about it."

They reached a dive shop and went inside. It wasn't crowded—just the clerk and two guys who didn't look like they were interested in buying anything.

"These look big enough," Gina said, pulling a set of fins off a display rack.

Jesse sat down and held one of the wide and stubby fins up to his foot. "Yeah, these'll fit."

The girl behind the counter looked over. "You are big man," she said in a sultry Russian accent. "Those are not for you."

She wore a short skirt and a low-cut blouse, and was tall, almost statuesque. She had short, black hair cut bluntly to just above her shoulders all the way around, boxing in her face with straight bangs that fell below her eyebrows.

She appeared fit, and Jesse thought she'd probably be pretty if she didn't have so much makeup on, especially the red lipstick.

"What would you suggest?" Gina asked, asserting they were together.

"Wait here," the Russian woman said, then disappeared into the back.

"She's going to try to upsell you some piece of crap," Gina whispered.

The clerk came out with a box that was at least three feet long, with the word Mares in big, bold letters.

She unabashedly looked Jesse up and down. "Strong legs, yes?"

He nodded, and she opened the box. "These are brand-new," she said, taking one long fin out and handing it to Jesse. "They are for free diving, not with scuba. Bend it. Only very strong legs can make these fins work the way they are designed."

Jesse put one hand inside the foot cup and pushed down on the fin near the midpoint. It was very rigid, not like the typical rubber fins, and the edges seemed to be made of some kind of hard but slightly flexible plastic.

Then he slowly slid his hand out to the end, more than two feet beyond. The rigidity decreased to the point of being very flexible at the tip.

Jesse was reminded of a picture he'd seen recently of a diver swimming toward the surface, long fins double-bent in S figures, providing great upthrust as well as down.

"How much?" he asked.

"For you, *krasivyy*," she said, smiling, "only one hundred American dollars."

"Got another pair in a size…" He turned to Gina. "Think Rusty's what? An eight?"

"Seven," she replied. "Mine fit him, and I wear a men's seven sometimes."

"These and the same in a seven?" he asked the clerk.

Her smile broadened.

"*Da!*" she exclaimed, then disappeared behind the counter into the back room.

"Are you sure about this?" Gina asked, picking one of the fins up and examining it. "I've never seen anything like these before and that's a lot of money."

"I saw them on the cover of a dive magazine just last week," Jesse replied. "Jean-Michele Cousteau tested them and was impressed, but said they were better suited for free diving."

The clerk returned with another long box, which she placed on the counter. "With tax, that will be two hundred and twelve dollars."

Jesse reached into the right cargo pocket, where he'd deposited Bering's roll of twenties. He peeled off twelve and handed them to the overdressed clerk.

"Keep the change," he said, then dropped the wad of cash back into his cargo pocket.

He didn't feel any guilt at spending money he'd basically stolen from the pot dealer. The only remorse he felt was that someone had worked hard to earn it, only to blow it on pot. He'd taken the cash *out* of the illegal market and put it back into the open market. And to top it off, he was using it to get what he needed to put more criminals behind bars.

"Thanks," he said, reaching for the two long Mares boxes.

She put both hands on his for a moment before he lifted the boxes.

"It is nothing, *krasivyy*," she said, letting her long nails rake Jesse's hand. "Come back again, please."

Jesse and Gina hurried out and turned right, heading south on Greene Street back toward the marina.

"She wanted you," Gina said. "I was about to scratch her eyes out."

Jesse chuckled. "If I'd been alone, she wouldn't have shown the slightest interest, just like she ignored those other two guys. She was only doing that to rile *you*."

"If I hadn't been there, she'd have been all over you."

"The one thing most women want, especially Russian women, is what another woman has."

She laughed. "Oh, now you're the expert on Russian women?"

Jesse looked down at her and grinned. "Only the one who was a repeat character on *Hogan's Heroes*." Then he pulled her close. "You don't have anything to worry about."

"Well, I'm going to find out what '*krasivyy*' means," she said. "And if it means what I think, she'll be blind by tomorrow."

Chapter Thirty-Four

When they got back to the boat, Jesse noticed there were large groups of people reboarding the cruise ship through the gates to the south.

Rusty and Juliet had the water hose and shore power disconnected, and all but two dock lines had been coiled and were hanging on the safety cables.

"Whatcha got there, bro?" Rusty asked, pointing at the boxes. "Got a coupla M16s in there?"

"New fins," Jesse replied, opening one of the boxes.

"Whoa!" Rusty exclaimed, lifting one of the next generation Mares fins out of the box. "These are the ones Cousteau tested!"

"Should make the swim a lot faster and easier."

Gina looked toward the gated area. "The ship will be leaving in less than an hour."

She'd no more than said the words when Jesse heard—or more accurately—felt a low rumble from deep inside the cruise ship.

"I'll go let the dockmaster know we'll be back later tonight," Gina said, then smiled at Jesse. "Or early tomorrow. You still owe me."

Less than an hour later, *Pleiades* motored out of the bight, keeping well to the east of the slow-moving cruise ship backing away from the dock. They got the sails up quickly and were soon well past it.

Jesse stood beside Gina at the helm, noting the knot meter on the dash. "She's three knots faster under sail than on the engine."

"Just to get us past that pig," she replied, jerking a thumb toward their stern. "When we turn east, we'll have to drop the sails and run the engine."

Jesse looked up at the wind vane on the masthead. It indicated the wind was abeam and slightly to the stern, but he knew that their forward speed pushed that back slightly. He looked down at the compass—their course was due south, which meant the wind was probably dead out of the east.

"Or we could just sail farther south for a better wind angle to sail back," Jesse replied. "We're not in a hurry. We have four or five hours to get there."

Rusty laughed as he leaned back and put an arm around Juliet. "I think the worm's turned."

Gina looked up at him. "*Pleiades* doesn't have radar. We usually sail close to land."

"We won't have to go far beyond sight of land," Jesse offered.

"Ain't no weather in the forecast," Rusty chimed in. "I checked before y'all got back. Wind's s'posed to stay steady all evenin'."

"It could get choppy out closer to the Gulf Stream," Gina warned, turning the wheel slightly to the left. "I hope you know what you're doing. Trim for upwind. We'll take a chunk out of the return course while it's calm."

Rusty was already moving toward the primary winch to haul in the jib, and Jesse quickly pulled in the slack on the main sheet, then used the winch handle to haul the boom in closer.

When he rejoined Gina, Jesse noticed the boat had slowed slightly.

"She's not the fastest going upwind," Gina said.

Jesse imagined a triangle with three equal sides, the base being the short route on engine power, and the right side was the course they were on. They'd travel twice as far, but at two knots more speed, and he figured the base leg couldn't be any more than three miles.

"How far would it be motoring in a straight line?" Jesse asked.

"From the marker we passed five minutes back to right offshore of Smathers is just a hair over three nautical miles."

Jesse turned to Gina. "It'll only take about half an hour longer."

"Then I vote we sail on," Juliet added. "The diesel is loud, and it stinks."

"So, you're a navigator, too?" Gina asked, looking up at Jesse.

He turned his head upward toward the wind vane; it was pointing about thirty degrees off their course. Then he checked the knot meter and compass again.

"Not really," he replied. "But I am pretty good with geometry. If we hold this course for forty-five minutes, we'll travel about three miles at this speed, right?"

"Almost exactly," Juliet replied.

"In forty-five minutes, we can turn to the opposite wind heading and if we sail another forty-five minutes, we should arrive just west of the beach. It's an equilateral triangle with the sides being three miles. Then we can start the engine and motor east while we take down the sails and look for a place to anchor."

"We won't even reach the edge of the Stream in just three miles," Rusty said. "It's a good five or seven to the wall. So, it ain't gonna get much worse sea state than this. Now, out there in the Stream—with the wind blowin' the opposite direction of the flow, it'd be pretty rough."

The farther the boat moved away from Key West, the choppier the water became. But, just as Rusty had predicted, it wasn't unmanageable, and was in fact quite exhilarating.

After forty minutes, they could no longer see the island. To the east, the sky was beginning to turn purple, and a nearly full moon was almost to its zenith.

The sun was shining fully under the starboard side of the bimini top, even with the boat heeled over several degrees. It was getting closer to the horizon with each passing minute.

Gina glanced down at the clock. "Time to tack," she said, then turned the wheel.

"Need me to do anything?" Jesse asked.

"You said a reciprocal wind angle, right?" she asked, as the sails luffed, and the bow passed through the wind. "It's a self-tacking jib."

"That should put us where we'd be had we motored for three miles," Jesse replied. "A little west of Smathers Beach."

Gina looked up through the plastic section of the bimini, checking the wind vane. "Did you figure in the current?"

He looked down and arched an eyebrow questioningly. "We didn't reach the Gulf Stream."

"Yeah, but there's still a little bit of an eastward-flowing current," Gina said. "Think we should come off the wind a few degrees to compensate?"

"How fast is the current?" Jesse asked, picturing the triangle in his head again.

"In close like this," Rusty said, "about half a knot."

In his head, Jesse moved the top of the triangle to the left a little, figuring the drift would have taken them three-quarters of half a nautical mile for the forty-five minutes in the half-knot current.

"Yeah," Jesse said. "Open it up to about forty-five degrees of wind angle. We drifted almost half a mile from what I figured. Got any binos?"

"We're out of sight of land," Gina said.

"But not the control tower at the airport. It's close to the beach, right?"

"Just beyond the east end," Gina replied, standing and looking northward. "Take the wheel."

Gina hurried down the companionway as Jesse rested his hands lightly on the wheel, feeling the opposing forces of water on the keel and rudder and wind in the sails.

When she came back up, Jesse pointed ahead and slightly to the left. "Look just a little left of the bow. I think we're still off by a few degrees."

Gina raised the binoculars and steadied herself with one hip propped against the forward bulkhead.

"Almost spot on," she said, lowering the glasses and looking up at him. "Dead reckoning at its finest. Come left ten degrees."

Jesse turned the large, stainless-steel wheel slightly, watching the compass and glancing up occasionally at the wind vane.

"That's it," Gina said, looking through the binos again.

"Fifteen degrees on the compass," Jesse said. "But we'll drift another half mile on the return leg, too."

He turned the wheel a little more and waited for the compass to reach ten degrees magnetic. There was a piece of paracord wrapped in a dozen loops around the wheel, which he guessed was the neutral rudder position, so he brought that to the top of the wheel, then used Gina's bungee cord to lash the wheel in place as he'd seen her do.

"It's almost sunset," Jesse said. "Let's let Otto run things for a few minutes."

"Otto?" Juliet asked. "Oh, I get it. The rubber band autopilot."

"We still have some sandwiches left over," Rusty said. "I put 'em in plastic bags in the cooler tray."

As Rusty was headed down the companionway ladder, Gina called after him. "Don't forget to take them out of the plastic before coming up." Then she turned to Jesse. "Do you know how big the largest sea turtle ever seen weighed?"

Jesse shook his head. "I'd be guessing but probably over a thousand pounds. Biggest I've ever seen was probably three hundred."

"Almost two thousand," Gina replied. "It had most likely weighed more, but by the time it weakened and drowned, it probably hadn't eaten in weeks because of a plastic bag lodged in its throat that it mistook for a jellyfish. It had another twenty pounds in its gut."

"Of plastic?" Jesse asked, surprised.

Gina looked up at him. "There's fifty million tons of plastic floating out here."

As the sun slowly began to slip below the horizon, the four of them kicked back in the cockpit, quietly munching and enjoying nature's color show.

"Have you ever seen the green flash?" Gina asked Jesse, as *Pleiades* sailed steadily northward.

"That's just a myth, right?"

"No, bro," Rusty replied. "I've seen it, and Pop's seen it five times."

"JJ and I saw it once too," Gina said. "Remember, JJ? We were all out on Gregor's Boston Whaler at Party Island."

As they watched the sun sink closer and closer to the horizon, Jesse remembered other sunsets he'd seen, often with Pap. The old man said the "golden hour" just before sunset was the best time to reflect on the day's works.

And this is the last sunset of the decade, Jesse thought.

He looked down at Gina and wondered where they'd be at the end of the next decade.

"They say that if you close your eyes just before the sun sets,"

Gina said softly, staring westward, "then make a wish and open them, if you see the flash, your dream will come true."

"Did yours?" Jesse whispered, looking at her profile.

She looked up and smiled. "You're sitting in it."

They both turned their attention back to the setting sun, and just as the last of it was about to disappear, Jesse closed his eyes. When he opened them, the sun disappeared with a wink.

But he didn't see any flash.

Chapter Thirty-Five

◆―――◆―――◆―――◆―――◆

As the evening grew darker, Gina used the binoculars every ten minutes or so to judge their location and distance from the airport control tower near the east end of the beach. Twenty minutes after they'd tacked, the binos were no longer needed, as the well-lit control tower was clearly visible.

Soon, even the lights along the southern shore of Key West could be seen, and Gina was able to pick out a few other landmarks.

"Do you see where the yellow streetlights along South Roosevelt stop at the west end?" Gina asked, pointing just to the left of the bow.

Jesse recognized the evenly spaced yellow lights for what they were—streetlights. Squatting slightly to look under the foresail, he could see where they ended.

"Got it," he replied.

"Put the bow on that last light," Gina instructed. "That's where South Roosevelt turns and becomes Bertha Street at the west end of Smathers Beach."

Jesse turned the wheel a little and waited until he could see the end of the streetlights just to the right of the foresail. "How far away is it?"

"You don't know, Navigator?"

He looked at the clock and knot meter. "Less than a mile? It looks farther away."

"It a beanie island, mon," Gina said, in a sort of Jamaican accent.

He laughed. "I take it 'beanie' means small here?"

"According to Lawrence," Gina replied. "He's a local Jamaican cab driver, about our age. What's the depth?"

Jesse looked down at the bottom finder. "Water's twenty feet deep."

She looked over to check the depth finder herself. "Twenty feet *under the hull* where the transducer is mounted. So, add that to what the depth finder says for water depth. The keel's two feet below the transducer. So, when it says five feet, there's only three under the keel,"

"Keep an eye on that," Rusty said. "When we got eight or ten feet under us, we'll be less'n a quarter mile off the beach. That's about where we want to anchor."

"I'll take over," Gina said, sliding between Jesse and the wheel. "I need you at the mast to help with the main when I turn upwind."

"Aye aye, Captain," Jesse said, relinquishing the helm.

"I'll let it down slow," Juliet said, as Jesse climbed onto the cabin roof. "Just try to get it folded as neat as you can over the boom as it comes down."

A few minutes later, Gina started the engine, then waited another couple of minutes before putting it in gear and turning *Pleiades* almost directly into the wind.

"Let the wind push it one way," she shouted to Jesse. "Then you fold it the other."

As the sails began to luff, Rusty started pulling on the furling line, hauling in the foresail, while Juliet slowly lowered the main. All Jesse had to do was shove the big mainsail over to one side as it came down, then let the wind push it back toward him, creating nice, folded layers across the boom.

BAD BLOOD

Once Rusty had the headsail furled, he grabbed a flashlight and moved up to the pulpit, shining it down into the water.

"Turtle grass," he called back, moving the light farther ahead and sweeping it back and forth. "As far as I can see."

"Keep looking," Gina called out to him. "I'd rather not disturb the grass."

Jesse climbed down and stood beside Gina at the helm. There were two other sailboats already anchored, one closer to the beach and the other a little farther out than *Pleiades*.

Gina pointed toward the boat nearer to the shore. "That small one has a swing keel, so they can get shallower."

After a few minutes of motoring, when they were near the center of the long, white sand beach, Rusty pointed to the left.

"Sandy patch to port!"

Gina spun the wheel and the boat turned ninety degrees. Then she straightened it again for a moment, watching Rusty's flashlight beam on the water.

When it was pointed almost dead ahead, she made another sharp turn to the right, then reduced speed to a crawl.

It was obvious to Jesse that Rusty and Juliet were no strangers to Gina and Rachel's boat, and that he was the only one who needed to be told what to do.

"Twenty feet," Rusty called. "Ten feet... Stop!"

Gina shifted to reverse and brought the boat to a standstill, then took it out of gear.

"Neutral," Gina called forward.

Rusty put the light down and turned the windlass handle enough to release the safety chain and catch. Then he cranked the handle, letting the anchor drop to the bottom before he pulled the handle out.

Rusty rose and looked back toward them. "Anchor down, handle out."

Gina shifted to reverse as Rusty watched the chain clanking noisily over the rollers, his light shining on it.

"Twenty-five-foot link," he called out.

Gina continued backing.

After a moment, Rusty looked back. "There's fifty. Give her five more clankety-clanks and we'll have a good scope."

A few seconds later, Gina reduced power and shifted to neutral again. Rusty latched the windlass and reattached the safety chain. Then Gina backed up, with the engine revving to seat the anchor in the sandy bottom.

"That should do it," Gina said, moving the shifter to neutral and killing the engine. "Great job, everyone!"

Jesse glanced at the clock. "It's not even twenty-one hundred. We have more than three hours."

Rusty climbed back down into the cockpit. "Me and you oughta tag in and out on those binos," he said. "See if we can see any of the players arrive."

Jesse had told Sergeant Johnson his idea earlier that day, and they'd both explained it in more detail to Rusty, who agreed. It was an adaptation of something their squad leader had been drilling into them since they'd reported to the unit.

Since we dwell on the ground, our brains have adapted to look down and around at our surroundings, discounting the vertical.

"Horses and other hooved animals got used to open prairies!" Sergeant Livingston often shouted as they moved through the North Carolina pine forests. "Their pupils evolved to be long and horizontal for looking around! Cat's pupils are long and *vertical*, to see up! Be a damned cat, Marines! Check those trees!"

Jesse figured the average person, being a land-dweller, would look for threats coming from all around them, except out of the water. And it was that marine environment that the Marine Corps took advantage of so well.

He'd already noticed that there weren't many places in the Florida Keys where you couldn't see a boat at anchor, so he didn't feel they were overly conspicuous sitting in a slow boat, out in the open.

"Should we turn on the anchor light?" Gina asked quietly.

"Yeah," Jesse whispered, noting the other two boats anchored on the windward side of the island had lights on. "Not doing it would look suspicious."

The moon and the lights from shore provided plenty of illumination for them to move around on deck. Jesse took the binoculars up to the roof of the cabin and sat down with his back to the mast, watching the beach.

He grinned when he saw Johnson climbing out of an old Dodge pickup, which was backed into a spot near the east end of the beach. He dropped the truck's tailgate and pulled a couple of fishing rods out and leaned them against the bumper. Then he turned around and hopped up onto the tailgate.

He wore a ballcap and baggy clothes and didn't appear in the least like a cop on a stakeout. He even had a cooler and what looked like a beer can sitting beside him. Jesse doubted there was beer in it.

"Johnson's already here," Jesse whispered to the others. "Far east end. A white Dodge pickup."

Rusty sat on the cabin top beside him and looked out toward the beach. "That's a long swim, bro."

"Breathe after a wave passes," Jesse said, not taking his eyes off the beach. "We'll use the waves for cover."

"What waves?" Rusty asked.

"The surf's over a foot," he replied. "We'll just have to stay down until we reach the surf zone. Or pop up like a sea turtle."

A car pulled in and parked a little east of Johnson. Two men got out, then one opened the trunk and they both pulled rods and reels out and started putting them together. Once assembled, they each lifted a tackle box out and started past Johnson.

Jesse saw the sergeant's mouth move rapidly as they walked past him, but neither man seemed to notice.

"Two more cops just arrived," Jesse said. "They're heading toward the center of the beach."

Over the next twenty minutes, he saw a few more men arrive on foot, several minutes apart, and each of them walked past Johnson, receiving quick orders.

There was a rumble from the west end of the beach and Jesse moved the binoculars that way. A motorcycle turned into a parking spot, then turned all the way around, and the rider pushed it back with his feet after shutting off the engine.

"First tango just arrived," Jesse said softly, watching the man move toward the beach.

The parking area was well lit, and a little light spilled into the middle part of the beach but left most of it visible only by moonlight.

"What's he look like?" Rusty asked.

"Maybe six feet," Jesse replied. "Heavy-set and bald. He might be one of the guys who were with Sideshift at the motel."

For a moment, Jesse lost him behind a stand of sea grapes, then saw him walk out onto the beach in the moonlight, staying close to the vegetation. He found a recessed spot in the bushes and sat down, his body angled toward the middle of the beach, watching, but oblivious to anything in the water.

Chapter Thirty-Six

◆———◆———◆———◆

Over the next hour, either Jesse or Rusty was watching through the binoculars, checking out every car that parked and every person that walked the beach. They pinpointed where the cops had positioned themselves, most of them toward the center of the beach and spread out, each doing odd, fishing-related things. One guy had a spiderweb of monofilament hanging from his reel and was pretending to untangle it by the light of a kerosene lantern.

They also spotted two more who could easily fit the gang mold sneaking around the dune. A second biker had joined the first at the west end of the beach, where he also found a spot on the sand near a clump of small palms, a good thirty feet from the first. A third had arrived in a pickup and had taken a position near the east end, also trying to conceal himself from scrutiny. At least from anyone on land.

If the cops picked up on their presence, they didn't show it.

"It's twenty-three hundred," Rusty whispered, as Jesse watched a car pull into the middle parking area and stop. "Somethin' should be startin' soon, don't ya think?"

The front passenger door opened, and a giant figure got out. When he turned toward the light, Jesse grinned.

Sideshift had a big black eyepatch covering his left eye.

The car rocked as someone inside moved and the back door on the driver's side opened. It rocked again, and then an even larger figure emerged from the backseat.

The gang leader was early, and he had another goon with him, plus whoever was driving the car and hadn't gotten out yet, not to mention the three guys already on the beach. Six players so far.

"Sideshift just arrived," Jesse whispered. "And he's got an even bigger guy with him."

"Bigger?" Rusty asked. "Only one guy I know like that. Name's Lil' Pete and he's close to four hundred pounds, but mostly fat."

Jesse watched the two men stop at a table and sit down for a minute. Then the fat guy moved back near the parking area and sat on a bench.

Their positioning told Jesse their intent. They were going to try to lure him to the middle and surround him.

He lowered the field glasses and looked at his friend. "You ready?"

"Let's go swimmin'," Rusty replied, his voice low and menacing.

Quietly and deliberately, the two moved to the cockpit, where the girls helped them pull on one-piece wetsuits. Jesse wore one that belonged to Gregor, who was only a few inches shorter. It fit tightly, and the legs were a little short, but the sleeves only reached mid-forearm.

"Still better than nothing," he said.

"I'll send the signal when you go in the water," Gina said nervously.

They strapped weight belts on, with just a few pounds of lead attached to compensate for the wetsuit's buoyancy.

Gina and Juliet watched in silence as Jesse and Rusty both strapped dive knives to their ankles.

"I hope you don't have to use that," Juliet said. "You're just going to sneak up on them and clobber them, right?"

"That's the plan," Rusty replied. "This is only in case of a net tangle or somethin' like that."

The two young men stood, and Gina was suddenly in Jesse's arms, while Juliet hugged Rusty.

"You be careful," Gina whispered. "Don't take any chances."

They kissed, then Jesse moved over to the starboard side deck, where a ladder hung over the toe rail. He sat down and slipped the fins on, then his mask, and quietly went down the steps, facing away from the boat.

Once he was in the water, Jesse moved aside, kicking with very little effort as he pulled the neck of his wetsuit away and allowed cold seawater to flood the inside. It would quickly warm from his own body heat and would help keep him warm the whole time they were in the water.

Rusty climbed down and, under the cover of darkness, the two of them moved along the hull to the front of the boat and held onto the chain as they both looked toward shore.

The green and red navigation lights came on. They were the *second* signal to Sergeant Johnson that they were starting their swim. The first would've been three clicks on the VHF mic on channel 68.

"There's some rocks over there," Rusty said, pointing. "We should be able to make that underwater easy enough."

"Then do another survey and maybe split up there," Jesse added. "I'll take the two guys on the left."

"What? You don't think I can handle two?"

Jesse grinned at him in the darkness. "I know you can. But they're a good ten or fifteen yards apart, and I can move faster."

"Ya got a point there," he conceded. "Then we move to the center for the big guys."

"Remember," Jesse cautioned, "we have to let them attack first. The cops'll take care of them after that. But where they're positioned, they can't see the three sentries."

Rusty nodded as they hung on the chain, both beginning a slow breathing exercise, taking deep breaths and letting the air out slowly to saturate their blood with oxygen and slow their heart rates to be able to extend their normal breath hold.

Jesse nodded, and they both slipped beneath the surface and started kicking slowly in the direction of the rocks.

The new fins were extremely efficient, and the moon provided enough light for them to stay together swimming halfway between the surface and the bottom.

After nearly a minute, Rusty looked over at Jesse and trickled a little air out of his nose.

Jesse nodded, then angled toward the surface, moving over behind Rusty. They both began exhaling used air as they rose, propelling themselves upward with the fins.

Rusty broke the surface first, gulped air, and went back down immediately.

When Jesse passed the spot where Rusty'd surfaced, he lifted his head, inhaling quietly, and spotted the rock no more than fifty feet away.

He submerged again and they continued kicking; the whole thing took no longer than a turtle would take, inhaling a couple of breaths, and if anyone were watching, Jesse hoped that's what they'd think they were seeing.

After half a minute, the rock became visible ahead, and they angled toward the south side of it, away from the beach.

Staying close together, with hands on the jagged limestone outcrop, they raised just the tops of their heads and eyes out of the water.

Jesse saw no movement on the beach, no sign of threat or discovery.

He raised his head slightly more, exposing his nose and mouth.

Rusty did the same, right beside him.

"Nobody saw us," Rusty whispered, looking toward the west end of the beach and slow breathing again. "I'll only need to get about fifty yards to flank him and be out of his peripheral vision, then a little more to come outta the water behind him."

Jesse's swim would be farther. He'd have to make it almost a hundred yards to reach a point where he'd be perpendicular to the guy's sightline.

Surfacing before then might give him away.

He'd done a hundred yards underwater before, but the mention of how the fins tired the famous oceanographer's legs had him wondering.

"I'll wait in the surf zone until I see you come up out of the water," Rusty said. "Ready?"

"Let's do it."

They each took two more slow breaths. Then Jesse nodded and submerged, turning to his left as Rusty went the other way around the rocks.

The water was only about eight feet deep, and Jesse struck out with both arms held tightly against his sides and his face down, watching his moon shadow glide across the bottom.

There were patches of turtle grass and small clumps of corals beneath him, and even though it was night, he could easily see twenty feet ahead by moonlight.

With his old fins, he could just count his kicks and know how far he'd traveled. The number of kicks it took to cover twenty feet was something every diver learned sooner or later. But that was with regular fins and scuba gear. He figured he'd probably use a quarter fewer kicks to cover the same distance with nothing but mask, fins, and the weight belt.

His kicks were long and powerful, and he could feel a lot more resistance in the oversized fins than he was used to. The water moving over his body seemed faster than he'd ever felt on previous swims. The quadriceps muscles in his legs, the long powerful ones on the front of the thighs, began to burn from the exertion.

As he neared forty seconds, he dialed back the effort, trying to conserve oxygen.

At fifty seconds, his lungs began to spasm, so he slowly released a third of the air they held.

Finally, at nearly sixty seconds, he had to surface. He rose slowly, facing what he hoped was the beach, until his eyes and nose were above the water. He took a slow breath, then exhaled fully.

He'd way overshot his mark.

Chapter Thirty-Seven

◆―◆―◆―◆―◆

Submerged once more in the dark embrace of the water, Jesse swam slowly toward the beach. Both he and Rusty had been no strangers to night swimming before being assigned to Force Recon, and he felt no fear or trepidation.

The darkness and the water were his allies.

He had swum well past both of the men hiding near the dune. He figured he'd covered nearly 150 yards and now he'd be coming up well behind them.

When he reached the surf zone, Jesse carefully removed the fins and pulled his mask below his chin while lying in two-foot-deep water with only the top of his head exposed. In daylight, he'd be clearly visible from anywhere on the beach—a large, dark shape in the water—and under the light of the moon, anyone walking near the water's edge would at least see his head.

But the beach was empty.

He waited, scanning the dune line with his eyes, and listening. The surf wasn't loud, but the waves were coming almost parallel to the beach, so the sound of the small breaking waves was almost continuous.

When the next wave began to break, far to his right, Jesse rose and ran in a crouch toward the safety of the vegetation growing on the dune.

Dropping down onto one knee in the sand, he looked far down

the beach and saw Rusty running out of the water, beyond the third guy. There was no other activity. No shouts. No gunshots. All three men were so intently watching the middle of the dune area, where they expected to see him, that neither had seen past the other.

Jesse slowly removed his wetsuit and deposited it with his gear under a clump of sea grapes. He could see the back of the nearest guy, but the other one was positioned deeper in the vegetation, higher on the dune. He knew the geography between the two, though, so he started his slow, stealthy move.

The first guy never even knew he was being stalked when Jesse side-fisted the base of his skull, causing him to crumple silently onto the sand.

Then, when he moved around the shrubs the guy was using for cover, he could see the next man.

Still five feet away, a shell cracked under Jesse's heel and the man heard it, snapping his head around in alarm.

But it was too late, because Jesse pounced as soon as the sound was made, landing a solid right to the side of the man's head as he struggled to get to his feet.

The biker grunted loudly as Jesse followed through with a knee to the same spot.

Baldy rolled over sideways; his eyes closed.

Both of the lookouts at his end of the beach were down, but Baldy's grunt might have been heard. So Jesse circled back around the sea grape cluster, certain in the knowledge that Rusty was on his way toward the center of the beach.

When Jesse emerged, Sideshift was standing right in front of him, twenty feet away, holding a gun in his hand. Beyond the gang leader was the bigger guy, who he could now see was only heavier, not taller.

Instantly and instinctively, Jesse's mind calculated the distance between the two men and determined the fat guy wasn't going to be a part of what was about to go down. There just wasn't any way a guy that big could get to Sideshift in time to help.

Beyond him, Jesse saw Rusty in a dead run through the cluster of cops, and he completely discounted Lil' Pete as a threat.

A shot rang out as Jesse dove to his right, rolling upright behind a thick palm tree.

"Fuck it," he heard Sideshift snarl. "I don't need no damn gun and I don't need two eyes, you little shit."

Jesse looked around the tree and saw the big man tuck the gun in his pants and start walking menacingly toward him.

"When I get done bashin' the shit outta you," Sideshift growled in a low voice, "I'm gonna have a good ole time with your little blond girlfriend. She's gonna be the star in Amber's and my next porn flick."

Just as he saw Rusty leap sideways through the air, feet first, Jesse stepped out into the open, six feet away from the giant.

There was a loud gasp and whoosh of air as the fat guy went down, Rusty right on top of him, landing a flurry of unneeded punches to the man's head.

Jesse and Sideshift stood glaring at one another. The biker smiled, stained teeth yellow in the glow of the lights. "I think your little buddy just died."

"Not hardly, ya big ape," Rusty snarled, rising to his feet as the cops began running toward them.

Sideshift's hand moved suddenly to the gun at his waist.

At the same instant, Jesse was already moving, taking a long stride toward the man with his right foot, then leaping into a spinning back kick.

His left heel met bone with a sickening crunch.

Landing on his feet, Jesse crouched, both hands up, as

Sideshift's head lolled to the side, blood already flowing from around the eye patch.

The big man went to his knees just as the first cops arrived, guns drawn and covering the two fallen bikers.

Sideshift seemed to teeter on his knees for a second, then his left leg flexed uncontrollably, and he fell face first into the sand with a heavy thud.

"Don't move!" one of the cops shouted, pointing a gun down at the prone figure, twitching on the sand. "Put your hands behind your back!"

Sergeant Johnson joined the first cop, his gun also trained on Sideshift's body as he kicked the gun away from his hand.

"He's not going anywhere," Jesse said softly, rising, and staring down at the gang leader. Then he looked over at Johnson. "He'd already fired once and was about to shoot again. I didn't have any choice."

Johnson knelt in the sand and put a hand on Sideshift's neck, feeling for a pulse. Then he looked up at Jesse. "You two get out of here."

Rusty moved over beside Jesse. "Is he...?"

"Yeah," Johnson said, rising. "He's dead. Get lost. You were *never here.*"

Jesse looked past the deputy, seeing Amber Henderson get out of the car Sideshift had arrived in. She took two steps toward them, a rifle coming up in her hands.

"Gun!" Jesse shouted as he crashed into Johnson, just as a bullet tore into the deputy's shoulder.

A half dozen cops, already tense and on edge, turned toward the sound of the shot and opened fire.

Chapter Thirty-Eight

◆━━━◆━━━◆━━━◆━━━◆

Deputy Johnson got up, seemingly unhurt by the shot from Amber's rifle. He had a tactical vest under his fishing shirt. Then he told Jesse and Rusty once more to leave and say nothing about what happened.

The two Marines wasted no time trotting out to the waterline.

Jesse looked back, still shaken by what'd happened.

"You a'ight?" Rusty asked, putting a hand on Jesse's shoulder.

He glanced back at the scene again. The cops were already putting yellow tape around the area where the two bodies lay on the ground.

"Yeah," Jesse replied. "I'll be okay."

"Go get your gear," Rusty said. "We'll meet up in the water."

"Okay," Jesse replied, then turned and started running toward the west as Rusty ran in the opposite direction.

It wasn't supposed to happen like that, Jesse thought. What had Brisco meant about making Gina into a...

They looked alike! Carly and Gina could pass for sisters.

Jesse found his gear and headed to the water, pulling the mask down around his neck as he waded out deeper to put the wetsuit and fins on.

All five bikers, plus the woman, had been armed, and now two were dead and the others arrested and would be headed to the hospital before booking.

He hadn't meant to kill the man. His instincts had taken over when the gun came out. His target had been the man's weak spot. He hadn't even considered that it would be a death blow until he'd seen the blood pooling around Brisco's head.

In knee-deep water, Jesse looked back toward the scene. Police cars with lights on had arrived, along with an ambulance. When the water was to his thighs, he floated on his back and put the long fins on, then began to kick, angling toward Rusty, who was already swimming out.

When they met up, about halfway between the beach and the boat, Jesse heard a splash and looked over to see the dinghy in the water alongside *Pleiades.*

"What the hell're they doin'?"

"You okay?" Jesse asked.

"Scrape on the knee," Rusty replied, as they both watched one of the girls climb down into the small boat and start rowing.

Rusty turned to face Jesse as they started back-floating toward the dinghy. "What about you, bro? You killed a man."

"I put down a rabid animal," Jesse replied. "And I think that's how Johnson wanted it to end all along."

"And what about the woman?" Rusty asked, as the splashing of oars got closer.

"Jesse!" Gina called out, her voice urgent but quiet. "What happened? We heard gunshots."

Rusty and Jesse stopped swimming and grabbed either side of the dinghy's bow as Gina scrambled forward.

"Are you okay?" she asked.

"We're fine," Jesse replied, as he and Rusty moved back on either side of the boat to the middle. "Sit tight in the bow till we get aboard."

"Ready to board," Rusty said from the other side.

"Board!" Jesse ordered, then kicked hard as he pulled himself up onto the dinghy's side, then extended his right arm.

Rusty did the same thing, and they grasped one another's wrists and finished the maneuver, rolling into the boat facing different ways.

"What happened?" Gina asked.

"Sideshift and that Amber chick are dead," Rusty said, pulling his fins off. "And everyone else was arrested."

"Amber Henderson?"

"Yeah," Jesse said, as he got his fins off and sat up on the middle seat, while Rusty manned the tiller. "We have to go see Carly."

"Wait," Gina said, reaching out and taking one of the oars. "We can't get there in this, or in *Pleiades*."

"She's right, bro," Rusty said. "We need wheels."

"Swim back to the boat, Jim," Gina said. "We'll take the dinghy to Higg's. There's a phone there."

Rusty looked at Jesse. "How long you gonna be?"

"Maybe half an hour," Jesse said. "There are things she needs to know before she hears about it on the news. Gina too."

"Me?"

"I'll tell you both at the same time," Jesse replied. "I still have to sort it all out in my head."

Rusty gave him a knowing look as he pulled his fins back on. "A hard row oughta do that."

"Happy New Year," Jesse said with a grin.

Rusty nodded and shifted over to the side. "*Vaya con Dios*," he said, then fell backward into the water.

"What the hell does that mean?" Gina asked, moving past Jesse to the little tiller.

"It's Spanish for 'go with God,'" Jesse replied, as he started rowing.

"I know *that*," she hissed. "What'd he mean by the rowing should do it. Do what?"

"You steer," Jesse said, starting to get into a steady rhythm he knew he could sustain. "Hard work lets me think. Give me time to process everything I just learned."

"But what did you mean by—"

"Steer," Jesse said. "Don't talk."

Gina slumped back, pouting, but kept the tiller pointed in the direction she wanted to go.

Jesse looked past her toward the east, his moon shadow falling across Gina's knees each time he leaned forward to take another sweep with the oars.

It had to be close to midnight—seven hours until dawn—the first day of a new year, and he was going to spend it paddling a dinghy.

How could he have missed it? He'd seen Chuck Bering at Louie's Backyard, trying to hide behind a menu. He didn't know him at the time and hadn't realized it was the guy in the Cordoba until he stepped in front of him on Mallory Square and punched his lights out.

That was when their attention turned away from Carly. When Amber gave up trying to kill Carly's husband to make her more dependent and malleable. When the biker gang found the girl they wanted.

Carly was being manipulated. And now they'd found another possible stand in.

"That's enough," Gina whispered. "We're almost on the beach."

Only when he stopped rowing did Jesse feel the tension in his shoulders—the tightness of a hard workout. He turned his head and saw that they were near the foot of a pier.

"We can hide the boat under the pier," Gina said, as Jesse swung a leg over and stepped out. "The phone booth is on the corner, just off the pier."

Jesse took the dinghy's line and pulled it toward the giant pilings the pier was built on. Then Gina jumped out, and together they pulled it up onto the sand.

"Are you sure it'll be okay here?" Jesse asked, as they trudged up the loose sand toward the dune.

"Probably," Gina replied. "Are you going to tell me what that meant earlier? How this involves me?"

"When we get to Carly's house," Jesse replied. "I'm still piecing a few things together."

They found the phone and Gina called her friend's wife, telling her where they were, and where they needed to go, then hung up.

"He'll find us along Atlantic Boulevard," she said, taking his hand and leading the way east, back toward Smather's Beach.

Jesse walked along quietly, still sorting snippets of information out in his head. After walking a block, a horn honked, and the same blue Thum Taxi pulled to the curb.

Jesse opened the back door and let Gina get in.

"Twice in a weekend," Nick Thacker said, looking back over the front seat. "Happy New Year, Gina and Jesse."

"Same to you, Nick," she replied, sliding over so Jesse could get in.

"Where to? Schooner Wharf? More than a half hour left."

Jesse noted the time on the car's dashboard—2320.

"Carly and Scott's house on Stock Island," Gina replied. "And can you wait there for us and bring us back here to the pier? My dink's on the beach."

"Most likely," he replied, putting the car in gear. "Won't get busy again till after midnight, anyway."

He turned right onto Bertha, then made a quick left onto South Roosevelt.

"Wonder what happened here," Nick said, craning his neck. "Think somebody drowned?"

The taxi rode past the scene in silence, the police lights flashing inside the car bathing their faces in blue and red.

Four men were loading a stretcher into the ambulance. Jesse could tell by the shape of the covered form that it was the guy Rusty had drop-kicked into next week from a dead run.

Beyond them, headlights from a police car shone on the riddled and bloody corpse of a dark-haired woman in a black dress—Amber Henderson.

A few minutes later, they reached the house where Carly lived and Nick used the radio to tell his wife that unless she had an emergency call, he was going to wait there.

"We won't be long," Jesse said, climbing out.

Carly was standing at the doorway, one little boy in front of her and another trying to hide behind her.

"What happened?" she asked, as Jesse and Gina approached.

"Can we talk inside?" Jesse replied.

"Yeah, sure. Come on in." She stepped back, bumping into the older son. "Caleb, take your brother to your room and play."

"But, Mom," he whined, "the ball's about to drop."

"We won't be long," Jesse told the boy in a reassuring tone.

As the two kids trudged toward the back of the house, Carly waved Jesse and Gina in. "Can I get you anything? A beer?"

"We're fine," Gina said and paused. "There's been a shooting."

"We heard it on the news," Carly said. "Have a seat. The local news actually broke in on the New Year's Eve show while Tanya Tucker was singing." She looked back and forth between Jesse and Gina as they all sat down. "What happened?"

Jesse took a deep breath. "Amber Henderson is dead."

"What?" Carly cried out. "When? How did it happen?"

"She wasn't who you thought she was," Gina said.

"Gina's right," Jesse agreed. "And she wasn't here with any fashion magazine either."

Chapter Thirty-Nine

◆━━◆━━◆━━◆

After Jesse finished explaining the events leading up to the shooting at Smathers Beach, he questioned Carly about the attempts on Scott's life, and determined that he'd correctly guessed that Amber hadn't been anywhere around Carly during all four encounters.

"It wasn't a man who attacked Scott with the knife," Jesse explained. "It was Amber, wearing a man's hoody. The angle of the stab meant it had to have been someone no taller than about five feet."

He went on to explain how the outlaw motorcycle gang was involved in trafficking models into porn, with help from Amber, and how they were both targeted because of their looks.

The two women sat in stunned silence.

"So, why would she want Scott dead?" Carly asked, her eyes moistening. "He hardly ever even said anything to her. And she never once came on to *me*."

"It's part of the process, I guess," Jesse replied. "The, uh, film producer wanted a specific... type of model. Someone who looks like the two of you. Amber needed to get you to become dependent on her so she could coerce you into doing it. And in Gina's case, the bikers were just going to abduct and force her."

"You can say the words, Jesse," Gina said. "The porn mogul wanted a petite blonde—someone not in the business—for a forced lesbian gang rape scene with Amber Henderson and a bunch of bikers."

Jesse felt his face flush. "Well... yeah."

Carly looked blankly at Jesse. "Is that what guys get off watching?"

His face flushed deeper. "No! Well... I don't know. Some, I guess."

"Amber's dead?" Carly asked. "I can't believe it. You're sure?"

"I watched her go down in a hail of bullets from at least four cops."

She leaned forward and covered her face as she started sobbing, and Jesse didn't know what to do or say.

Gina moved over to Carly's side and hugged her closely. "It'll be alright," she whispered soothingly. "You couldn't have known."

"So, it's over?" Carly asked, looking up with tears in her eyes. "Scott can come home?"

"Call Deputy Sergeant Bart Johnson tomorrow," Jesse said. "I'm sure they recovered the bullet from his vest, and I'd bet my last dime it'll be a match to the one they dug out of your neighbor's tree."

A horn honked out front.

"We have to go," Gina said. "Are you going to be alright?"

"It's a lot to take in," Carly replied, drying her eyes with a tissue. "But looking back, I can see it now. She'd spent the night and left less than an hour before Scott that day he was shot at. And you think it was actually her?"

"Yes," Jesse replied. "The dancers she met and did cocaine with at Chuck Bering's place live in this same neighborhood and Amber probably stashed the rifle and just hid out there until the police were gone."

"We left her with the boys to go for a walk on the beach."

"And it was late," Gina said. "The kids were asleep."

Jesse looked the woman in the eye. "So, she slipped out, drove to where she knew you would be, and waited."

The horn honked again.

"Yeah," Carly replied, standing. "I'll be okay. Nick must have another fare."

Jesse and Gina rose, and Jesse went to the door, holding up one finger to the driver. "Remember," he said, turning back to Carly, "call Sergeant Johnson in the morning. He might not be on duty, but if you tell the dispatcher you have information about the shooting, they'll patch you through somehow."

Gina and Carly hugged at the door, and Jesse was again impressed by the similarity of the two women.

"Back to the pier?" Nick asked, as Gina slid across the back seat.

"What time is it?" she asked.

"Twenty till," he replied, as Jesse got in and pulled the door closed.

"Yeah, back to the pier, Nick," Gina replied. "As fast as you can get there; I have an appointment."

A moment later, he crossed the bridge back onto Key West with a green light ahead of them at Roosevelt, and less than five minutes after leaving, they arrived at the pier.

Jesse took three of the twenties from the wad in his pocket and handed them over the seat. "Keep the change, Nick. And thanks."

Gina was already running toward the beach alongside the pier, and Jesse sprinted after her.

"What's the rush?" he called out, as she began tugging on the dinghy.

"I don't want this year to end on a bad note," she said. "Help me get it into the water."

Together, they lugged the dinghy off the beach, and as soon as it was floating free, she climbed in, and Jesse pulled it deeper.

When the water reached above his knees, he climbed in too and started rowing, while grinning at Gina working the tiller like a third oar.

"Row faster!" she whisper-shouted.

Jesse put his whole body into it, launching the little boat up onto its own bow wave with every stroke.

Gina stopped the back-and-forthing on the tiller and guided the little boat toward *Pleiades*, resting at anchor in the moonlight.

It only took a few minutes of hard rowing to reach the boat, and as they came up on the port side, Jesse noticed all the lights were off.

"That y'all?" he heard Rusty call from the bow.

"Yeah," Gina replied, scrambling up the ladder, then tying the dinghy off to a stanchion. "What time is it? Did we miss it?"

Rusty stood and pulled his pocket watch out as Jesse climbed up the ladder.

"Five till," he replied. "We got both of the beanbags out."

Jesse followed Gina to the foredeck and found Juliet lying back in a large, black, beanbag chair with a wine glass in her hand, gazing up sheepishly at Gina.

"I'm afraid we raided your stash," Juliet said. "It's only been chilling for half an hour though."

"Perfect!" Gina said, then turned and pushed Jesse backward. "Go get two more glasses from the cupboard beside the sink."

Jesse hurried down to the galley and found the glasses, then returned to find Gina sitting on the other bag, with plenty of room beside her.

Rusty and Juliet were snuggled together, looking up at the night sky and talking quietly.

"Here you go," Jesse said, offering Gina a glass.

She picked up the bottle and poured it half full, then the other. "Sit down."

"Aye aye, ma'am."

He sat next to her and leaned back, looking around as Gina wiggled closer. Rusty didn't have his watch out.

"How will you know when it's midnight?" he asked.

Just then, a bottle rocket soared up into the air from somewhere back in the neighborhood beyond the beach, exploding with a crack. Then another, and two more. In seconds, they were erupting all along the shoreline.

Gina took his glass and placed it on the deck, along with her own, then rolled on top of him, kissing him passionately.

Car horns blared from shore, as well as from one of the other boats at anchor, and far to the west came deep blasts from several large yachts' air horns. All the honking was a backdrop to more small fireworks launched from islanders' backyards, mostly little bottle rockets, but some rose more than a hundred feet, illuminating the sky with red and green sparkles.

Gina pulled away, smiling down at him as her hair dangled in his face and rockets exploded behind her. "Happy Key West new year, Jesse."

He pulled her back down on top of him again and kissed her deeply, all thoughts of shootings, knives, poison, bombs, and dead bikers gone from his head.

Finally, Gina rolled off him and stood up. "We're going to bed," she announced to Juliet. "It's been a... uh, long, hard day."

Rusty and Juliet both laughed.

"Yes, it has," Rusty said. "Happy 1980, bro!"

Gina pulled him aft along the side deck, then ducked under the bimini. Jesse followed her down into the salon, pausing to look back at the beach for a moment. The flashing lights were gone, and people were firing Roman candles over the sand.

"Come on," Gina urged him.

He ducked under the hatch and followed her through the narrow passage to the aft cabin, where she pulled her top off over her head and then started tugging at the drawstring of Jesse's swimsuit, quickly pulling them down to the deck.

"Close the door," she said, looking up at him with eyes ablaze with passion. "There will *not* be any interruption this time."

Chapter Forty

◆──◆──◆──◆──◆

It was a deep dive, over a hundred feet once they went down to the stern of the shipwreck, where they found a huge jewfish by the prop at a hundred and five feet.

They'd spent fifteen minutes exploring the deck and wheelhouse of the old tugboat, taking pictures of one another at the wheel with Gina's underwater camera before descending over the stern to find the big fish hiding behind the rudder.

Jesse checked his dive watch, a big, cheap thing he'd picked up in Key West. He'd gone back to the dive shop alone, and sure enough, the Russian woman had basically ignored him, except to ring up the sale.

Now, he checked his air gauge. Still over a thousand pounds of pressure left. He reached over and grabbed Gina's as the four of them hung on the anchor line for a safety stop.

She was down to five hundred.

He jerked a thumb toward the surface, fifteen feet above them.

The others nodded, then they all started a slow ascent, rising toward the boat's hull fifteen feet above.

When he reached the surface, Jesse hit the auto inflator on his buoyancy compensator to float effortlessly.

"I've never seen one so big!" Gina shouted, inflating her BC fully.

"That thing had to be at least six hunert pounds!" Rusty added.

The four of them kicked their way back toward the stern of Rusty's boat, masks pulled down under their chins.

Jesse tossed his fins through the transom door, then climbed up with all his gear on while the others removed theirs in the water. He quickly shrugged out of his vest, put the tank on the rack, and used a bungee to hold it in place before moving to the side of the door to help Juliet, then Gina climb aboard.

"What a great dive!" Juliet exclaimed. "Did you *see* all the growth on the foredeck? It's only been down there a little over two years."

"And you don't know what it's called?" Jesse asked Rusty.

"No clue, bro," he replied. "When I found it, there wasn't nothin' growin' on it, so it hadn't been there long. I only told a coupla people about it, and nobody knows of any tugs that size missing anywhere in Florida. I've gone over it stem to stern and couldn't find a name or anything."

"Maybe a drug runner?" Jesse grinned. "Another mystery?"

"Ya don't always gotta know all the whats and whys to exploit a resource," Rusty said. "Wanna guess how many snappers was on that wreck?"

"Dozens," Jesse replied. "And a lot of hogfish, too."

"I fished it once a week before the Corps," Rusty said. "Never failed to bag my limit within an hour. Now a buddy of mine does."

Jesse looked beyond the bow, where dark clouds were starting to build, miles to the west. "Looks like your dad was spot on again. How's he know and the weather report doesn't?"

"The forecast on the news covers a big area," Rusty replied, as he started the outboard. "In a broad sense, this'll be a beautiful Keys evenin'. Them clouds'll build quick and rain out even faster. It's where it rains out that ruins the evenin' in a small area, and this time they'll reach saturation when they get to the middle of the Seven

BAD BLOOD

Mile Bridge."

"Yeah, but how?" Jesse persisted, as he moved forward to get the anchor. "How's he know when a cloud is going to reach a point where it starts to rain?"

"Pop's lived his whole life right there in that house, bro," Rusty said, as Jesse started hauling up the long anchor rode. "Forty-four years a watchin' the water over Key Vaca Bight. He's only been outta the Keys a handful of times, and like his dad before him—and me too, I guess—we spent most of our lives on the water. Ya get to know the feel of things and how everything around you relates to everything else when you're that close."

Rusty coiled the line as Jesse hauled it in, finally reaching the chain part of the rode. His boat only had three hundred feet of anchor line and fifty feet of chain, so it wasn't really adequate for anchoring in a hundred feet of water, but any current was directly opposed by a light breeze, and the sea was flat calm. The anchor hadn't dragged an inch.

It was still a long haul, though.

Finally, they got the anchor aboard, and Rusty took the helm as the girls stretched out on the forward-facing bench in front of the console.

The day had warmed into the seventies, at least. And the water temperature had been warmer. He asked Rusty about that when he put the boat in gear and turned northwest.

"Still colder'n a well-digger's ass, if ya ask me," he said. "The Stream ain't fixed. It can move closer and farther, and when it gets in close, the water's warmer."

"Makes sense," Jesse said, as Rusty increased speed, bringing the boat up on plane, where it glided smoothly across the water with barely any sense of movement.

Jesse moved forward to ask if the girls needed anything.

"We're good," Gina said with a smile, big blue sunglasses covering her eyes.

Twenty minutes later, Rusty slowed and idled into the narrow canal, where they turned the boat around and got it tied up to the dock.

Rusty and Jesse began unloading and rinsing all the dive gear, while the girls went up to the bar to get some sandwiches.

It'd been more than two days since the incident on Smathers Beach, and none of them had said anything to anyone about it, not even to Rusty's parents.

Jesse had thought about it over and over, trying to come to grips with the fact that he'd not just killed one man, but was at least partly to blame for Amber Henderson's death as well.

"We got three days of sunshine after this little blow," Rusty said, looking toward the darkening sky. "I reckon we oughta start tryin' to figure out the how part of gettin' back to the base pretty soon."

"We drive the Mustang," Jesse said. "I included that in the deal with Shorty on Monday and gave it to you, so I'm not out anything. And since you work for me now, you drive."

"Works for me," Rusty replied, then sat down on the gunwale. "How ya feelin' about the other day?"

Jesse sat down next to his friend, elbows on his knees. "I'm okay. I know that if the same situation came up a hundred times, I'd do the same thing each time."

Rusty looked past the bar and what remained of the bait shop, then stood up quickly. "That's a good thing, then. Cuz, here comes Deputy Johnson."

Jesse reached over and grabbed his T-shirt off the boat's dash and pulled it over his head. Then together, he and Rusty started toward the patrol car pulling into the parking area.

The doors opened and Sergeant Johnson got out of the

BAD BLOOD

passenger side, while his son climbed out of the driver's seat. The sergeant said something to Tony and started walking toward them.

His arm was in a sling.

"I thought you had a vest on," Jesse said, as they got closer.

"They can stop a bullet," Johnson said. "But not the impact and momentum. Broken scapula."

"I'm sorry to hear that," Jesse said, and truly meant it.

Johnson extended his good hand. "It might have been in the back of my neck if you hadn't knocked me aside. Thanks."

Jesse shook his hand. "Don't mention it."

"I won't," he replied, nodding toward the boat. "That's why I'm here. Is that your new boat, Jim?"

"It is," Rusty replied.

"Let's go over there and sit down a minute," Johnson said, leading the way.

When they reached the dock, Rusty pulled a boat box closer, and they all sat down, the two younger men on the gunwale of Rusty's boat.

Johnson looked Jesse in the eye. "How are you holding up, son?"

"I'm okay," Jesse replied, wondering if he was going to be arrested.

Johnson cleared his throat. "Following up on a tip from a concerned citizen," he began, "the forensics guys ballistically matched the slug from my vest to the one dug out of a tree next door to Scott Ingersoll's house from an unrelated attempted murder a couple of weeks ago. We determined that the shooter had a grudge against Mr. Ingersoll and that case is now closed with the shooter dead."

Jesse nodded knowingly. "I never meant for anyone to get killed."

"The autopsy reports were filed this morning," Johnson

continued, "as well as the finding of the peer board. *Both* police-involved shootings were deemed justified."

Jesse and Rusty looked at one another, then back to the deputy.

"Both?" Jesse asked.

"For the record," Johnson said, shifting his weight on the box and clearing his throat again. "And what I'm about to tell you is actually *in* the reports of all officers involved on the scene when Monte Brisco and his cohorts were confronted at 2330 on New Year's Eve on Smathers Beach. My report stated that when I encountered Brisco, he drew a revolver and opened fire. At which point I, and I alone, returned fire, hitting Mr. Brisco in the head, and killing him instantly. One of Key West's officers saw a woman with a rifle, and yelled 'Gun!' just as she fired. But the officer was faster and pushed me aside, saving my life, as other officers on the scene opened fire and killed Amber Henderson."

"That's... not what happened," Jesse said, even more confused.

"That's *exactly*... what happened, son," Johnson said. "I was temporarily relieved of duty until this morning, when the peer board got the autopsy reports as well as the final statements of everyone who was on the scene. With all the corroborating evidence, I was reinstated and Peter Knowles, also known as Lil' Pete, along with the other members of the Sun Devils, don't remember anything. They were all arrested on various charges, including felony possession of several guns, and they will all be imprisoned for at least the next twenty years as repeat offenders."

"I don't get it," Jesse said. "Why would you and the other cops stick your necks out like that? And why would the doctor performing the autopsy think a bullet did what I did to Brisco's face?"

As the girls started down across the yard, Johnson looked up at Jesse and gave him a sad smile. Hearing the girls laughing, he glanced back for a second, then stood and tipped his hat at Rusty.

"Tell your mom and dad hi for me, Jim. And tell your buddy who the coroner is." Then he turned and started to walk away. "You boys enjoy the rest of your leave."

Jesse was totally confused. "Who is the coroner?" he asked Rusty, as the girls passed Johnson.

"Pop told ya how Bart's wife left him and their kids, remember?" Jesse nodded.

"Her older brother, Bart's brother-in-law, is the coroner," Rusty said, watching Johnson get into the patrol car. "His son was killed in Nam."

"What did he want?" Juliet asked.

Rusty squinted against the sunlight, as he looked up at her. "Just lettin' us know everything's cool," he replied, putting his shades back on.

Gina took Jesse's hand and pulled him up from the gunwale. "Let's walk before we eat."

They strolled to the end of the dock, then down to the boat ramp.

Gina was quiet.

Finally, she stopped and looked up at him. "How are you dealing with it, Jesse? Knowing that you killed someone?"

It was a blunt question, and Jesse sensed that she too was struggling with what had occurred on the beach the other night.

"When something like that happens," he replied, searching for the words he'd been thinking about for two days, "it becomes... reactionary chaos; fight or die. They made first contact and we survived."

Afterword

I find I'm really enjoying writing these stories of Jesse's younger life, likely because the memories from my own time in the Corps at that age are so vivid in my mind. Those were simpler times, unencumbered by cell phones, GPS, and computers, when we made mistakes and learned by trial and error instead of asking Siri and Alexa the same question we asked last week. We memorized phone numbers, directions, and people's names. The connections we made were face-to-face instead of through Facebook. The only tweeting was from the birds, and we took the time to stop and listen.

Jesse has matured a little more since boot camp and he's been promoted again. Soon, he'll be off to NCO School, where he'll become a non-commissioned officer and learn how to lead men in battle.

We got to meet Arthur Brooks in this story, if only for a short moment. You might remember him from the opening scene of *Fallen Out*, when he retired Jesse from the Corps. He was a colonel in that first book of the original series and the commanding officer of Jesse's battalion. Here, he's a lieutenant, just a few years older than Jesse. In later stories, we'll meet him again, as well as Tom Broderick, Tank Tankersley, and of course, Russ Livingston and his son, a very young Deuce Livingston.

And Gray Redmond.

If that name from chapters one and two seemed familiar to you, but you can't find it mentioned in any of my twenty-seven books in the original series, it's because he's not there. This introduction will become clearer in Jesse #28, *Apalach Affair*, which will be released on September 1. I might have jogged a few memories with the title.

Gray Redmond is Maggie Redmond Hamilton's dad.

If you're asking yourself who Maggie is, then I've got a wonderful surprise for you. She is the main character in the late Dawn Lee McKenna's *Forgotten Coast Series*.

Dawn and I had talked many times about sharing characters in a scene, but the closest we ever came was appearing as ourselves in one another's books. Wayne Stinnett was a salty old oysterman in her first book in the series, *Low Tide*, set in Apalachicola, Florida. He'd served in the Corps with Maggie's father, Gray Redmond. In *Fallen Honor*, Dawn McKenna was the Key West fortune-teller who shot the coke dealer and saved Jesse's life.

Many of Dawn's characters will be in *Apalach Affair*. My family and I went there for a vacation research trip last March and I met a few of them. She often used real people around Apalach as her characters and the town loved her.

Cap Daniels and I have been working with Dawn's oldest daughter, Kat, who recently obtained control of the rights to her mom's books and has republished them. Dawn and I found Cap's books shortly after he'd written the first Chase Fulton novel, and we introduced him to our readers. That seems like a lifetime ago, now.

Anyway, Kat republished her mom's books as a legacy and to help support herself and her three younger siblings, two of whom are still in school. It took over two years, but Kat's done it. So, if you're wondering what all the hoopla is about, that's it. Dawn's books are back, and I wanted to see where Dawn's characters might be today, five years after the series ended. So, I had to introduce Gray in this book for his reintroduction in *Apalach Affair* to have the impact I hope it will have.

So, if you haven't read them yet, please check out Dawn Lee's books on Amazon. I promise, you won't be disappointed.

I loved letting my mind wander back in time nearly half a century for this book, back to my youth, where I could dig up nuggets of wisdom and lessons for Jesse to learn and remember. In these young Jesse books, he isn't the rock-hard, all-knowing, retired Marine gunny depicted in the original series.

He's just a kid learning about life, and being thrust into very serious situations. He's only a kid chronologically, though. All those things he seems to know by heart in the original series are just being planted in young Jesse's mind for the first time in these stories.

Is it easy for a sixty-five-year-old man to write through the eyes of an eighteen-year-old? Not as easy as you'd think. But I feel like I'm starting to get in touch with the young man I used to be with every chapter. However, I do find myself having to stop and look something up that I can't remember. I mean, it was a long time ago!

A special thanks to the many learned individuals in my core reading group who get my raw manuscript before it goes to my editor. Tom Crisp, Glenn Hibbert, Alan Fader, Dana Vilhen, Kim DeWitt, Mike Ramsey, Jason Hebert, and Drew Mutch helped with some of the geography of the time period. My tech consultants didn't get much exercise in this one though, but many found inconsistencies and helped flesh out the setting as it was forty-four years ago, not long after I first visited the Keys.

A very special thanks to my wife and family for putting up with my imaginary characters being part of the dinner conversation all these years. They've become as real to Greta and Jordan, who have read all my books, as they are to me. They help me bang out plot lines and twists while we're relaxing in the pool.

During our recent week in Apalach, we all felt something unique about the place and are planning to return there. We stayed in a VRBO on the beach on St. George Island and walked where Maggie walked to investigate the murder of a man who'd raped her decades earlier. We went to other places too, and they offered ideas for the next book.

I live and work for my family. Well, it's also fun talking to imaginary people, like we did as children.

Milli turned one year old while we were on St. George, and she is a devout beach dog now. Apalachicola is a dog-friendly town. Just about anywhere people can go, they can take their dogs, including the beach.

Thanks also to my editor, Marsha Zinberg, my final proofreader, Donna Rich, my narrator, Nick Sullivan, and my assistants at Aurora Publicity, Sam, Ash, Cam, Jen, Mel, Amy, Adriane, and Brian. Without your knowledge and assistance, my writing would be much slower and the final result, a far cry from what you make it, and what my readers have come to expect.

Finally, I'd be very remiss if I didn't extend my deepest gratitude to you, my readers, for escaping from your busy lives into my imaginary world for a little while. You've stuck with me through twenty-five years of Jesse's life and now we're working on the twenty years prior to that.

These stories are my life now. I couldn't stop if I wanted to, and I consider you to be my extended family. Thank you.

Wayne

Also by Wayne Stinnett

The Jerry Snyder Caribbean Mystery Series

Wayward Sons Voudoo Child Friends of the Devil

The Charity Styles Caribbean Thriller Series

Merciless Charity Enduring Charity Elusive Charity
Ruthless Charity Vigilant Charity Liable Charity
Reckless Charity Lost Charity

The Young Jesse McDermitt Tropical Adventure Series

A Seller's Market Bad Blood

The Jesse McDermitt Caribbean Adventure Series

Fallen Out Rising Storm Rising Tide
Fallen Palm Rising Fury Steady As She Goes
Fallen Hunter Rising Force All Ahead Full
Fallen Pride Rising Charity Man Overboard
Fallen Mangrove Rising Water Cast Off
Fallen King Rising Spirit Fish On!
Fallen Honor Rising Thunder Weigh Anchor
Fallen Tide Rising Warrior Swift and Silent
Fallen Angel Rising Moon
Fallen Hero Rising Tide

Non Fiction

Blue Collar to No Collar No Collar to Tank Top

The Gaspar's Revenge Ship's Store is open.

There, you can purchase all kinds of swag related to my books. You can find it at

WWW.GASPARS-REVENGE.COM